PERFECT
Harmony

Emily Albright

Amberjack Publishing
New York | Idaho

AMBERJACK
PUBLISHING

Amberjack Publishing
1472 E. Iron Eagle Drive
Eagle, Idaho 83616
http://amberjackpublishing.com

Publisher's Cataloging-in-Publication data
Names: Albright, Emily, author.
Title: Perfect harmony / Emily Albright.
Description: Eagle, Idaho : Amberjack Publishing, [2018] | Summary: Seventeen-year-old Pippa Wyndham, a top cellist, faces stiff competition in her senior year from cocky Declan Brogan, a transfer student from a fancy conservatory who shares her determination to be the best.
Identifiers: LCCN 2018005075 (print) | LCCN 2018013514 (ebook) | ISBN 9781944995836 (eBook) | ISBN 9781944995829 (pbk. : alk. paper)
Subjects: | CYAC: Cello--Fiction. | Competition (Psychology)--Fiction. | Friendship--Fiction. | Dating (Social customs)--Fiction. | Family life--Oregon--Fiction. | High schools--Fiction. | Schools--Fiction. | Oregon--Fiction.
Classification: LCC PZ7.1.A4316 (ebook) | LCC PZ7.1.A4316 Per 2018 (print) | DDC [Fic]--dc23
LC record available at https://lccn.loc.gov/2018005075

Cover Design: Jaclyn Reyes
Cover images: Suhyeon Choi, Mark Golovko, Aaron Burson

For Ryan.
I'm so blessed that this band geek found
her choir nerd.

Prologue

When I started learning the cello, I fell in love with the instrument because it seemed like a voice—my voice.

—Mstislav Rostropovich

My cello is my voice. It's my world. My whole life, it has allowed me to express all my sadness, frustration, happiness, dreams, and wishes inside its haunting strains. It has been the one place I could always turn to no matter what I was feeling. Today, however, marked either the beginning of my future or the end of my lifetime goal.

The final audition of the summer was upon me. I'd applied to numerous music schools: Juilliard, NYU Tisch, Oberlin, Berklee . . . basically the majority of them, and I'd spent the summer making audition tapes and traveling to live tryouts. But this one right here, this was the one that really mattered. Goddards. The premiere school for musicians, dancers, and actors. It'd been my only goal for as long as I could remember.

As I sat in the hallway, staring at the closed double doors, waiting my turn, I couldn't breathe. Muffled music hit my ears, and my stomach started to revolt and churn. Cello in my hands, I tried to focus on my music and picture it in my mind. Blank.

"Breathe, Pippa." Mom's hand covered mine with a comforting warmth. "You're going to do great."

Mom got it. She was a concert pianist. She'd been here before.

This morning we'd made the trek up to Seattle for the open audition Goddards was holding. As long as they had your application, you were welcome. And they'd had mine since early junior year. Way before my brother and friends had sent any in. I knew what I wanted. Always had. Thankfully, most of the schools requiring live auditions staged them all across the country. A New York trip wasn't in the cards for our family this summer.

I was playing it smart though, and I still applied to backup schools.

Hopefully, I wouldn't need them.

Because my goals were set in stone: Always be the top cellist. Graduate from Goddards. Join the New York Philharmonic. Okay, I may need to work my way up to the New York Phil, but I'd get there eventually.

This plan of mine had been in place since I was little. There was nothing that was going to stop me from achieving it. That is, as long as I remained the best. I know the other students in the cello section seemed not to give a fig who was section leader, but I sure did. I wanted that first chair spot to stay mine. It'd been mine since the first year we'd started competing for chair positions in middle school. It mattered.

A lot.

The doors creaked open and a short girl carrying an oboe exited and stared at the floor as she walked past us. She looked slightly green.

"Ms. Wyndham?" The man at the door, wearing a dress

shirt and khakis, looked up from his clipboard and met my eyes. "As soon as you're ready."

I stood, straightened my dark pants, and shot one last longing look at Mom.

With a wink and nod, she mouthed, *you got this.*

Deep breath in, I walked through the door and stood before the judges. Dear God, please don't let me screw this up.

CHAPTER *One*

Music is the universal language of mankind.

—*Henry Wadsworth Longfellow*

At the tender age of seven, I met the boy who I knew, with absolute certainty, I was going to marry. He ran me over. So I guess you could say I was literally hit by love.

It was early afternoon, and my family had pulled our trusty mini-van up to our new house in Portland. As I stepped out, a boy on a blue bicycle plowed into me. From a heap of tangled limbs and bike parts, his watery blue eyes met mine, and the rest of the world spun away. He immediately asked if I was okay, despite his own bloodied elbows and knees. He was easily the cutest boy I'd ever met. Since that moment, I'd been a lost cause. Unrequited romance for one, please.

Ten years later, and I still had it bad. Only now Noah Foss had traded in his bike for a Jeep and was cuter than ever. He was also the captain of the basketball team, Mr. Popularity, and the Tweedledee to my twin brother's Tweedledum. So basically, he ticked off every box in the totally-out-of-my-league reality checklist.

Although he *had* been my first kiss. Kind of. Let's just say we were a pair of eight-year-olds motivated by curiosity.

"Pips, come on. Move your butt or we're gonna be late." My BFF and nearly next-door neighbor Quinn stood at my side, rushing me along.

I slammed my red locker door, twirled the combo knob, and followed her to our English class. We slid into our seats just as the bell rang. The perpetually perky Ms. Peters was nowhere to be seen.

Noah and my brother Phillip sauntered through the door looking like they hadn't a care in the world. Typical. Phillip sat in the front row, where Peters had moved him for not paying attention, and Noah made his way to his seat beside me.

"Morning, Pips." He did a quick incline of his head in the quintessential dude nod.

"Hey." I played it cool. Seeing Noah at the start of my day always got my heart racing in the best possible way. I turned to Quinn on my other side and gave her a cheesy look of bliss. She just shook her head and clicked her pen. We went through this ritual nearly every morning.

"Five minute rule," one of the muscled jocks called from the back row while high-fiving his buzz-cut buddy next to him.

I chuckled and rolled my eyes. Like Ms. Peters would ever skip a class. We wouldn't be so lucky. A staccato series of clickity-clacks sounded from the hallway. The unmistakable sound of authority hoofing it our way.

"Good morning, class." Ms. Peters stepped through the door, the scent of powder and mint clinging to her filled the room. Not far behind her came a tall, lean boy. Ruffled dark hair and dark eyes made a stark contrast to his pale skin. His black leather jacket was unzipped, and strapped to his back was a large, hard-shell, gunmetal-gray case. I immediately knew what it was.

A cello. That meant he could be competition. The only question was just how good was he?

My eyes narrowed. He'd better not try anything. I had worked my ass off to get first chair at school and the Oregon Youth Symphony. My cello was my life. He was edging dangerously close to my turf. Scratch that, he was invading my turf.

"As you can see, we have a new student."

The tall boy's eyes scanned the classroom and paused momentarily on me, unsmiling.

Ms. Peters continued, "This is Declan Brogan. I have no doubt you'll all make him feel welcome here at Marshland."

Declan shifted the weight of the case on his shoulder.

"Pippa." Our teacher turned to me, a smile on her wrinkled face. If I had to venture a guess, I would've said she had to be on the other side of 100. She'd been teaching here forever. "Would you please show Mr. Brogan where he can store his instrument?"

"Of course." I stood and pulled the sleeves of my gray sweater down. These late fall mornings left a damp chill in the air that lingered in the school until midafternoon. As I walked past Declan and into the hall, I caught a whiff of something woodsy mingled with raindrops. I wrinkled my nose, perturbed that he smelled nice. "Follow me."

He fell into step beside me without saying a word. Curious what his story was, I glanced up at him, realizing he was way taller than I'd originally thought. "So, are you new to Oregon or just Marshland?"

"Oregon." His voice was deep and smooth.

"Where'd you move from?" I pointed to a stairwell on our right, and we headed down. Posters and banners for the winter formal were stuck to the red brick walls with sticky-tack, lacy snowflakes dotted around the signs scattered throughout the school. Though the building itself was absolutely ancient, it'd undergone a major renovation last summer. Now it boasted a mostly new and modernized interior.

"New York City."

"Whoa, that's a major change. Are you happy to be here or miserable?" It would've made me miserable. It'd suck to move during your senior year and leave all your friends and world behind.

He turned and looked at me, a wry twist to his lips. "What do you think?"

I raised an eyebrow and went down the stairs to the main level, then crossed the length of the school so we could access the basement. "Well, judging by the fact that I've yet to see you smile, and you look like you'd rather drive your bow through your forehead than be here, I'm gonna go with miserable."

A slight smile played at the corner of his mouth. "And we have a winner."

Walking from the basement landing and down a long hallway, we arrived at the music room. I led him up the tiered, industrial-carpeted stairs, weaving around empty chairs toward the back corner and into the orchestra's storage and practice room. The band kids had an identical room on the opposite side. The rooms were large with no windows and boasted storage spaces, ranging in size, lining the walls. The central area of each room was reserved for practicing. Mr. Woods would send us in here during class by section if there was a passage we needed extra work on. In our advanced orchestra we had five cellos, and we had to fit them into the three large cubbies assigned to our class's section, making it two to a cubby. Except mine; mine was the only cubby with room to spare.

Marshland boasted one of the largest and best music

programs in the state. There were even a few kids who trans-
ferred in for it. In my orchestra, I only knew of a handful
of violins who'd done that, but there were definitely more of
those kids in the band.

"Here, let me scoot mine over. You can slide yours in
beside it."

He stopped and rested his hands atop the shiny gray
surface, watching me. "You're a cellist?"

Holding my polished black case upright, I watched him
straighten and slip his cello into the open spot. His case
stood slightly taller than mine, which made sense; he was so
much taller than me, and cellos came in a variety of sizes.

"I am."

Stepping back, his chocolatey eyes twinkled as he looked
me over. "You any good?"

I popped my hip and smiled. "Section leader."

"Don't get too comfortable up in that first chair." He
leaned toward me and wet his lips. "You won't be there much
longer."

I raised a brow, my upper lip curling in distaste. "Excuse
me?"

"Back home, *I* was section leader. I plan on keeping that
position here. You've just been keeping the seat warm for me.
Thanks, Princess."

Jerk. I pursed my lips and laid on a sarcastic, saccharine
tone. "Wow, that was fast. Way to go, I already can't stand
you."

His brows rose as swiftly as the smirk appeared on his
face. "And yet I'm totally okay with that."

"Whatever you do, don't worry," I reached out and
patted his arm. "You'll get used to second chair in no time.
Everyone else does . . . *Princess*." I spun on my heel and left.

"Pippa, what are you doing in here?" Mr. Woods walked
through the door, carrying a stack of what appeared to be

freshly copied sheet music. His dark hair was streaked with unruly strands of gray that matched his beard. He looked as though he'd just rolled out of bed.

"Morning, Mr. Woods. I was just showing the new guy where he can put his cello." Internally, I laughed. If this Declan kid thought he'd take first chair from me, I'd show him exactly where he could shove his cello.

Hands tucked into his jean pockets, Declan caught up with me on the bottom step.

"Another cello, eh?" Woods smiled and glanced between us. "I wonder if you'll be any competition for Miss Pippa."

With a chuckle, I glanced at Declan. "Mr. Over-Inflated-Ego sure thinks he will be."

"Well, I hope you at least warned him." Mr. Woods smiled. "Pippa won't go down easily, she'll put up quite a battle. She's the principal cellist with the Oregon Youth Symphony, as well."

Declan peered down at me, his eyebrows lifted and he had a slight tilt to his lips. I couldn't tell if he was impressed or silently laughing at me, which was annoying as hell.

"When can I challenge her?" he asked, eyes on me as he spoke, before turning back to Woods for an answer.

"We don't do challenges here. It doesn't promote a unified orchestra if you're constantly battling each other. However, midyear I hold a round of optional challenges, but that's not until the first week of February."

"Got it." Declan rocked back on his heels.

"You two should get to class. I'll see you this afternoon." Mr. Woods went up the tiers to his office and shut the door behind him.

With a jump, I landed on the concrete floor and left. Declan padded softly behind me. I was anxious for sixth period—curious to hear just how good he was.

I zipped up the one flight of stairs then calmed my irritated stride until we were side by side. Silently, we walked past the office. The lady at the counter waved at me, and I lifted my hand in reply. Her daughter played the violin, and last year she and I'd performed a duet at a competition. Shannon and I had been complete opposites. She was tall, and I so wasn't. She was super slim, I was just average. She was tanned, I was pasty. I could go on and on. Next to her, I'd felt invisible.

Declan cleared his throat, drawing my attention. "So, how long have you been playing?"

"Since I was five. You?"

Taking his hand from his pocket, he rubbed the back of his head, ruffling his brown hair. "Four."

Of course.

We walked back up to the third floor. Ms. Peters's class was the very last door at the end of the hall. I pulled my lip balm from my pocket and ran it across my dry lips. From the corner of my eye, I noticed Declan watching me. What on Earth was he thinking?

Aside from his being arrogant and obnoxious, I didn't quite know what to make of him, and I didn't like it. He put me on edge.

Declan paused in front of the open doorway, gesturing for me to enter the classroom first. He followed close behind.

Quinn raised a slender brown brow at me as I slid into my seat. I just shrugged and shook my head.

"Declan, you've got a choice between the two open seats." Ms. Peters smiled.

A desk in the front row beside Phillip was empty, and so was the seat behind me. Declan nodded and walked past the option in the front row.

Undisrupted, Ms. Peters continued with her lesson on *The Scarlet Letter*. Going to the cupboard, she pulled out a worn copy and delivered it to Declan as she walked down the aisle. Her long, pale-blue chiffon scarf dragged over my desk.

"Alright, you need to have this finished by Friday. There will be a test, ladies and gentlemen. Use the last twenty minutes of class to read quietly." She made another lap around our desks before returning to her large oak one at the front of the room.

Noah reached over and tapped my shoulder. I looked up from the pages at him. With a stealthy movement, he lifted his phone and wiggled it, mouthing at me, *check your phone.*

My heart skipped a beat as I leaned down and grabbed my cell from my bag and held it under my desk. What could he want?

Noah: Want to study together on Thursday?

My lips parted. Well, that's definitely a first. In ten years of massive crushing and dreaming, Noah had never asked me to do anything with him. At least not alone.

Me: Sure.

I looked over at him and saw him reading my text. His eyes crinkled at the edges, and he turned around and gave me a thumbs-up. The tempo of my heart raced double-time as he put his phone in his pocket and turned his focus to doodling in his notebook, his blond hair slipping over his forehead.

I took a deep breath, trying to calm myself down. It didn't work. Excitement thrummed through me, filling my senses. Play it cool, that's what I had to do. This wasn't a big deal. It was studying, that's all.

It wasn't like Noah didn't already spend all of his free time at our house anyway. Despite living at the end of our street, he rarely went home. He practically lived with us. Dad always teased that he was an honorary Wyndham. So this really wouldn't be all that different, would it? When he and Phillip weren't at basketball practice or whatever afterschool sport was in season, they could usually be found hanging out on our couch, stuffing their faces.

But this time it *was* different. This time he was coming over to see me. Me! My fingers clutched the cuffs of my sweater, and I brought my fist up to cover my way too bright smile. I just barely managed to hold back the excited squeal that was dying to get out.

It's not a big deal.

Who was I kidding? It was a huge deal, colossal in fact.

CHAPTER *Two*

*Music expresses that which cannot be put into words and
that which cannot remain silent.*

—*Victor Hugo*

My final class of the day was orchestra, and I was
running late thanks to my history teacher. Rushing down the
polished concrete hallway and through the door, I skidded to
a halt when I saw Declan sitting in my chair, the first chair,
on the second tier.

Oh. Hell. No. This dude had messed up my day every
time he crossed my path. From English to chemistry, where
I'd gotten stuck as his lab partner. This was the final straw.
He was going down.

"All right, Mr. Brogan, would you mind playing a
passage from a piece you're working on? Let's make sure
you've been placed in the correct class." When Mr. Woods
spoke, the rest of the class went silent, no longer playing or
tuning.

"Not at all."

My shock having worn off, I regained my mobility
and wove through the violins and violas toward the prac-

tice room. The enemy's dark eyes flicked up to mine, a wry smile on his lips. I kept my face neutral, not wanting to give him even a moment of satisfaction while he quickly tuned. Although I tried to hide my irritation, the steam coming from my ears may have given it away.

Inside the practice room, I tossed my messenger bag near my cubby and pulled my case out. Laying it on the floor, I knelt and unpacked Francesca.

Yes, I named my cellos. And no, that's not weird. This one's named after my grandmother on my mother's side who's also a cellist. She's the reason I started playing in the first place. Although most people call her Frankie—Grandma that is, not my cello.

Adjusting my endpin, the metal post on the bottom, to the mark I'd made, I winced as a beautiful strain of music hit my ears.

Declan.

My eyes fluttered closed, and I listened. It was lovely. The tone rich and strong, his instrument sang under his finger-tips. Evidently, he knew what he was doing. This was bad.

Shit.

I inhaled sharply.

He's really good.

Cello in hand, I stepped through the doorway and watched. No music on my stand, he played the opening strains from Bach's "Cello Suite No. 1," arguably one of the most famous and well-recognized cello solos in the world. Chances were if you watched TV, you'd heard the tune. Declan played it perfectly and a little quicker than normal. It was clear he knew what he was doing.

When Declan finished, Mr. Woods smiled, his fingers steepled in front of his lips. "Lovely. Thank you, Mr. Brogan. I do believe you've been correctly placed. Would you and Miss Wyndham mind staying after class? I'd like a word with the two of you."

With a nod at Mr. Woods, I wondered where the hell I should sit. Thanks to the seat thief, I was lost. Silently, I fumed and headed to the back row of the section, mentally running through ways to get rid of the jerk. My stand-partner, Lucy, sat beside him. She was sweet, beautiful, and currently making cow eyes at Declan. The traitor.

I sat my black folder full of music down on the stand near an empty chair. The head was loose and flopped forward, dumping my music on the floor. That basically summed up my day. I even got the crappy music stand. Laying my cello on its side, I crouched down to pick up my scattered pages; taking a moment and closing my eyes, I slowly exhaled.

My life had been perfect before Declan showed up. He'd been here one freaking day and suddenly my world was a topsy turvy kind of unstable. Which was a huge problem for me because I thrived on stability. As I rubbed at my fore-head, I realized that everything I'd worked so hard for was now threatened. If I wanted to get into Goddards, the most selective and top music college in the nation, I *had* to stay section leader. And I wanted to study at Goddards more than anything. Anger boiled under my skin. This wannabe usurper wasn't going to take it away from me. No way in hell.

The rustling of papers reached my ears and permeated my consciousness. I opened my eyes to see Declan kneeling down beside me, gathering my scattered sheet music.

"You okay?" he asked as he handed over the messy pile of black and white pages, a smug smile on his lips.

I nodded and snatched it from him, stuffing it haphazardly in my folder. "Thank you. And yes, I'm fine; it's just been a long day. I'm tired."

When we stood, he grinned and dropped his Black Hole rockstop, a rubbery hockey-puck-looking thing the endpin sat in to keep the instrument from slipping, in front of the chair I'd been about to claim.

"Thanks for letting me borrow your chair, Princess." He studied the fingerboard of his instrument before looking back at me with a snicker. "It'll do just fine, when I take it from you."

My eyes narrowed as I closed the distance between us and looked up at him. "Let's get a couple things straight. First, you keep calling me Princess, and I'll snap your bow. Second, keep on dreaming there, City Rat. I know it's a good thing to have goals, but you can forget it. You're not gonna take my chair. But do enjoy the view from back here. I'll wave from first."

His eyes had a mischievous sparkle to them as he stepped back and watched me tuck my sleeve of music under my arm. I wasn't certain, but it seemed like he was enjoying my irritation. With a twirl, I navigated through my section, careful not trip on anyone else's endpin—that's the last thing I'd need, to faceplant in front of Mr. Arrogant.

"Alright kids, pull out the Holst piece." Mr. Woods rifled through his sheet music. "Jupiter" was by far my favorite of all the planet movements. We'd eventually be joining together with the advanced band to perform it.

"Declan, I want you on a first part. Just pull a chair on the end, next to Pippa. You can share with her until I get copies together for you."

I squeezed my eyes shut and blew out a heavy breath before I scooted toward Lucy, who'd slid down as far as she could. She straightened her stand and flashed Declan a winning smile. We were snug, which could prove tricky with string instruments. Hopefully we wouldn't impale each other with our bows.

Hmm, on second thought . . .

Declan plunked a chair down by mine, reaching up, he

maneuvered the stand so it sat between us. I angled my back toward Lucy, hating that his chair was technically in the section leader's spot.

I hung my bow from the lip of the stand so the hairs faced the ground. From my pocket, I pulled an elastic to secure my long hair. If I didn't, it'd tangle in the pegs or get in the way of my fingering, and when the music called for me to slide down the fingerboard, well, that wasn't pretty. And it hurt like a motherplucker too when you ripped out that much hair. Flipping my locks into a loose topknot, I looked at Declan, who was watching me. "What?"

He shook his head. "Nothing, you just missed a piece."

I followed his finger and noticed a dark auburn haze just to the side of my vision. Reaching, I secured it in place, grabbed my bow, and got into position as the first notes sounded. To my left, I heard Declan playing with ease.

Goosebumps spread in a wave over my skin. Playing in large groups always moved me. The music coursed through every facet of my body, leaving shivers in its wake. The way we worked together to make something so beautiful never failed to blow my mind.

After playing the piece once, we went back and worked on a few tricky passages. Then we waited while Woods worked with the violas, tuning them once more before they started. Only a few minutes left of class, we ran through it one last time before Mr. Woods lowered his baton. "Great job. Pack up, get outta here. I'll see you all tomorrow."

Declan stood and carried his cello up the tiers to the storage room. Following, I went to my case and sat beside him.

"I'm gonna go out on a limb here and guess that you're the Miss Wyndham who Mr. Woods wants to see after class with me, aren't you?" He loosened the hairs of his bow before securing it in the lid of his case and eyed me.

"Yup, that'd be me. Lucky, lucky me." I pulled the elastic holding my ponytail out and stuffed it back in my pocket. My hair tumbled over my shoulder, and I threw it back with a head toss. Fastening the velvet strap over the neck of my cello, I closed the lid. The bell rang as my last clasp clicked into place. Most of the other cellists left their instruments in the storage room, but I wanted mine with me. I had to practice, and I had other rehearsals and lessons that I needed it for, which meant I lugged it in every morning and back out every evening. Bag on my shoulder, I carried my cello to Mr. Woods's messy office, waiting for Declan to follow.

"Ah, Pippa, give me a second." Woods held up a finger and turned to rifle though his drawers of music. His office walls were lined with mismatched filing cabinets and stacks of paper. Unused instruments took up one corner. "Cello, cello, cello." He clicked his tongue and adjusted his wire-rimmed glasses on the bridge of his nose.

Declan stopped beside me, his hands resting atop his case, and checked his watch. It irritated me that he didn't leave his instrument at school like the others. Stupid, yes, but I still felt it.

"Aha! Here it is." Handing a piece of music to me and one to Declan, he said, "I've always thought this would be fantastic for you, Pippa."

The cover page read "Passacaglia" by Händel-Halvorsen. I flipped through it, intrigued. "Isn't this normally for a violin and cello?"

Mr. Woods nodded. "It is, but I saw a cello duo perform this piece, and it was amazing. When I came across the sheet music, I grabbed it. I've had other students attempt it, but I have a feeling the two of you could really make it come to life."

Declan stopped flipping through the pages and leveled a look at Mr. Woods. "You want *us* to duet?"

"From what I can tell, you play almost as well as Miss Wyndham. And you're expected to do two pieces for Solo and Ensemble. Normally that'd be in spring, but this year they're holding it in early February. It's a large percentage of your grade. You need a solo, and this could work as your ensemble piece."

I started to hand the pages back. "I'm already doing a duet with Lucy."

"Lucy's decided to quit orchestra after winter break. It interfered with her cheer schedule. I'm surprised she didn't tell you." Mr. Woods scratched his bushy beard.

"Me, too." I pulled my arm back. She and I had sat beside each other for years. It'd be weird not having her there. Maybe this was why she'd been stalled on picking a piece. I glanced around; the music room was now empty save for the three of us. God, I really didn't want to duet with *him*.

"I think it's going to be brilliant." Mr. Woods smiled and crossed his arms over his tacky sweater–clad chest.

Declan didn't say anything. With a nod, he swung his cello onto his back and left.

"Thanks, Mr. Woods." I waved and followed after Declan, whose long strides made it difficult to catch up. How damn tall was he anyway? "Declan, wait up."

Sighing, he stopped halfway past the student parking lot. "Do you need something?"

Cello over my shoulder, I put my hands on my hips, grumpy about the whole day and now annoyed with his sudden attitude. "Look, I get it. Getting stuck together as lab partners in chemistry was bad enough. I don't want to do this duet with you anymore than you do. But we should figure out when we're going to practice."

He ran a hand through his unruly hair, looking annoyed. "Can we do this tomorrow? We have 'til February, you know.

Plus, I'm gonna miss my bus if I don't hurry." One of his arms lifted in gesture to the bus stop on the main road and dropped back down.

I looked toward the street and saw the familiar white and blue city chariot loading a line of students. "Fine, whatever."

Turning on my heel, I walked over a patch of grass to my black Honda Pilot. Opening the back hatch, I slid my case along the gray carpet and slammed it shut. At my car door, I stopped and watched Declan board his ride.

This is gonna be a long year. A really long and probably miserable year.

In my seat, I took a deep breath and slid my key in the ignition. It was amazing that I hadn't hyperventilated yet with all the heavy breathing I'd been doing. My phone chimed from my bag, when I pulled it out there was a new text.

> Quinn: You-know-who ran into Jenna and me after school. He was wondering where you were. :D

I knew exactly who she meant. And a flutter of delight settled in my stomach. Finally something to actually smile about.

> Me: Really?

Warm fuzzies enveloped me. Noah was probably at my house right now. It was a Monday, which meant no practice tonight.

> Quinn: Yup! Maybe it's a sign, lol. He wants you. ;P

> Me: Right, a sign you're insane. On my way home. Later.

I tossed my phone in the leather passenger-seat and took off, grateful this horrible day was finally ending. At the stop sign to the parking lot, I did a mini happy dance in my seat. No doubt a healthy dose of Noah in my near future would make everything infinitely better. He could probably take my mind off the battle I had on my hands, at least for a little while.

CHAPTER *Three*

Music can name the unnameable and
communicate the unknowable.

—Leonard Bernstein

I stood at the kitchen sink drying the dishes before sliding them into the cabinets while watching Noah and my brother through the window. They were playing basketball in the driveway. The best part? Noah had taken his shirt off, despite the chill in the air.

Watching as he did a jump shot, I bit my lip. Seriously, could he get any hotter? Without looking, I put the plate away, banging it into the edge of the white cabinet and nearly dropping it.

"Sweetheart, would you pop outside and ask Noah if he's staying for dinner?" Mom leaned into the kitchen from the living room doorway. Her last piano student must've just left. Dark auburn hair fell over her shoulders, and I smiled. No matter how busy she was or what was going on around her, she always looked so put together.

With a nod, I turned my focus back to my task and slid a glass home. "What are we having?"

"Lasagna and garlic bread."

"Let me finish here, and I'll go ask." I tucked the last cups away and sorted the silverware. Sighing, I gave a longing glance out the window. If only.

"You ever going to tell him?" Mom asked, peeking in the oven and checking on the bubbling lasagna.

My stomach lurched and I turned to face her, eyes wide with feigned innocence. "Tell who what?"

Her eyebrows rose. "Oh, I don't know. Maybe tell Noah that you think he's just the bee's knees." She finished with a silly, lovesick look on her face, teasing me.

"You're such a dork." I shook my head. "And no. I don't plan on outing myself to him anytime soon. It'd be too weird. Maybe someday." I shrugged. "When Phillip wouldn't flip out." I tossed my dishrag down and headed for the back door.

"Oh, hey, tell Phillip I expect him to actually clean the bathrooms tonight. He can't keep putting it off."

"Will do." I bounded down the back steps onto the grass. We lived in an old two-story craftsman home surrounded by trees. I loved it here. All the attention to detail in the woodworking made it homey. I rounded the corner to our detached garage. Laughter met my ears as I spied them.

"Hey, Noah?"

He clutched the ball between his hands and turned to me. "What's up?"

"Mom wants to know if you're eating here tonight—it's lasagna." I tucked my hands up my sleeves, the chill biting through my sweater. I didn't know how he could go shirt-less—not that I was complaining.

Smacking the ball, and a little out of breath, he said, "Sure, why not? My dad's out of town and Mom's probably got a meeting."

"'Kay, I'll tell her." I twirled, intending to dart back into the house then stopped. "Oh, Phillip, Mom also said you better do the bathrooms tonight."

He scrunched his face in distaste. "I'll trade you for dishes?"

"No way." I laughed and turned to leave.

"Hey, Pips?" Noah called.

"Yeah?"

He tossed the ball to Phillip and walked over to me. "Why don't you come play with us?" He clapped his hands once then rubbed them together, looking like he was excited for something.

"Me? Uh, yeah, so not athletic, in case you've missed that all these years." I backed away from him with a scoff.

Advancing on me, he grabbed my hand and pulled me to the driveway. "Come on, you can be on my team."

I opened my mouth to protest, but nothing came out. First him wanting to study with me and now this? What the hell was going on? Whatever it was, I'd take it.

"She's not lying. All the athletic ability came to me." Phillip laughed and held the basketball between his arm and hip. "I don't think you even got a drop of it." He tugged his red tee away from his sweaty chest, fanning it a couple times.

"True, but I got all the brains, talent, and looks instead." I grinned sweetly as he squinted his eyes and stuck out his tongue. "See? Proof." I looked at Noah and gestured at the face Phillip was making.

"She has a point, man." Noah chuckled and stole the ball from Phillip's grasp. "Come on, how about a quick game of H-O-R-S-E?"

I shook my head as Noah bounced the ball. "No, seriously, sports aren't my thing."

"We'll go easy on you." He tossed the ball to me.

Inhaling, I stared at it, feeling the bumpy texture under my fingertips. "Super quick." I threw the ball back at him.

Noah caught it, got close to the basket, and tossed the ball in with a soft snick of the net. "Your turn." He passed it back to me.

My feet stood firmly planted where his had just been. I glanced over at Phillip standing near the ivy-covered fence, arms crossed and smiling like I was great entertainment.

Deep breath, I held the ball with both hands at my chest, elbows out, and pushed off. The ball hit the chipped rim and bounced off, banging against the garage door. "*H*, this'll be over quickly."

Phillip caught the ball and walked over to take his turn, snickering.

"Hang on, man." Noah pressed a hand to Phillip's chest before grabbing the ball. "That was a warm-up. We've been out here playing for a while, so she deserves at least a warm-up shot."

He handed the ball back to me, his fingers grazing mine. I shivered at the realization of just how close Noah's bare chest was to me.

"It's not going to help." Phillip took a step back. "She doesn't even know how to hold the ball."

I glared at my brother. "I'd like to see either of you hold a cello."

"Do you mind if I give you a couple pointers?" Noah moved closer.

"Sure." I spun the ball between my fingers.

"First, you've got to widen your stance and bend your knees." He gestured to my feet as he walked to stand behind me.

Warm hands pressed against my shoulders and slid down the length of my arms, grasping just above my wrists. My eyes widened. His touch made it nearly impossible to breathe. His hands on me, and his bare chest pressed into my back made my mind swirl.

What exactly was I doing again?

"Bring your hands up higher, no shooting from the chest. Use this hand to follow through."

Words. I knew he said them, I just couldn't focus on them. Thank God Noah couldn't see my face right now. Flames of shyness licked at my pale cheeks, staining them crimson. It was bad enough Phillip had a perfect view of it all. The wry look on his face told me just how funny he thought this was.

"Jump when you take your shot; that should help," Noah added.

I mutely nodded. With him so close, my voice had vanished.

"You ready?" His mouth was mere inches from my ear.

When I shook my head yes, he released his hold on me and stepped back.

Eyes clenched shut, I said a quick prayer and hoped I wouldn't make a fool of myself.

Sucking in a deep breath, I looked up and followed his instructions. With a little jump, I released the ball. It sailed from my fingertips, hit the backboard, bounced on the metal rim, and spun around the ring before dropping through.

My mouth popped open. "Did you see that? I did it!"

"That was awesome." Noah swept me into a hug.

I gasped with surprise.

"That was a total fluke." Phillip roughly patted Noah on the back and pulled him away from me, raising an eyebrow at him. "My turn." Phillip retrieved the ball.

Noah and I stood to the side.

"Pips, can I get your help?" Mom's voice called from the kitchen window.

I tucked my hands in my jean pockets. "Sure, Mom."

"Oh, and boys," Mom added, "get to a stopping point and come in and set the table."

Phillip groaned. Noah just nodded and grabbed the ball from my brother's hands with a laugh.

"Well, gentlemen, this is me leaving on a high note." I waved before jogging for the door.

"Would you mind washing and chopping the veggies for a salad?" Mom asked when I got inside. She looked like she'd just finished loading her dirty cooking dishes into the washer.

I stood again at our white farmhouse sink under the window, washing, peeling, and slicing an English cucumber all while keeping an eye on the guys.

"I take it lover boy will be joining us?"

"Yup." I didn't have to look at her to know she was smiling. It was threaded all through her voice.

Outside, Noah and Phillip had stopped playing and looked like they were having a heated discussion. My brother held the ball on his hip again and gestured to the house, his face screwed up.

What had happened since I left?

Mom pulled the lasagna from the stainless wall oven as I slid the sliced cucumbers into the salad bowl.

"Go get the boys." She pulled her cell from her pocket. Calling Dad was my guess. He'd been putting in a lot of late hours at the office recently. He was the creative director for an ad agency downtown. They'd recently landed a huge account, and he'd been working overtime. Mom understood, but that didn't mean she was happy about it.

Hopping down a couple of the back steps, I called out, "Dinner's ready, come inside."

Phillip tossed the ball into the grass and hustled over to me. I watched it roll until it stopped under the bush that in the spring would be covered in little pink blossoms. It made the yard smell divine.

Noah walked halfway toward us and stopped. "Phillip,

you sure you're cool with me staying?"

I looked at my brother. He'd frozen and looked at the ground, his shoulders rolling forward.

"Dude, I don't want to talk about it. I want no details. Zero. Got it?" Phillip turned and gave Noah a pointed look.

"You guys okay?" I asked, confused.

Phillip looped his arm over my shoulder. He stood at least a head taller than me. I hated it almost as much as I hated him being born first. Three minutes makes a big difference when it comes to the family hierarchy.

"We're good. No worries, Pipster." Phillip reached up and ruffled the top of my head, messing my hair. He only did it because he knew how much I hated it. I smacked his hand away as he said, "Come on, Noah."

Noah flanked my other side and smiled when I looked at him. His chin, covered in light blond stubble, had a faint cleft in it. I thought it made him look manly.

At the circular table nestled into the eating nook of our kitchen, I sat beside Mom. Before my lifelong crush could slide in next to me, Phillip took his spot. The scent of the cold air and dry leaves radiated off both the boys. It made me thankful for our warm house.

"Thanks for having me for dinner, Mrs. W." Noah passed the salad bowl over Phillip to me.

"Of course. Your mom's fed Phillip more times that I can count. You're like another son." She smiled at him, her green eyes twinkling. "How was school?" Mom asked.

Phillip and Noah both answered positively.

I more or less grunted.

"Pippa?" Mom turned to me, a bite of lasagna suspended en route to her lips.

Shrugging, I said, "It's nothing."

"What happened?"

"There's a new kid." I looked up at her and sighed.

Mom's brows lowered. "And that's bad?"

"He's a cellist. And he's good . . . really good. Mr. Woods wants us to do a duet for Solo and Ensemble."

"That sounds nice." Her head bobbed as if she thought this sounded like a positive thing. "I'm not seeing why you're so unhappy."

"The jerk told me he was going to take first chair from me. Then when I tried to talk to him about practicing our new duet, he didn't seem to care. He's also my new chem lab partner, as well as being in my English class. It's like I can't escape him. He was everywhere today and I just . . . I don't like him." I picked at my lasagna. "And he calls me Princess, which I *hate*."

"You're talking about that dark-haired guy that came in with Ms. Peters this morning, right?" Noah sipped his water.

I nodded.

"He didn't look happy to be here," Noah observed.

Phillip popped a large forkful of lasagna into his mouth. "I didn't really pay much attention to him."

"Shocker there." I picked through my salad and filled my fork with cucumbers and swirled them in a puddle of Italian dressing. "He's just a cocky, egotistical jerk."

"I hope you'll be nice to him, Pippa. Make him feel welcome. He's got to be lonely and pissed off that he had to move his senior year. I expect you to be kind, even if he does try to take your chair."

Screwing up my face in distaste, I said, "I'll tolerate him and be polite, but if he thinks he's stealing my chair, I'll kick his ass back to New York."

Mom didn't like my answer. Her scowl suggested she didn't like my language either. "You don't have to like him, but you do have to behave like a Wyndham. Kindness is essential in this world, especially when there's so little of it left. And don't swear, young lady."

"I know, Mom." I should've felt at least a little remorse for my irritation with Declan. I knew he was going through a lot. But honestly, I didn't really care. My seat, no, my *life* was at stake here.

I wouldn't give up easily.

Declan had a fight on his hands.

CHAPTER *Four*

What is best in music is not to be found in the notes.

—*Gustav Mahler*

At my locker, I slumped against the metal door and watched Noah flirt with the head cheerleader, Sydney. She was cute, nice, and entirely too perky for this early in the morning. Laughing, she put her hand on his arm. Her brown ponytail bounced against her tight, green tee.

"Look away, it's too painful." Quinn arrived, blocking my view with her infectious smile. Lexi was at her side. They'd gotten chummy years ago when Quinn and I had been on the outs. Usually she'd only pop up whenever we weren't talking, which made me curious why she was here now. She was basically Quinn's backup BFF. One thing was certain about Lexi, she wasn't my friend. At all. She made that very clear whenever she was near me. Even the sneer she wore whenever we made eye contact suggested she'd rather I get hit by a bus than share the same air with me.

"You're right. I know." I ignored Lexi's perma-scowl and turned to finish unloading my bag, then reloaded it with the notebooks for my first two classes, English and chemistry.

"Morning, ladies." Jenna sidled up to me. We'd been friends almost as long as Quinn and I had.

"Morning," I said in unison with the other two.

Quinn entered the combo to her locker, which happened to be right next to mine. "So, any prospects for Winter Formal?"

I laughed. "No. You?"

Winter Formal was the second weekend in November. Just four weeks left to score a date.

"In my dreams, Phillip's asked me numerous times." She stuffed her worn bag in the bottom, grabbed a notebook, and shut the door with a metallic clank. "In real life, no one's asked."

Lexi crossed her arms over her chest. "I already got asked, but I told them no. I know someone better will ask me."

I glanced at Jenna, who just rolled her eyes. We'd known each other since the fourth grade. She and I always seemed to find ourselves on the same page, which was oftentimes a refreshing change of pace from Quinn. Jenna and I'd also never had a falling out. Our friendship was easy.

"Well," I said as I looked to Quinn, not sure how to reply to Lexi. "If we don't have dates, we'll just go together." I closed my locker and turned, smiling at her and Jenna.

"Deal," Jenna said with a nod.

Quinn grinned, her navy framed glasses sliding down her small nose. "You'd be way more fun than any guy would be."

"You know it." I looped my arm with hers and laughed.

Down the hall, Declan sauntered toward our first class. I slowed my gait, not wanting to deal with him today.

"What are your thoughts on the new guy?" Quinn's multicolored rubber bracelets slid down her arm as she pushed her glasses back up with a finger.

"He's competition."

Jenna looked in the direction we were all staring. "What new guy?"

"That one." Quinn pointed him out.

"The hot one." Lexi's eyebrow raised, and she fanned herself.

"God, is he ever." Quinn nodded at Lexi. "And Pips, you'll just have to show him not to mess with such a badass cello player as yourself."

"That's my plan."

The warning bell rang and Lexi leaned in to whisper something in Quinn's ear. She then darted off down the hallway without another word.

"See you guys later." Jenna waved, her blonde curls bouncing against her shoulders.

I released Quinn's arm before entering Ms. Peters's classroom. Posters of literature's greats lined the walls, with their faces and quotes. But they weren't what I was looking at. Declan's eyes met mine as I walked to my seat. He inclined his head in greeting.

Ignoring him, I sat at my desk. His eyes were burning a hole through the back of my skull, I swear. I glanced at Noah, who winked at me, making me smile. I loved it when he did that.

"Morning, Pippa," Declan's deep voice rumbled from behind me.

I leaned over and grabbed my notebook and pen from my bag. As I sat back up, I briefly met his stare before I faced the front. "Morning."

From the corner of my eye I could see Noah sizing Declan up.

Declan's warm breath hit my ear, startling me. "Did you have a chance to look over that duet piece?"

"Nope," I threw over my shoulder dismissively. I opened

my copy of *The Scarlet Letter*, hoping my reading would ward off more questions from him. Last night, I'd decided to be polite but only that. We would never be friends, and I was more than okay with that.

Ms. Peters came in, heels clicking, and stood before the whiteboard. Her presence ensured I wouldn't have to deal with any conversations Mr. Obnoxious might try to start.

When the bell rang, signaling the end of first period, I stuffed my book into my bag and stood.

As Quinn and I reached the hallway, Phillip stopped me.

"Hey, Pips, can you give me a ride tonight after practice?" My brother adjusted the backpack on his shoulder, giving me his puppy dog eyes. He'd bought his car with money made from his summer job. It wasn't much to look at, but it was his. Which, apparently, was important to him. Then again, he never had shared all that well. By default, I got the car Mom and Dad had intended for us both to use. I had no complaints whatsoever.

"What happened to your car?" I asked as Declan slipped around me. He turned to watch me before walking off.

"Nothing. I'm just letting Mike borrow it. He's got a shift at Oaks right after practice and couldn't get a ride. He was gonna skip, but I told him he could take my wheels and swing it by the house later."

Mike worked at Quinn's mom's restaurant, The Live Oak Grill. She'd bought it a year after her husband's death and business had been steadily booming.

"Um, I wasn't planning on staying after school. Why can't Noah give you a lift?"

He jutted a thumb toward Noah, who was standing right next to him. "Turdbucket here has an appointment or something."

"An interview," Noah clarified.

I looked between them and nodded as Celeste, another

cellist, slid past me and smiled. I returned the gesture and said, "Fine, I suppose I could. Why not?"

"Thanks, you're a peach. Best sister ever."

I shook my head in amusement and turned away. The four of us walked in the direction Declan had just gone.

"Do either of you have Winter Formal dates?" Noah asked, holding onto the black strap of his book bag that crossed his chest. The gray fabric of his tee stretched taut across his well-defined pec muscles.

My mind flashed to him yesterday, shirtless in my driveway. Wait, what had he just asked?

Quinn saved me and answered for us. "Unless you count each other, nope, not yet. Who'd you ask?"

The tips of my Converse caught my attention. I didn't want to hear who the lucky girl was. Probably some cheer-leader, like he usually asked.

"No one yet."

Really? I looked up at him, eyes wide.

"What?" Quinn shook her head and stared. "I'd have thought you'd have something lined up a long time ago."

He shrugged. "Wasn't sure who to ask this year. It's our senior year, I've got to make this one count."

My brother rolled his eyes and looked down the hall like he no longer wanted anything to do with this conversation.

"Well, Captain Basketball." Quinn had called Noah that since he'd gotten the position last year. "Something tells me no matter who you ask, they'll say yes."

We stopped at the stairwell, Phillip, Quinn, and Noah were going straight, I was heading down a flight. "I'll catch you guys later."

As I stepped away, I heard Quinn ask Noah, "Come on, you really have no idea who you want to go with?"

Unfortunately, I couldn't hear his reply. Going with Noah would be a dream come true. But as I lived in the real world, I knew it could never happen. I didn't run in his crowd. He was jock, and I was an orchestra dork and way more academic than he was. It certainly didn't stop a girl from dreaming though.

I slipped into the chem lab just as the bell rang.

"Cutting it close, Miss Wyndham."

"Sorry, Ms. Pollock." I sat beside Declan at our table. In front of us sat a worksheet and instructions for our lab experiment along with several transparent cups filled with clear liquids. Laying next to it were some pH strips and a color chart showing different levels of acidity.

"Alright class, today we're going to do an easy experiment on acids and bases." Ms. Pollock took a seat on the long table in the front of the room. She ran through her lecture, then gave us instructions. Our job was to test the liquids' pH and write our findings about each.

I grabbed one of the worksheets and wrote my name at the top, then slid Declan's to him. "Which one should we do first?"

Grabbing the first cup, he took a sniff. "Ammonia, yuck."

I picked up the second glass. I didn't need to get it too close before I knew what it was. "Vinegar."

The third fluid didn't have a smell.

"And water." Declan leaned over his paper and wrote a heading for each glass in the blank space. He wrote in an impatient chicken scratch that reminded me of most boys I knew.

I picked up a pH strip and dunked it in the ammonia. It immediately turned blue.

"You want to practice after school today?" Declan asked as he jotted down the results.

"Not sure." The morning sun was shining over the tree-tops and into the windows that ran the length of the class-room. I enjoyed the warmth of it on my back.

"Do you have other plans?" he asked, dipping a new strip into the vinegar.

I tapped the eraser of my pencil against my lip, watching his long fingers pull out the now red indicator. "I've got to give someone a ride after basketball practice."

"I didn't peg you as the basketball playing type." He studied me, his mouth slightly open.

Shaking my head, I chuckled. "No, I'm not on the team. That'd be a disaster."

"Well, why don't we get some rehearsing in while you wait for them?"

I finished writing our findings for the vinegar on my sheet and turned to him. "Um, I was actually thinking of watching practice."

His face scrunched up, making his brown eyes sparkle with a mischievous glint. "Ugh, how boring."

"Not boring." My brows drew together in irritation. Although, even I had to admit it was only entertaining if Noah was there.

"What's so boring, Pippa?" Ms. Pollock stopped, looking down at us over her long thin nose, unamused.

"Oh, uh, nothing, Ms. P." I smiled up at her. "I said, 'not boring.'"

Hands clasped behind her back, she stared at me. "How about a little less talking and more working?"

As she walked off, I turned to Declan, who, judging by the amused look on his face, had enjoyed my discomfort a little too much.

"Was that fun for you?" I whispered.

He nodded. "Little bit, yeah."

I quietly wrote my paragraph and sat there wishing he'd just disappear. Why did he even have to show up in the first place?

"So, what about practicing?" Declan leaned toward me

and kept his voice low.

"Don't you have a bus to catch?"

An entertained smile spread across his lips, one side hitching higher than the other. Grudgingly, I admitted he had a nice smile. His bottom lip was also fuller than the top. I only noticed because he'd caught it between his teeth.

"There's always a later bus."

"Wow, yesterday you made it sound like your bus was the only one that stopped there. Ever." I slipped the last test strip into the water.

"Well, if I miss my bus, I'm sure you could give me a ride. You do that, right?"

"What?"

"You're giving someone a ride tonight, so why not me?"

I sniffed a whispered laugh and pulled the strip out. "Um, because last time I checked, you weren't my brother. Or have I missed a really big announcement? Are we actually triplets?"

Declan's cheeks pinked up to his ears. "Ah, your brother." He softly chuckled. "Wait, are you a twin?"

I nodded.

Ms. Pollock clapped her hands. "Alright, class, put your papers on the front desk, clean your stations, and let's pack it up."

Declan held out his hand for my paper. I handed it over and watched as he walked it up. He had a similar build to Noah: tall and slender, yet muscular. He turned, his eyes meeting mine and I quickly averted my gaze, focusing on packing my bag. I was glad I wouldn't have to see him again until sixth period.

Apparently I wasn't that lucky. The next time I ran into Declan was at lunch. Quinn, Jenna, and I sat in the hall by our lockers as he sauntered by. Chatting his ear off was Quinn's backup BFF, Lexi. She played the clarinet in the band, and I'd heard she was actually pretty good. I wondered how they met. Laughing, she placed a hand on his forearm.

Declan's eyes darted to me, then away. Lexi had dated the drum major of the marching band all last year. There were quite a few stories of things they'd done in the band storage room when Mr. Woods wasn't paying attention. Whether they were true or not, I couldn't say. Nor did I care.

Something about seeing her with him annoyed me, which irritated me even further.

"Hey." Lexi waved at the three of us, her eyes slivering at the edges.

Declan nodded, twisting and untwisting the cap of his water bottle. They walked on and I turned to watch until they hit the stairwell and started going down.

"She's trying to stake her territory early." Quinn shrugged, her light brown hair slipping over her shoulder. "Gotta give her props for going after what she wants."

"You really think she's interested?" I glanced back to where they'd just disappeared, the light coming through the windows bounced off the white walls and made me squint.

"Uh, duh! He's hot. I think a lot of girls will try and take a whack at him." Jenna took a bite of her sandwich and looked longingly down the hall. A chunk of dark hair fell over her eyes, but she didn't bother to move it.

"Really?" I asked and popped a chip in my mouth.

Quinn's eyes widened. "Oh yeah."

♪

Inside the storage room I grabbed my cello from its cubby and sat it on the floor and popped open the case. Declan was already in there doing the same. His black hoodie was zipped up, but at the collar I could see the green of his t-shirt underneath.

He smiled at me. "You know, you never gave me an

answer."

"About what?" I set my bow aside and lifted my cello.

"Practicing after school." Standing, he tightened the hair on his bow.

I held onto Francesca and lowered the lid of my case. Still kneeling, I sat back on my heels and looked up at him. "I'll be here, so I guess we could start working on it."

"Great." He nodded and went to take his seat as I stood and followed.

"Ah, Declan. I have your music." Mr. Woods handed him a large black folder. In the bottom right corner, in silver letters, it read *Marshland High School*, just like they all did.

"Thanks." He tucked it under the arm holding his cello.

"Why don't you sit on the other side of Lucy?" Mr. Woods gestured to where she sat, tuning to the note the first chair violin was playing.

We each took a seat next to her. She turned to greet him, undoubtedly with an eager grin on her lips. I twisted my hair up and examined my fingernails to check their length. If they grew too long, they'd break when I'd strike the fingerboard and would be snaggly and tender the rest of the day.

Mr. Woods went to the podium and sorted through his pile of sheet music. "Let's start with some Shostakovich today."

Music opened and ready, I watched for Mr. Woods's signal. When his baton hit the first beat after his countdown, we played. The music swirled around the room and crashed over me.

There was nothing better than this, right here.

We ran through it, stopping to work on a section for the basses. As we played again I peeked at Declan a few times. His face looked intense—he was really into it.

After working through a couple more pieces, Mr. Woods set his baton down and closed his music. "Alright, pack it up.

Great rehearsal."

I glanced at Lucy as she grabbed her music and stood. Declan's eyes caught my gaze, and I turned away to fiddle with the loose sheets in my folder and pull out our new duet.

Practicing was definitely a more productive way to spend my time rather than ogling Noah for the next two hours. Pulling out my phone, I texted Phillip and told him to meet me in the music room after practice.

The room cleared out quickly. Mr. Woods finished writing something on a sticky and attached it to the piece we'd just worked on. Stepping down from his podium, he glanced at the music on my stand. "You two practicing? Glad to see it. Use the room for as long as you need. I'll be here a few more hours."

"Okay, thanks." I turned toward Declan.

"You ready?" he asked and shifted into the chair next to me, slipping his music onto the stand Lucy had just left behind.

I nodded.

He leaned over, a wry smile on his lips. "I'm assuming you want first."

Keeping my expression passive, I gave a nonchalant shrug. "Why don't you take it? You should get a chance to be first at something at least once this year."

A deep laugh left his throat. "Oh, well in that case, you might want to keep it. I'll be taking first chair from you, Princess. Don't worry about me."

"Ha, good luck with that." I adjusted my cello and leaned it against my shoulder. "Both parts are equally challenging; take your pick." Sitting straighter, I tried to act like I didn't care and that him calling me Princess hadn't just prickled every nerve in my body. Really, I did want first. I just didn't want him to know it. Actually, scratch that. What I *really* wanted was for him to vanish into thin air.

"Fine, I'll take second." The corners of his lips curled up, and he looked away from me.

Despite being a gigantic pain in my ass, I couldn't deny Quinn, Jenna, and Lexi were kind of right about him being cute. He did have a great smile, but that's all I'd concede.

I grinned and shook my head. "Let's take it slow. I haven't run through it yet."

"Neither have I."

After counting us in, our instruments harmonized beautifully. My eyes followed along the sheet music, goosebumps covering my skin as a shiver shot through me. We both made mistakes, but we stayed in sync to the end.

"That wasn't bad." Declan flashed me another one of his crooked grins.

"Nice job, guys." Mr. Woods leaned from his office and gave us two thumbs-up. "You'll have that nice and polished by February."

"Let's go over this section again?" Declan pointed with the tip of his bow to the page.

I nodded. As our cellos sang in unison, I couldn't stop the delighted smile from filling my face. I was actually having fun. I'd never done a duet with someone so on my level before.

We stayed and practiced until Phillip found us. Dropping his bag by the door, he sat on the bottom step and listened as we finished a tough passage. When we stopped, Declan looked over at Phillip, unsmiling and quiet.

"Hey, Phillip." I waved with my bow. "Give me a sec and I'll go pack up."

"No worries." Phillip scratched his scruffy cheek and rested his elbows on his bare legs, still in shorts from his practice.

I hurried into the storage room and opened my case. I slipped Francesca inside as Declan knelt beside me.

"You know, you're really not half bad." He secured the neck of his cello.

One brow lifted as I looked over at him, loosening the hair on my bow, then wiping it with a soft cloth to remove any residual rosin. "Um, thanks, I think."

His hands paused on his clasps. "That was intended as a compliment."

My case secured, I stood and slung my messenger bag over my shoulder before slipping my cello on my back. "Okay, then I'll concede that you don't suck as much as I had hoped you would."

"Touché." He stood looking pleased, his accompanying laugh rich and warm.

I bounded down the wide steps toward Phillip, giddiness coursing through me. "You ready?"

"Let's go." Phillip grabbed his bag and led the way. Declan followed after us.

When we reached the nearly empty parking lot, Declan continued on for the bus stop, past the tall naked maple tree. "See you tomorrow." He waved and tucked his hands in his black leather jacket.

"Bye." My breath curled steamily in the evening air, illuminated by the parking lot lights.

Phillip and I got in the SUV, the heater still on full blast from this morning. Only now it was shooting freezing air at us. With a push of a button, I turned it off.

"You know, you didn't even introduce me to the new guy."

"Oh please, he's in our English class. Besides, I'm sure there'll be a next time. We're bound to be practicing and studying together a lot." My nose wrinkled at the unpleasant thought.

"You guys sounded really good." His seatbelt slid home with a click. "Does he play as well as you?"

Sighing, I didn't know how to answer, so I shrugged and grunted. Declan was good, really good. But stacked up against each other, which one of us would come out on top?

If I wanted the future I'd painstakingly planned out, it better be me. Goddards didn't accept second best.

CHAPTER *Five*

I've found that no matter what life throws at me, music softens the blow.

—*Bryce Anderson*

The short drive to the school did nothing to warm my car from the overnight chill. Not ready to face the day, I sat idling in the parking lot, hands to the heater vent, urging it to get warm. Today was Thursday. That meant Noah was coming over to study for our English test. My pulse raced at the thought of Noah and I together, *just* us.

A quick peek at the empty bus stop, and I shook my head at my silliness. Killing the engine, I got out and pulled my cello from the hatch.

Francesca on my back, I zipped up my black fleece jacket, wishing I'd grabbed my heavier coat. The sound of hydraulic brakes from the city bus hit my ears. Smiling, I didn't stop. I watched as two underclassmen crossed my path heading for the side doors. They were laughing and talking loudly, reminding me of Quinn and me.

"Morning, Pippa." Declan caught up easily and slowed his long stride to walk beside me.

"Morning." We took a few steps in silence before my curiosity got the better of me. "So, why the city bus and not a school bus?"

His shoulders lifted. "Because I'd rather be hit by an actual bus than have to ride a school bus."

"Okay then." I nodded, smiling. "So do you have to pay a fare for your case?"

Laughing, he looked straight ahead. "Amazingly, no."

"Good to know; my baby's never ridden public transit." I giggled, then added, "Only the best for her."

"Ah, so she's high maintenance—just like you, Princess."

I scoffed, still hating his nickname for me. "I am *not* high maintenance."

At the double crimson-colored doors, he pulled one open and waited for me to pass through. I looked up and offered a small smile to convey my appreciation. We walked down a flight of stairs side by side. The halls down in the bowels of the school had few students milling about this early.

In the music room we walked up the four tiers and saw Lexi coming out of the band storage room. She stopped in front of us, leering at Declan. "Hey, Pippa. Morning, Declan, I'll see *you* in trig." She wiggled her fingers in a wave as she took a step toward the exit.

So that's how they knew each other.

"Yeah, see ya," Declan answered.

With a wink, she bounced through the doors.

I glanced back in time to see her turn and check Declan out when he wasn't looking. Shaking my head, I flipped back around. Declan had almost made it to our storage room, but I quickly caught up to him. Laughing, I slung my cello off my back.

"What's so funny?" He reached out and held his cello steady as I slid mine in.

"Nothing." I shook my head. I didn't have an explanation for it, but after our practice last night, something had subtly changed. I was a smidgen more comfortable around him. Don't get me wrong. He was still the enemy, and we weren't even close to being friends. But truthfully, I think it was our constant bickering that had altered things.

"Then why are you laughing, Princess?" He crossed his arms and watched me.

"Seriously, stop with the nickname already." My request only made him grin. "How did you not pick up on that?" I gestured behind me with a thumb.

His brow scrunched in confusion. "I have no clue what you're talking about."

"Lexi's totally crushing on you."

With a wave of his hand, he brushed my comment off. "I don't think so. It's called being friendly." With a sardonic smirk on his face, he added, "You should try it sometime."

I pushed his shoulder. "Ha ha. And no, it's called flirting." He followed me out, our footsteps muffled by the gray carpeting. At his scoff, I said, "You can believe whatever you want, but I've known Lexi since first grade. She likes you." Smug smile on my face, I pushed the door open with my hip.

Declan rolled his eyes and shook his head. "You need to stop by your locker?"

I nodded, allowing the change of subject. "You?"

"Nope, I've got everything with me." He held onto the strap of his black backpack looped over one shoulder, and tucked his other hand into the pocket of his jeans.

At my locker, Declan waited patiently while I shuffled my books from my bag and grabbed the stuff I'd need to replace it.

"Hey, Pips." Quinn appeared, pushing her glasses up her small nose. Craning her head back, she looked up at Declan.

Smiling, she added, "Hey, Dec."

"Morning, Quinn." He grinned as he peered down at her.

Last night I'd called Quinn and gushed about our practice and bemoaned how good a player he was.

"Heard your practice went well last night."

Declan nodded and leaned back on his heels. "Yeah, it was pretty good."

"Pips, we still on for tonight?" Noah leaned around my open locker, clasping it in his hands, and nearly bumping into Declan in the process.

Nodding like a bobble head, I smiled. "Yeah, sure, of course. I'll see you after school."

"Sounds great." Beaming, he gave a little clap to the door, making the metal sing. Much like my heart at the moment.

My stomach fluttered as he sauntered away and stopped to high-five a teammate. I get to be alone with him. Sighing, I turned around to a scowling Declan and a pleased Quinn. With a tight smile, I closed my door and scrambled the lock. "Let's get to class."

♫

"He *likes* you."

"What? Who likes me?" I looked around the back of my black SUV, knowing I'd find Quinn leaning against the driver's side door. School was out, and I was loading up my cello.

She walked toward me, the dimples in her cheeks evident. "Declan."

Chuckling, I said, "No, he doesn't. Trust me. He only likes irritating me."

"Totally likes you."

I gave her my best unamused face. "I play well, but we're only a good match musically. That's it. Even *tolerate* would be too strong a word for us."

Quinn crossed her arms over her light gray jacket as the breeze rustled the colorful leaves on the trees and made the ones lining the parking lot swirl in a chilly dance. "Look, I know you only have eyes for Captain Basketball, but I'm serious. When you mooned over Noah this morning, Declan noticed. You should've seen the look he shot Noah. He's *not* a fan, I'll tell you that much."

I scrunched my nose and reached to pull the back hatch down. "Okay . . . or maybe Noah just rubs him the wrong way."

"Right, Noah rubs him the wrong way because *you* like Noah . . . duh."

"And how long have these hallucinations been happening? You should probably tell someone." I shook my head, my boots crunching over loose stones and leaves on the asphalt. "I'll see you later, Quinn."

"Call me after the study session with Romeo." She waved, walking toward her little red car.

Waving back, I climbed into my SUV, excited to see Noah. We'd never been alone before—Phillip was always around. But tonight, we'd be studying, and my brother would want nothing to do with that.

I pulled from the lot and stopped, waiting to turn, blinker clicking a steady beat. Glancing at the bus stop, Declan was there. His eyes met mine and I looked away, my stomach somersaulting. Probably just my excitement for my study date.

Quinn seriously had no idea what she was talking about. Declan was the one person who had the potential to destroy everything I'd been working toward. We'd be lucky if we were able to walk away from this as merely bitter acquaintances. Him? *Like* me? *Pfft.*

On the road, I passed a few friends and waved. When I pulled into our driveway on our tree-lined street, I parked next to Noah's empty soft-top Jeep. Climbing out, I smiled at my reflection in my window, the excitement inside me nearly bubbling over. Around the corner of the house I found Noah sitting on the back steps, leading to the door we always used, book bag at his side.

"Where's Phillip?" I was always last getting home.

Noah stood and smoothed down his jacket. "Um, I think he's helping Coach with something. You ready to study?"

"Yup." I grabbed the knob on the back door and gave it a twist and pushed. Locked. That's weird. It explained why Noah hadn't just gone inside. Mom was always home after school. She was usually giving lessons. Maybe they'd canceled. Unlocking the door, I led the way inside and tossed my keys on the kitchen counter. "Mom?"

Silence greeted us.

Noah sat his bag on the table and plopped down on the bench. "Guess it's just us."

"Looks like it." I sat across from him, nervousness crawling through my body. I pulled out my tattered and dog-eared copy of *The Scarlet Letter* and set it on the tabletop, my notebook followed. I moved the ceramic bowl of green apples to the side.

"Wow, that's taken a beating." He pulled out his still pristine copy.

I eyed his and laughingly picked it up, the pages zipping under my thumbnail. "Well, yeah, I've actually opened mine and, you know, . . . read it."

"Yeah." He scratched the back of his head, looking guilty. "There's a slight possibility I didn't . . . really . . . read it." His shoulders rolled in a guilty-but-aren't-I-cute slump. "I watched the movie though."

"Noah!" My mouth popped open. "I'm not a miracle worker. There's no way you'll be ready by tomorrow. I'd start reading if I were you." I slid his book back across the table to him.

"You're super smart. I was hoping you'd tell me how the book differs from the movie. Get me on the right path."

I shook my head. So this was all about his grade. It'd been silly to hold even the slightest hope otherwise. "I've never seen the movie; I doubt I'd be much help. Sorry."

He caught his bottom lip between his teeth and slowly let it release. "It's streaming on Netflix. Come on." He stood, notebook and book in one hand; grabbing mine with his other, he yanked me into the family room.

My heart nearly skidded to a halt as I looked at our twined fingers. Just as swiftly, he let go of me, turned on the flatscreen, and pulled up the movie in record time.

"Okay, sit. Here's the remote, stop when you need to and tell me what really happened."

My gaze dropped to the remote in my hand. "Are you serious?" I looked up at him, stuck on the right thing to do. "Why should I do this? You should've read the book, and you know it."

"I know, you're right." He took a step away from the TV and knelt in front of me. "I've been so busy with the team and my other classes that this kinda slipped through the cracks. School isn't my thing, you know that. But I promise it won't happen again. I just need you to help me this one time." Hand over his heart, he met my eyes, smiling. "Plus, it's Demi Moore. You can't go wrong there."

I did know that school wasn't his thing. When he'd applied to colleges last spring, he'd really struggled with the idea of even going. Looking at his bright baby blues, I could feel myself relenting. He was just too cute with his dimple in one cheek and sweet smile. "Fine, sit. I'll help, but just this once." I held up one finger to make a point, hoping I had a tough look on my face to show I meant business.

"Deal." He sat beside me on the cream-colored couch then tossed several of the throw pillows toward the unoccupied corner.

With a sigh, I leaned on the arm, tucking my legs up underneath me. Hitting play, I watched as the movie incorrectly began with Reverend Dimmesdale going to an Indian funeral and Hester Prynne arriving in the new world and meeting the reverend.

I hit pause. "Okay, to start, the book has an anonymous narrator. It's *not* from the perspective of Hester's daughter. The opening scene in the book is Hester on the scaffold by the pillory, holding her baby, being punished for adultery. The movie is showing us Hester and Reverend Dimmesdale meeting, which wasn't in the book."

"Wow, that much wrong in just five minutes? I'm in trouble." Noah leaned closer to me.

Glancing his way, a frizzle of energy pulsed through me and I chuckled. "Yeah, you are."

The back door banged shut. "Pippa? Where's Phillip? Hello, Noah," Mom called.

"Hey, Mrs. W," Noah said, sitting up straighter. "Phillip's still at school."

Out of breath, Mom appeared in the doorway, unbuttoning her coat. "What are you two up to?"

"Slacker here didn't read the book for our English class. He's hoping I can get him a passing grade."

Mom shook her head with a disapproving mom smile. "Noah, I know you know better."

"I do. I've already promised Pippa I wouldn't do it again." He held his hands up in surrender and glanced at me, looking ashamed.

"Alright, continue on. Noah, stay for dinner, I'll call your mom."

I hit play again, occasionally pausing to correct an inaccuracy. By the time the credits rolled Noah had nearly two pages, front and back, filled with notes.

"I think you just saved my life, Pippa." He tossed his notebook down and closed the distance between us, patting my knee with a warm hand and resting it there.

"No, I just saved your grade." I patted the top of his hand, trying to ignore the tingles his touch sent racing through me. I planted my feet on the hardwood floor, needing to ground myself. "And now you owe me."

His fingers gave my knee a quick squeeze. "Anything. I'd do anything for you, you know that."

"Aw, you're sweet."

His eyes met mine and a grin curled his lips. "Pippa, what would you think about going—"

"Are you two done yet?" Phillip, who'd been home only mere minutes, came and wedged himself between Noah and I, crunching on a handful of chips.

Sighing, Noah sat up straight and scooted to make room. "Yup, I think we just finished. Anything else, Pips?" He leaned around my obnoxious brother to look at me.

"If you feel good about tomorrow, then we're done." I stood and pulled my sweater together, wanting to whack Phillip on the back of his head.

Noah nodded. "Thanks for everything."

I went to the kitchen and grabbed plates and silverware, intending to set the table. Phillip's familiar laugh hit my ears. Smiling, I went to grab the linen napkins in the drawer near the door to the family room, partly because it was easier to listen in from there.

"Thanks a lot, man. You couldn't have waited a couple minutes longer?" Noah's words gave me pause. What were they talking about?

"Not my fault you're not as smooth as you think you are." Phillip's voice faded out as they bounded up the stairs.

Noah not smooth? Since when? And what on Earth had he been about to ask me?

CHAPTER *Six*

Music touches us emotionally, where words alone can't.

—Johnny Depp

I sat in the hallway by my locker with Quinn and Jenna. Lexi was nowhere to be seen. Not that I minded in the least. She and Quinn were having another one of their tiffs. I had no clue why. They had a very on-again, off-again relationship. Taking a bite of my sandwich, I looked up to see Declan coming our way. He had an easy swagger in his step, his Chucks tapping against the concrete floor.

"Hey, Pippa." Declan nodded when he spotted us. "Practice tonight?"

My peanut butter and jelly glommed together in a ball in my mouth. Swallowing, I nodded. "I guess I can stay after school, or we could go to my house."

"Cool, we'll sort it out in class."

"Sounds good." I smiled and watched him walk away.

"What was that?" Quinn asked from my left, an amused smile on her lips.

I scrunched my face, confused. "What was what?"

"You totally checked out his ass as he walked away."

"I did not!"

Jenna licked the back of her plastic pudding spoon and nodded, her blue eyes sparkling. "You so did." She snickered. "To be fair, he's got a really great tush. I'd have looked too, if my back hadn't been to him."

"I did not check out his butt, thank you very much." I stuffed the half-uneaten sandwich in the plastic baggy and stood, taking the few steps down the hall to toss my brown-paper sack. When I returned, I sat back down.

"Look, he likes you, and he's hot." Quinn sipped her soda.

I rolled my eyes. "No, he doesn't. He puts up with me because we don't have any other choice. Stop trying to make something happen there."

Jenna's thin lips twitched. "And yet, you don't deny he's hot."

A heavy sigh left my chest. "Okay, I'll admit, Declan is *sorta* cute, but he's nothing like Noah." My mind tripped back to this morning in English. We'd gotten our quiz results from Friday and Noah had gotten a B. After class, he'd picked me up in a hug and spun me around.

If he hadn't held onto me, I may have floated away from sheer happiness. I'd been in a daze ever since.

"I know you like Noah, but you guys are *so* different. He's all jocky, you're all artsy. You're brains, he's brawn. You have plans for the future. Does he? Plus, he's always dated from the cheerleader crowd, and the last time I checked, you didn't exactly run with those girls." Quinn stood and walked to the trash and back. "All I'm trying to say is that you and Declan . . . fit."

I stood and Jenna followed. The bell signaling the end of lunch was about to ring, but since my locker was right behind me I didn't have to go far to get my books.

"Yeah, so never gonna happen. Right now, he's seriously

55

my enemy. And since he plays so well, he always will be." I shook my head. Miffed by her opinions, I opened my locker, pulled out my books for the last half of the day, and stuffed them into my bag. "I'm heading to class. I'll see you guys later."

There were just so many things wrong with the idea of Declan and me together. It irritated me that she couldn't see it. How could I possibly date a guy who wanted to take everything away from me? He was one of the few who had the power to shatter my dreams. And I wasn't about to let my guard down just because he was kind of cute.

♪

Declan silently walked beside me to my car. Mr. Woods had to leave early, so we couldn't use the music room to rehearse. The thought of bringing Declan to my house made me nervous.

Opening the back of my SUV, we slid our cellos in. Declan smiled as he reached up to close the hatch.

"Pips," Quinn called from her car across the parking lot and waved me over.

"Here, get in," I said to Declan as I hit the button on my key fob. "I'll be right back." I jogged over to Quinn, fearing what was about to come out of her mouth. "Don't you dare say anything about him liking me."

Her lips popped open with innocent indignation. "Me? Never." She giggled. "I get it, he's not an option for you. My mouth will be forever shut on the topic. What I was gonna say was maybe bringing Declan to your house might get a rise out of Noah. He's probably there with Phillip right now. Seeing you two together might make him jealous, which could be a good thing. And just so you know, if you wanted to, you could totally hint to your brother that he should ask me to Winter Formal. I totally wouldn't mind."

"Like I'd use Declan like that." I shook my head and long strands of hair fell over my shoulder. "I may not like him, but I've resigned myself to be nice. And if you want Phillip to ask you, why don't you pop by and talk to him yourself? Or even better, *you* could ask *him*." I used my hands to motion like my brain had exploded, then turned and headed back to my car.

Through the windshield I could see Declan watching me. Looking away, I tucked the stray strands of hair, which the wind had picked up and tousled around my face, behind my ears.

"Everything okay?" he asked as I climbed in and buckled up.

"Yup, peachy." I shivered as I started the engine. "You ready?" At his nod, I drove off; a strange nervous energy reverberated through me.

"How'd you do on the English quiz?" I asked, needing to end the awkward silence.

"I got a hundred percent. You?"

I shot him a smile. "Same."

Foot on the brake, I stopped for a couple students in the crosswalk. The tall boy with shaggy red hair I recognized from the basketball team. I think his name was Neal. He waved and smiled, which I returned.

In the driveway, I killed the engine next to Noah's Jeep. Phillip had parked his blue sedan in the street. Grabbing our cellos, Declan and I walked past Noah and Phillip practicing in the driveway. They had a game tonight. I was surprised to see them here.

"Why aren't you two at school?"

"The game's later than normal, and Coach wanted us to get dinner. We have to be back in two hours." Phillip pinned the ball between his arm and hip.

"Hey, Declan." Noah ran a hand through his short blond

hair while giving him a judgmental once-over.

Declan did the dude nod and turned to me. "We should get rehearsing."

I nodded. "If I don't catch you two before the game, good luck tonight."

In the kitchen, Declan put his cello down and removed his coat while looking around and absorbing his surroundings. "Nice. My mom's always liked these kind of houses. We're living in a condo right now until she has the time to house hunt."

"That's kinda cool."

"No." He shook his head. "It's really not. Our neighbors are loud and obnoxious. It's almost like being back in New York."

Studying him, I noted a sadness in his brown eyes. "I bet you'd go back to New York in a heartbeat if you could, wouldn't you?"

"I would, but my dad doesn't have the time for me." He shrugged. "His new wife Missy and their daughter keep him pretty occupied."

I wanted to dig deeper, but the last thing I needed was for him to think I was prying. Footsteps on the stairs stopped all conversation. Mom came down the back set, pushing her hair off her face.

"Hey there." She eyed Declan. "Judging by the cello, I'd guess you're Pippa's new partner for Solo and Ensemble."

He held out his hand to shake hers. "Hi, I'm Declan."

Mom shook his hand, looking genuinely happy to see him. "It's nice to meet you, Declan. I'm Isobel. Let me know if you guys need anything."

Declan nodded and turned to me. "So, where are we setting up at?"

"Hey, Mom, can we use the studio?" I noticed she wasn't wearing shoes, which meant she was probably done with lessons today. It must be a light day.

With a nod she said, "Sure, Gavin's family is on vacation for two weeks, so it's open."

"Thanks." I looked up into Declan's brown eyes and pointed toward the front of the house. "Over here." Cello case in hand, I led the way to the bay-windowed music room at the front of the house. A baby grand piano sat in the coved space. Mom was actually a highly sought-after concert pianist. Not that she toured much anymore, but that was totally her choice. She'd cut way back when Phillip and I were kids, wanting to spend time with us. Now, between events in her sporadic touring schedule, she did lessons. I always thought she'd start touring again as we got older because the offers were seriously neverending, but she seemed to get a lot of joy from teaching and didn't want to give that up.

"This is great." Declan came in and pulled a white wooden chair from the side of the room and added it to the solo one sitting in the center.

Sitting Francesca down, I closed the double French doors and knelt down in front of my case, flipping the silver clasps open. "So, do you have college plans?"

Declan already had his cello out and stood, watching me. "Oh yeah, it was never a choice, not in my family anyway."

"Same here. What do your parents do?"

"Mom's a senior designer with a shoe company and my dad's a TV producer and total asswad." He stood by the chair he'd pulled over as I got up.

"So where did you apply?" I handed over the music for him to set on the stand and went to take my seat.

"Everywhere."

I nodded and smiled. "Feels like that, doesn't it? What's your first choice?"

"Goddards." He sat after I did and got his cello into

position.

"Of course. Mine too." I ran my bow over my rosin and looked up at the music.

"So, do you have any plans for the dance?" he asked, playing a note for me to tune to.

I shook my head and copied his note, turning the small pegs on the tailpiece, bringing our instruments into perfect sync. With a laugh, I said, "Right now, Quinn and I are each other's dates. What about you?"

He balanced his arms atop the curves of his cello and looked at me. "I haven't asked anyone yet. I don't really know anyone, well . . . aside from you." A soft laugh left his lips.

Averting my eyes, I cleared my throat. "You ready to run through this?"

He nodded and took up position. A little way into the piece, Declan stopped. "Let's run this section slower? We're not together here and it just sounds off."

Slowly we worked note by note through a few measures when a knock on the door interrupted us.

Peeking his head in, Noah smiled at me. "Pips, can I talk to you for a second?"

"Sure, what's up?" I asked, clasping my cello and bow in one hand as I itched my nose. Rosin dust always made it tickle.

Noah's eyes darted to Declan then back to me. "Um, could you come out here? I'd like to talk to you in private."

I sat my cello in its stand and nodded, turning to Declan. "I'll be right back."

In the entryway, I waited, still holding my bow, as Noah reached behind me to close the frosted panel door. "Everything okay?"

Despite his wanting privacy, I knew Noah's every word would travel though the thin opaque French doors and right to Declan's ears.

"Yeah, it's fine, I um . . . I just wanted to ask you something."

"What's up?" I stared into his blue eyes. He looked nervous, which somehow made him even cuter, if that was possible.

"I was wondering if anyone had asked you to the Winter Formal."

I shook my head, my pulse jumping. "Um, no."

He crossed his arms in front of him and looked down at the dark wood floor. "Well, what would you think about going with me?" Slowly raising his head, he met my eyes.

I closed my now popped open mouth and nodded, unable to form words.

"Is that a yes?" A smile stretched across his face.

I nodded again, grinning. Me and Noah on an actual date. Holy. Shit.

"That's awesome!" He looked unsure whether he should hug me or shake my hand. "Um . . . I gotta run. Your brother's waiting in the car for me. We're gonna go grab dinner with a couple guys from the team." Unable to wipe the happiness from his face, he walked backward a couple steps then turned and darted out of sight.

Hand on the music room's knob, I'd only cracked the door open when Noah turned back and asked, "Oh, are you coming tonight?"

Facing him, I nodded again, but this time I found my voice. "I was planning to. I'm picking Quinn up in a little bit."

"Great, I'll watch for you."

I stood in the now empty entry, brain spinning with what had just happened. Quinn would never believe this. Deep breath in, I composed myself and went back to Declan.

"I take it you and Wonder Jock are now going to the dance together," he threw over his shoulder at me.

Lowering my eyebrows, I scrunched my face. "We are. How weird is that? I've known him forever, and he's my brother's best friend. I never dreamed he'd ask me out." Well, I'd totally dreamed about it, I just never thought it'd actually happen.

Confusion filled his face. "Isn't this what you wanted?"

"Why do you say that?" I grabbed Francesca and sat, not looking at him.

"Because of the way you salivated over him the other day." He loosened the hairs of his bow, only to tighten them again.

"I was not *salivating* over him. Good grief, Noah and I are friends. We don't think of each other like that." And I'm just a giant liar.

"Whatever you say, Princess. Let's get back to work."

CHAPTER *Seven*

After silence, that which comes nearest to expressing the inexpressible . . . is music.

—*Aldous Huxley*

Darkness surrounded my black SUV as I pulled up to Quinn's house and watched her jog down the driveway. When she opened the passenger door, a cold breeze pushed her in. Once she sat and settled, she blew her bangs off her forehead with a puff of air.

"You look awfully happy," she said, taking me in as she snapped her seatbelt into place. "What's going on? Ooh, did someone ask you to Winter Formal?" Her eyes widened, and she clapped her hands in front of her, hopeful.

Unable to wipe the perma-grin off, I bobbed my head. "Noah asked me." I covered my face with my hands.

"Wait, what?" She pulled my arms down, her hazel eyes wide in shock.

"Noah asked me to be his date for the dance."

Quinn squealed. "That's so great!" Her head tilted to the side. "So *not* who I was expecting, but it's great nonetheless. How'd he do it? You have to tell me everything."

I replayed the encounter for her. Every moment had been seared into my memory and probably would be for the rest of my life.

"This is incredible! I'm so happy for you. Well, happy and jealous as hell. Can you work your magic and get Phillip to ask me?" Her words came out in a rush, but that was pretty normal for Quinn.

Grinning like a fool, I just shrugged and gripped the steering wheel, the weight of the vehicle the only thing anchoring me to Earth. "I don't think Phillip's planning on going. He said something the other day about not having enough money for it." Truth was, after spending all his cash on his car, he was broke. Especially since his summer job had been temporary and ended when school started. That's why he'd been busy putting applications in all over town.

"Well, we still have to go shopping." Quinn grasped my arm in her hand. "I may not have a date, but I want an awesome dress."

"Definitely." I grinned and pulled out onto the road, eager to see Noah play tonight. Okay, I was just eager to see Noah, period.

"How was practice?"

"Good, I dropped Declan off right before picking you up. You know those new high-rise luxury condos?"

Quinn nodded and unwrapped a red, white, and gray chevron-print scarf from her neck. I loved that it was our school colors.

"That's where he and his mom are living until they find a house."

"That's cool. I wonder why he doesn't drive? I mean, if his mom has that kind of money, you'd think he'd have his own car."

I looked both ways as I took my turn at a four-way stop. "It sounds like his dad has a lot of money too. But I get the vibe that there's some serious bitterness there."

"Poor guy." Quinn's hands paused in the middle of playing with her scarf, and she turned to look at me, sitting up straighter. "I just had a brilliant idea."

"Well, don't leave me hanging." I laughed as I glanced over at her.

"I'm going to ask Declan to Winter Formal." She clapped her hands together then rubbed them vigorously.

Stopped at a traffic light, I turned to her, my eyes wide in surprise. "Wait, you can ask my sworn enemy, but you can't ask my brother . . . who you've known forever?"

A scoff left her throat as she pulled her glasses off and cleaned them against her scarf. "First, Declan isn't your enemy. And second, Phillip is in a totally different league, one I'm not on the level for."

"Okay." I tilted my head to the side. "I think you're being a chicken. You should ask Phillip if he's the one you really want to go with."

She eyed me, studying my face. "Well, unless you have a problem with me asking Declan."

The light turned green, and I pushed the gas, moving us closer to the school. "Aside from the obvious archenemy situation, no. Not at all. In fact, it'd probably be nice for Declan, since he doesn't really know anyone here yet."

Except me, as he'd reminded me only earlier today.

My chest felt funny and my stomach was on a downturn as well. Did her asking him bother me?

No.

Well . . . maybe.

Okay, yeah a little bit.

Why?

These prickles of irritation shouldn't be happening. I had a freaking date with Noah to look forward to. I should be firmly ensconced and happily floating on a freaking cloud.

Besides, Quinn deserved a hot date too.

Wait. Did I just really call Declan hot?

I thought a moment, analyzing my out-of-control internal monologue and coming away even more confused.

"You've stopped talking." Quinn burst into my thought bubble.

"What?" I shook my head.

"Pips, seriously, if you have a problem with me asking Declan, I won't do it."

I pulled the car into the dimly lit parking lot behind the gym and pulled the keys out. Turning to Quinn, I smiled and waved off her 'worries. "Don't be silly. Ask him out. It totally doesn't bother me. I promise. But what about Lexi? She's definitely interested in him."

"Right now, I don't give a fart about Lexi and what she wants." Sighing, she scrunched her nose. "And I'm really glad you don't mind, 'cause I'm totally gonna do it. But don't worry, I'll always be team Pippa."

"What happened with you and Lexi?"

She shrugged. "Mostly she was getting on my nerves. She's super needy and always so jealous of you. She gets mad at me all the time 'cause you and I are friends. The other day I'd just had enough and laid into her. So she's not talking to me now."

"I'm sorry." I slid my arms into my coat.

"It's not really your fault."

Looking up, students were filtering through the parking lot and into the gym. The visiting team's buses were parked off to the side. We were playing a Vancouver school tonight.

"You sure you're cool about me asking Declan?"

"Yup. Come on, let's go. I want to see Noah." I gave her an excited smile, wanting to end this Declan conversation once and for all.

Quinn met me at the front of the vehicle as I buttoned

my winter coat. Locking her arm in mine, we walked to the line of students illuminated by the yellow glow from the gym windows.

When we got to the door, we flashed our ID cards and followed the herd. Walking the edges of the wooden court, we climbed into the red bleachers and found seats behind the pep bad. It was silly, but I'd always wished I could be a part of it. Not that lugging my cello into the stands would be much fun. My lips curled at the mental image popping into my head. I could picture Declan and I fighting to keep the endpins from sliding on the thin metal walkway.

I scrunched my face and shoved Declan from my mind. How easily he'd popped in there bothered me.

Quinn sat down and I took a seat beside her, shedding my coat. As the bleachers filled, the team hit the court to warm up. Noah peered into the stands until he saw me, then he smiled and waved.

A warm tingle ran through me as I returned the gesture. Noah waving at *me*, searching *me* out. Unbelievable. A burning sensation took over my cheeks, the telltale sign that I was blushing up a storm.

"Captain Basketball sure looks happy to see you." Quinn bumped my shoulder.

Winter Formal couldn't get here soon enough.

♫

I stood in front of a rack of colorful and bedazzled dresses. The whole store was a sea of sequins and satin. Quinn and Jenna both carried an armful. I had two. Reaching up, I pulled a navy sheath dress and draped it over my arm. I glanced at Quinn as she scampered across the store from me, big grin on her face, happy as I'd ever seen her. She'd asked Declan this morning.

Emotions swirled through me. Ones I absolutely refused

to label.

Blissful look on her face, she floated over to me, her pile of dresses flouncing and sparkling with every step. How she hadn't dropped them was a mystery to me.

"You ready to try these on?" Quinn asked, a little breathless.

"Let's do it." Jenna giggled. Just today she'd been asked by some guy who I'd seen around but had never actually talked to.

I nodded, a small smile on my lips. This morning, Quinn had cornered Declan at my locker and asked him. I remembered the way his eyebrows rose and how he'd looked at me, as if asking if I had anything to do with this. I'd just shrugged and shook my head.

At his nod of acceptance, a churning, acidic feeling hit the pit of my stomach. I turned to my locker, giving them some privacy and me the time to sort out the proper reaction, which meant pasting on a grin. I would've much rather avoided the front row seat to their little moment all together.

"Yo, Earth to Pippa. You okay? You just froze up on us." Jenna waved her hand in front of my face.

Focusing on her, I smiled. "Yeah, I'm fine. Just got lost in a daydream, I guess."

"Dreaming of Noah? And what he'll think when he sees you in your dress?" Quinn's voice rose an octave and she practically had stars swimming in her eyes.

"Yup, you caught me." I laughed. Clearly that's what was on her mind.

Lips pursed, she managed to get a hand free long enough to give my shoulder a light smack. "God, you're so difficult sometimes. Come on, let's go try these on."

The blonde sales clerk opened doors for us. The store was nearly empty, as the mall closed in an hour. We'd been looking for dresses since school let out. I'd made Quinn promise this was the last shop tonight. If I was lucky, it'd be the last one period.

"Let me know if you ladies need anything."

I nodded, my stomach growling as I went into the room next to Quinn's. Jenna went in the door on the other side of me. Turning the lock, I spun to find a hook. "We've got to grab dinner on the way home."

"No kidding." Quinn's laughter cascaded over the wall. "Let's go to Oaks. My mom'll be there."

"Dang it, I can't. I promised my mom I'd be home by ten," Jenna's voiced grumbled. Her parents were über strict. I was a little surprised they were letting her go to the dance in the first place. It was one of the reasons why she'd been counting down the days until graduation and college since her sophomore year.

I quickly slipped into a dark-green dress. It was short and had a peek through at the waist. Immediately I started taking it off. "Ugh, no, you guys don't need to see this one."

Quinn's door squeaked as she opened it. "Pop your head out, what do you think of this one?"

Holding a black dress up to cover my bra, I cracked the door. The dress she had on reminded me of a peacock. Slim fitting and a beautiful dark purple, it had blue, purple, and green rhinestones at the collar. "It's actually really pretty."

"I think I like this the best of everything I've tried on." Twirling in front of the trifold mirror, Quinn stopped and giggled.

Jenna popped out in a hot pink number. "Ooh, I like that. It's very you. What do you think of mine?"

Quinn's nose scrunched. "Not my favorite."

"Try on the next." I shut the door and stepped into the black chiffon dress. The skirt was long and flowy. The top was snug and lacy. The back dipped down into a deep V and the lace sleeves stopped just above my elbows. It was simple and lovely. And best of all, I felt amazing.

An image of Noah popped into my mind and brought a smile to my lips. I pictured him standing in the foyer of my house and me coming down the front staircase. Why does every girl dream of making an entrance down a flight of stairs? Knowing my luck, I'd tumble down and land at his feet. Shaking the thought from my mind, I focused on his face and how he'd look when he saw me. His mouth would open, his eyes would pop, and he'd whisper, "holy cow"—or something like that—as he walked toward me.

A knock on my door startled me from my fantasy.

"You ready? Come on." Jenna sounded excited.

I stepped out, a huge grin on my face.

"Wow, Pips, that's gorgeous. It's so . . . you." Quinn twirled her finger to indicate she wanted me to do a spin. I obliged. "You have to get that. Noah's gonna love it."

"*I* love it."

"That dress was made for you." Jenna's eyes widened, her teal dress rippling on the floor behind her. "So gorgeous, and that back!"

I looked at myself in the big mirror. A motherly looking woman walked past and smiled. Her daughter, who must've been about thirteen, trailed behind, staring at us. I thought of my mom at home. She'd offered to come, but I'd told her we had it under control. Now I wished she'd come with us. "I'm gonna get this one."

Quinn stood beside me at the mirrors in an emerald green dress, turning from side to side.

"I like the peacock one better."

"You mean the first one?" she asked.

I nodded.

"Same here," Jenna chimed in.

"Me too." Her eyes twinkled. "I'm just gonna try the rest of these on real quick."

"Wait, what about this one?" Jenna did a turn, and Quinn gave her a double thumbs-up.

Looking Jenna up and down, I said, "I like it. The pale teal goes nice with your dark hair. It's really flattering."

"You know, Pippa, Winter Formal isn't a funeral." A familiar voice came from behind me.

Jenna and I spun to confront the intruder. "Lexi, what are you doing here?"

She stood with another girl who I recognized but didn't really know. Her eyes darted nervously between Lexi and me.

Flicking her brown hair over her shoulder, Lexi said, "Looking for dresses, of course."

"Who's your date?" Quinn exited the dressing room in a short yellow dress, putting her hands on her hips and jutting one out to the side.

"Kyle Pullman, on the lacrosse team." She looked pleased with herself.

Quinn nodded. "Well, good for you. I hope you guys have fun." Turning, she went to the mirror to examine herself, leaving Jenna and me to deal with Lexi.

"Come on, Rachel, clearly they don't have anything good here." Spinning on her heel, she walked off.

With a roll of my eyes, I went in my room and changed into my jeans, tank, and gray sweater. I didn't care what Lexi thought. This dress made me feel amazing. And I was thrilled I wouldn't have to try on any more. I put the rejects on the return rack. People who left dressing rooms messy drove me nuts.

My perfect dress in hand, I slid down the wall and sat near the mirrors. They could seriously use a couple chairs in here.

Quinn and Jenna sauntered in and out of their rooms in dress after dress. In the end, Quinn's peacock one won out. Jenna bought the long teal one with the modest train.

Dresses bought and bagged, we left.

"Do you think Declan will like it?" Quinn asked, clutching the garment bag in her hand as we walked down the long corridor, our footsteps tapping out a rhythmic cadence against the light-colored concrete floor.

"He'll love it." I smiled, distracted by the tall woman in front us carrying shopping bags. My attention pulled to the guy beside her in the black leather jacket. There was something familiar in the way he moved, and in his build—from his towering height to his perfect backside.

Is that . . . ?

He turned, and my heart gave an unexpectedly wonky and offbeat thump.

Declan.

Smacking Quinn on the arm, I whispered, "Why don't you ask him? He's right in front of us."

"Pippa? Quinn?" Declan stopped walking and waited for us to catch up. "What are you doing here?" The woman with him gave us a quizzical look.

"Dress shopping." Quinn held up her plastic garment bag with a smile. Jenna stood mutely beside her, grinning.

Declan nodded. "Ah. Mom, this is Quinn, my date for the dance on Saturday."

The tall woman held a hand out to Quinn. "Pleasure to meet you."

Quinn nodded. She looked unsure what to say, which was odd, considering she was usually such a chatterbox.

"And I'm sorry, I don't think we've actually been introduced." Declan gestured to Jenna.

"Oh, this is Jenna. Jenna this is Declan," Quinn said with her rediscovered voice as she gestured between the two of them.

He nodded, his eyes darting momentarily to me then back to Jenna. "Nice to meet you."

Once Jenna was introduced to his mom, he angled himself toward me, his eyes glinting playfully.

"And this is Pippa." His gaze didn't stay on me. Rather, he found a sudden fascination with his shoes.

"Pippa? I've heard a lot about you." A soft smile touched her lips. With a gentle tug, she straightened the front of her blue blouse then offered me her hand.

I shook it and chuckled. "No doubt he was complaining about getting stuck with me."

"Quite the contrary. Dec says you're incredibly talented." She looked to her son, pride evident in her face.

"Oh really?" I raised my eyebrows and grinned at Declan, who was now looking at me like he wished he was anywhere else in the world. I had to admit, a large part of me enjoyed watching him squirm. Despite how tempted I was, I decided not to tease him. "That's sweet. He's really talented too. It's fun playing with him."

Declan smiled and rubbed the back of his neck. "Thanks, Princess."

It was subtle, but there was a difference in how he'd said "Princess." I still wasn't a fan of the nickname, not by a long shot, but this time his usual mocking tone was gone. He'd actually sounded . . . friendlier. It didn't stop me from wanting to smack him for using it though.

"I'm looking forward to hearing your duet." His mom smiled and looked between us.

"Well, we still need a lot of practicing, but it'll be polished in no time," Declan answered, his gaze locked on mine.

The sound of a storefront gate closing hit my ears. The mall was nearly deserted.

"We should get going before the gate to Brunell's closes. I don't want to have to walk a mile to the car." Quinn jerked her head in the direction we needed to go.

"We're down at the other end," Declan answered.

"It was really nice meeting you, Ms. Brogan." I smiled.

"Likewise." Her brown eyes were soft and warm, just like Declan's. Even the way their mouths moved when they smiled was nearly identical.

Declan pulled his jacket together in the front and slid his hands into the pockets. "See you tomorrow."

"Later," Quinn chirped as I waved.

"Bye." Jenna lifted a hand, wiggling her fingers.

As we walked away, I turned to catch one last glimpse of him as my friends chattered at my side. Declan apparently had the same idea. It startled me to meet his eyes. His smile sent a tingle straight through me that settled low in my stomach. Weirded out, I flipped around and struggled to focus on what Quinn and Jenna were going on about.

"Do you want to go order our boutonnières tomorrow?" Quinn turned to the side and did a little gallop facing me.

"Dear God, if you're this excited about going with Declan, I can't even imagine what you'd be like if Phillip had asked you."

"I think I'd die, right on the spot." She ran a thin hand through her light-brown hair and pushed her glasses further up her nose.

Jenna just shook her head and looked at me to make a reply.

"Well, it's a good thing he didn't ask you then, I guess." Up ahead, the metal gate to Brunell's was partially down.

My head was a jumble of confused thoughts. I didn't like Declan. I couldn't. We weren't even friends. So why on Earth did he always manage to make me feel so out of sorts whenever he was around? He wanted my chair and everything I'd worked so hard for. He was my main competition for Goddards. I wasn't jealous of Quinn. I couldn't be.

And yet, her bubbly excitement was getting under my

skin. And the award for worst friend ever goes to: Pippa Wyndham. I blew out a heavy sigh. Happiness should be the only thing I felt for her right now.

"This is gonna be so much fun." She spun back around as we ducked under the gate to Brunell's. The guy standing by, waiting to close the gate, smiled at us. He had to be my dad's age. "We should double," Quinn squeaked with an added hop to her step.

"Um, I'm not sure what Noah's plans are. I can ask though." I pulled my keys from the pocket of my navy peacoat.

"Please do. He's probably got up a group to go, and well, since *I* asked Declan, I'm kinda groupless."

Jenna stood between us, looking from one to the other. "I could ask Patrick if Noah can't swing it."

Quinn smiled and nodded at Jenna.

"I'll ask him tomorrow." I shrugged.

Of course I'd do it for Quinn, but the thought of spending all night in the same group as Declan unnerved me. Which was totally my problem, and one that I needed to get over. I just wasn't sure I could.

CHAPTER *Eight*

Music is the strongest form of magic.

—*Marilyn Manson*

The bell chimed as we stepped into the entry of the Live Oak Grill. We'd parted ways from Jenna at the mall. Quinn's mom, Sarah, stood behind the cash register making small talk with a couple as they checked out. When she looked up, she gave us a little wave and grinned. Quinn and I didn't wait for her to seat us. We went to our usual table near the oak tree growing in the center of the restaurant—hence the name.

Draping our garment bags over the back of the booth, we sat. Several groups of people and couples filled the tables near us. Being as late as it was, I was surprised to see it so busy.

Thanks to Quinn's mom, Oaks was a clean and cozy environment. Next to the indoor tree, the coolest thing about the place was the retractable glass ceiling. At one time, this had been the home of an architectural firm; they'd done all the fun and funky modifications. I tilted my head back and sighed, taking in the inky night sky above us. During the summer months, the sides of the dome slid back, opening it up to fresh summer night breezes. It was beyond cool.

As kids, we'd managed to talk Quinn's mom into bringing us here after closing nearly every time I'd spent the night. She'd make us desserts and Cajun fries while we'd push the tables aside and spread blankets on the floor. Then we'd open the ceiling and try to stargaze with all the lights out. It was a little bit of magic in the heart of the city.

Quinn's mom headed our way, only stopping to briefly check on a couple customers. "Look at you girls. You look pleased. I take it you found something good?"

"Yup." Quinn grinned at her mom and turned on her sweet smile. "But we're starving, can we order first then show you what we got?"

"Of course. You want your regular?" At our nods, she patted my shoulder and spun toward the kitchen.

I followed the direction of Quinn's gaze as she pressed her lips tightly together, making them almost disappear. Her eyes had focused on the picture of her dad wearing his yellow fireman's turnouts, helmet unstrapped on his head, and a big smile on his soot-streaked face. She sighed and took her glasses off to clean them on her shirt. A candle sat off to the side of the frame and, as long as someone was in the building, it was always lit.

Almost ten years had passed since he died. Quinn was only eight at the time. A large fire in a downtown building took a turn for the worse and surprised the firemen when the roof collapsed. Quinn's dad and his partner were trapped inside, pinned by fallen debris. By the time rescuers reached them, it was too late.

One night when we were around thirteen, Quinn had confided, through a stream of tears, that she hardly remembered him anymore.

I glanced away from the picture to Quinn. I put my hand

over hers, giving it a squeeze. "You okay?"

"Yeah." Her voice sounded artificially perky as she slid her glasses back up the bridge of her nose. It'd been a long time since the picture of her dad upset her.

Mrs. Green came toward us with a tray of drinks. Her bob bounced around her face, her hair slightly darker than Quinn's light brown.

"Alright, ladies." She set our glasses down and folded her arms over her chest. "Let me see the pretties."

Quinn lifted her plastic garment bag and revealed her purple dress, making sure the colorful jewels at the collar were visible.

Reaching out, her mom brushed the soft fabric and smiled. "I love it. It's very you, Sweetie. You always did have a thing for purple. I love the colors of the jewels, like a peacock feather." Leaning in, she kissed Quinn on the forehead. "Okay, Pips, show me yours."

I pulled out my dress and let the black chiffon drape over the back of the booth.

"Aw, lovely. You girls are gonna be the belles of the ball. I can't wait to see pictures." Her fingertips brushed the lacy bodice, and her hazel eyes sparkled as she smiled. "I remember my high school dances like they were yesterday. Can't believe it's been over twenty-five years. God, I'm old." She laughed as she straightened her apron.

"Excuse me, Sarah?" An elderly gentleman to the side of us lifted his arm, signaling to her. One of the other waitresses went over, waving Quinn's mom off.

"Thanks, Bea." She gestured for her daughter to slide over. "So, Pips, tell me about this guy Quinn asked to the dance. I hear you know him well."

My shoulders lifted in a shrug. "Declan? Um, he's okay, I guess. I wouldn't say I know him well by any stretch of the imagination."

"Pips thinks he's trying to steal her first chair from her." Quinn smirked. "She's not exactly a fan."

"It's not just first chair. If he takes my seat, it makes my chances of getting into Goddards like . . . nil. They have such an incredibly tough selection process, and they only take the best. And they *never* take more than one person from a school. He could screw this up for me. It's a big deal, Quinn."

She raised her hands as if in surrender. "I get it. Trust me. You've talked of little else since he arrived."

My eyes narrowed, and I looked away. Her smiling face and nonchalant attitude rubbed me wrong, and I was getting pissed. Add it to her going to Winter Formal with Declan, and I would've rather been at home than here with her.

"Okay, ladies. You sort this out, I've gotta get back to work." Her mom stood and left us.

"You know, Quinn, I don't belittle your dreams. I know you want to go to the University of Oregon because your dad went there. That you want to study English and eventually be a professor of literature. I think it's great. I want you to do well and get your dreams, be successful. I would never brush you off if it was something you cared about."

Sighing, the smirk was still on her lips and in her eyes. "It's not that I don't want you to live your dreams, you know I do. I just think you can be overdramatic at times."

"Overdramatic? You seriously don't get it. The competition for a spot at Goddards is *crazy* intense. They only take ten cellists a year, out of the thousands who apply. They're the most selective music school in the world. God . . . " I looked away, unable to even look at her. There was no point rehashing it. I didn't want to do this with her; not here. I wanted to eat and go home.

"Don't be mad at me, Pips."

"I'm not."

"You're lying." She chuckled, which grated on my nerves.

"I'm tired and ready to go home. I've obviously bored you enough already with my worries. I'll just keep it to myself from now on."

Quinn's mom delivered our plates and glanced between us. "You guys doing okay?"

I nodded, popped a french fry in my mouth, then squirted a heaping helping of ketchup next to my burger.

"She's mad." Quinn shrugged at her mom, still with the ever-amused look on her face.

I met her gaze, fuming. "And you seem determined to make a bigger deal out of this than necessary. Move on. Eat your dinner."

Mrs. Green grabbed the water pitcher and poured a steady stream into my glass. "Enjoy your meals, and remember, you guys are friends. Be kind." She looked to her daughter as she spoke.

Taking a bite of my cheeseburger, I offered an unenthusiastic and microscopic smile. I would never shoot down Quinn's dreams. It bothered me that she clearly cared so little about mine.

♪

The dance was two days away, and tonight Declan was coming over to my house to practice. We were actually sounding pretty good. It had me considering different competitions we could enter. Ones with prizes. Possibly even the National Competition of Young Musicians. It not only offered a hefty check to each winner, but scouts from all the top music schools would be there. Most with scholarships to hand out. If I had to collaborate with the enemy, I might as well try and get something good out of it.

I stood alone at my red locker before the school day started and sorted my bag. Footsteps alerted me to an intruder approaching.

"Morning, Pips." Noah smiled, his thumb hooked behind the strap of his bag. "You excited for Saturday?"

Nodding, I smiled, happy to see him. "I am. It should be fun."

He leaned against Quinn's locker beside mine and ran a hand through his blond hair. "So, the team and I rented a limo, and we'll be going in one big group."

I'd had a hunch we'd be going with the basketball team, which meant most of the cheer squad would be with us as well. I was still a little lost as to why he'd asked me in the first place. I didn't fit with his normal crowd. To them, I was just Phillip's orch-dork sister.

Looking down, I caught my lower lip between my teeth as I realized I hadn't asked about Quinn and Declan joining our group. "Um, would you mind if one more couple came with us?"

"I guess we could squeeze one more in. Who'd you have in mind?"

"Well, Quinn asked Declan to go, and she'd really like to be part of a group, so she wanted me to ask you if it'd be okay." I met his gaze, torn between wanting him to say yes and wanting him to tell me maybe there wasn't enough room after all. I was still perturbed with Quinn from our dinner at Oaks the other night. We ended up just leaving it alone and hadn't revisited the topic since. Which was probably for the best.

He scrunched his nose, then sighed. "Yeah, sure, why not? Anything for you."

"Great. Thanks." Closing my locker door, I looked down the hallway wondering where Declan and Quinn were. I hadn't seen either of them this morning, which was strange.

Noah and I walked to our first class, and there they were, already in their seats. They were chatting and smiling at each other like they were the best of friends. Why didn't they come find me? At least Quinn could've. So much for her being team Pippa. I watched for a moment, putting on a smile when they both looked my way.

"Morning, guys." I sat and pulled a pen from my bag.

"Did she ask you?" Quinn leaned across my desk to talk with Noah, her bubbly nature turned up to full blast.

"She did, and it's fine. Why don't we meet you two at Pip's house when I pick her up?"

"Perfect." Quinn leaned back, her face lit up like a beacon. Turning to me, she added, "I'll just get ready at your house, okay?"

I nodded, trying to match her enthusiasm, but it just wasn't happening. One glance at Noah sent a small flutter of excitement coursing through me. I *was* excited to be his date. I'd only waited forever and a day for him to notice me and ask me out. The strange thing was, somehow I wasn't as excited as I had been when he'd first asked. A tiny part of me couldn't help but dwell on the fact that Quinn and Jenna were kind of right about one thing: Noah and I didn't match. Other than Phillip, what did we have in common? Zilch.

Now, with the addition of Quinn and Declan going to the dance together, I was settling into a funk. And I hated it. My normally blue skies were turning cloudy and gray with a high chance of drizzle.

Declan coming into town had done more damage than I'd anticipated. He hadn't just threatened all my dreams, he'd tweaked something in my feelings for Noah. Maybe it was the fact that I'd been so distracted with practicing like a mad woman, determined not to let Declan get the upper hand on me, that I really didn't care about possibly starting a relationship with Noah. Before this big city rat showed up, my life had been fabulous. I'd been perfectly happy.

Well, almost.

Ms. Peters dismissed us, and the rest of the day I spent huddled under my own personal rain cloud. Quinn knew something was up and kept asking me what was wrong. She wasn't buying it when I told her it was nothing. What I needed was to go home and be alone. Sort my jumbled thoughts. Mope.

I glanced at the clock. Orchestra was almost over, and then I'd be free to wallow.

"You still on to practice tonight? You don't really seem in the mood for it," Declan leaned in and whispered while Mr. Woods worked on a short section with the second violins.

His eyes, nearly the color of his cello, met mine, and I realized that I actually wanted him to come over. What was up with that? "I'm always up for practicing. I'm just a little grumpy today, I guess. Sorry."

"You don't need to apologize; we all have moods, Princess. You're allowed to." He winked and sat back into his chair, his cello leaned on its side on the floor beside him, his bow hung on his stand, hair facing the floor.

Three and a half weeks. That's how long he'd been here and how long it'd taken for my life to stop making sense. Three and a half measly little weeks.

The bell rang and Mr. Woods excused us. In the storage room, Declan knelt beside me and we made quick work packing up.

"Alright, Francesca, in you go," I muttered to myself.

Declan snorted. "Please tell me Francesca's the name of your cello."

I rolled my eyes at him and giggled. "Nope, it's what I've decided to start calling you. Come on, Frannie."

"I never understood why people name their instruments." Smiling, he stood and swung his case onto his back.

Following suit, I said, "Uh, because they're cool. That's why people name their instruments."

"So you're saying I'm not cool?" he asked as we left the rehearsal room and stepped outside.

"You're the one who said it, not me." I laughed as I pulled out my keys and unlocked the car from a distance. Joking around with Declan made that mopey little cloud following me lift.

He leaned into me and bumped my shoulder, making me laugh. "Well, I better think of a good name for my cello. I don't want anyone to think I'm not as cool as you."

"Everyone already knows I'm way cooler than you."

He scoffed. "Oh, is that so?"

"Yup." I looked up into his brown eyes and something deep inside me flipped. Averting my gaze, I stared at the toes of my shoes. This wasn't good. Not good at all.

CHAPTER *Nine*

When you play, never mind who listens to you.

—Robert Schumann

The engine of my SUV idled in the driveway of my house as I tried to figure out what was going on. In the open garage sat my dad's car, which was seriously bizarre. I glanced at the clock and turned to Declan, my face scrunched in confusion. "My dad's *never* home this early."

Pulling my keys from the ignition, we grabbed our cellos and headed inside. Declan trailed behind me into the kitchen where the sweet tinkling of a piano lesson met our ears.

I peeked in the living room only to find it empty. "Um, wait here. I'll be right back."

Declan nodded, and I set my cello aside, sprinting up the kitchen staircase. I tossed my backpack in my room as I went by.

"Dad?"

"I'm in the bedroom, Sweetie." His baritone voice echoed from the end of the hall.

I poked my head in my parents' room. It was decorated

in whites and creams, very serene. The complete opposite of how I'd been feeling lately. Dad stood on the threshold of the closet, undoing his tie and changing from his work clothes.

"Why are you home so early?" I asked.

"We finally finished, closed the deal, and I decided I needed to come home and see my family." He walked over, tie hanging loose, and gave me a hug.

"So we'll actually get to eat dinner together?" I sat on the corner of the bed and glanced out the tall windows that overlooked our front lawn. The last two weeks Dad had been getting home well after I'd gone to bed and had been out of the house in the mornings before I'd even woken up.

"That's the plan," Dad answered, this time from inside the walk-in closet. "Oh, your mom invited the Fosses over for dinner." His voice lifted into a teasing tone as he added, "So Noah will be here."

I heard Declan's voice coming from downstairs; he must be talking to Phillip. I needed to get back down there.

"Who else is here?" Dad tilted his head and listened.

"Oh, it's just Declan. He's here so we can practice."

"Declan, huh? Is he cute?" A wicked grin filled his slightly scruffy face, his blue eyes lighting up as if ready for mischief.

I couldn't tell you why, but Dad got a kick out of teasing me about boys. I shook my head. "You're not funny."

"I can't wait to meet him." He waggled his eyebrows and chuckled. "See if he's good enough for my darling daughter." He pinched my cheeks.

"Ugh, I'll see you later." I uncurled my legs from beneath me and hopped off the bed, done with his teasing and eager to get away. I did another quick stop at my bedroom, making sure it looked okay just in case we had to practice here. Everything appeared to be picked up. I went over to the bed and pulled up my purple and pink flowery bedspread and fluffed my pillows before bounding down the back stairs to join Declan, who was talking to Phillip.

"Hey, so, we can practice in the living room or my room, if you want. Or we could wait for my mom to finish her lesson and see if we can use the studio."

Declan's shoulders lifted. "I don't really care—you pick."

"Well, I'm off to do chores." Phillip gestured to the staircase, then turned to finish his previous conversation. "Have fun with Quinn at Winter Formal. She's a pretty cool chick."

My eyes widened at his reply. He thought Quinn was cool? That was the first I'd ever heard about that. Hell, I never really pictured him thinking about her at all, aside from the fact that she was my friend.

Just then, Mom opened the music room doors and walked her student out. When she looked my way, I gestured to the door she'd just come through, silently asking if we could use the space. She nodded as she rattled off instructions to a short, blonde girl who held a bag with song books peeking out over the side.

"Come on." I grabbed my cello and went to the music room. Pulling Francesca out, I slipped my copy of the sheet music from my folder and sat. Declan settled beside me and pulled the stand closer to the middle.

"You ready?" He played a steady tone at my nod so I could tune to him. His eyes stayed on my hands while I turned the fine tuning pegs at the bottom of the strings. When he looked up, he caught me watching him. Looking away, I combed my fingers through my hair and secured it in a band. He was silent. A tingly sensation unfurled up my neck and onto my rapidly warming cheeks. I could *feel* his eyes on me.

Clearing his throat, he said, "Um, want to just start from the beginning?"

I nodded and counted us in. Strains of music filled the room.

"Phillippa Wyndham." Dad barged in, the door banging against the wall. Declan and I both jumped and turned.

"Jesus, Dad, you scared me." I tightly pinched the frog of my bow as I placed my hand over my galloping heart.

"I just wanted to meet your new friend." He looked down at Declan, a cheesy smile spreading over his stubbled face.

Shit.

"I'm Phillippa's dad, Sam, and you are?"

Declan stood and wiped his hand on his jeans before extending it to my father. "I'm Declan Brogan, sir."

Is he nervous?

"Is this that new kid you were telling us about? The one who thinks he's better than you?" Dad eyed me with a mischievous glint in his eye.

Mortification spilled through every pore of my body. I knew he was teasing, but I was going to kill him. "You might say that."

Dad turned his attention back to Declan, super serious expression on his face. "So, *are* you better than my Pips?"

Declan's mouth fell open, but it took a moment for any sound to come out. "Um, well, I think you could say we're pretty evenly matched, sir." His eyes darted to me. "On the cello, that is." He looked back up at my father who was staring at him. Declan's hand streaked through his dark hair, ruining his messed-to-perfection look. "She's very talented—definitely keeps me on my toes."

"The best girls always do." Dad suddenly smiled and gave him a wink.

"Dad!" He needed to leave, *now*. "Time to go. We need to get back to work." If he survived the night, it'd be a miracle.

"Alright, have fun practicing." Goofy grin on his face, Dad backed out of the room and closed the door behind him.

Declan sat and took a deep breath then looked at me, his brows screwed together. "So, Phillippa, huh? Did your parents seriously name you guys Phillip and Phillippa?"

A laugh danced over my lips. "Yeah, they did. Super creative, right? One of the many joys of being a twin—matching names."

"Wow." He chuckled.

"You can see why I go by Pippa, right?"

He nodded his head in agreement. "Phillippa is a perfectly nice name, it's pretty. It's just when you know your brother's name that it gets a little . . . odd."

"Tell me about it. Phillip and I agreed years ago that they must've done it just to torture us."

A low chuckle rumbled in his chest, making me smile. Unable to maintain eye contact, I pointed to the music with my bow and gave it a tap. "Ready?"

"Yup." Still grinning, he turned to the stand and waited for my count.

We ran through the first section; the fast and bouncy bits were my favorite parts. As we approached the slow, melodic section, I heard the doorbell ring, but I didn't care. Not stopping, we ran straight through the plucked staccato passages. I shook my head and chuckled as I flubbed a couple notes.

When we played together, something incredible happened. The rest of the room sort of . . . melted away. It felt as if Declan and I were lost on an adventure, just the two of us. It was perfect. He shot me a grin that I caught in my peripheral vision. He played. I answered. Goosebumps peppered my flesh as we hit a groove. Together, as partners, we were pretty freaking amazing.

Stopping in a flourish at the end, we both spun around

to the unexpected applause coming from the now open double doors.

"That was amazing." Noah's mom, Nancy, stood with her arm threaded through her husband's. Beside her was Noah, wearing a proud smile as he looked at me.

"You guys sound incredible." Noah came over and bent down to give me a hug.

Shocked, I leaned my cello to the side and hugged him with my bowing arm. Over his shoulder, I caught Declan's eyes taking us in before he got up and walked to his case to pack up.

"Oh, we're a little early, you don't have to stop practicing. Keep playing, please." Nancy's bejeweled fingers fluttered in front of her, trying to stop him.

"I should probably get going. Pippa's my ride home, and I don't want her to miss dinner because of me," Declan answered, leaning down.

"Well, why don't you stay? Pippa can drive you home after dinner," Mom said as she came in, wiping her hands on a dish towel before giving Nancy a quick side-hug. Mom's green shirt against Nancy's orange one made them look like a deconstructed pumpkin.

Declan looked at me, as if to ask if I was okay with it. I shrugged with a nod. Having him stay for dinner might be sort of nice. On the other hand, having him stay for dinner with Noah had the potential to get super awkward.

CHAPTER *Ten*

Where words fail, music speaks.

—Hans Christian Andersen

Mom and I carried the plates of food from the kitchen to the long black rectangular table in the formal dining room. The seats were full, except two—one next to Dad and one between Noah and Declan. I knew which one was intended for me.

Inhaling deeply, I set the cutting board of garlic bread and the salad in the center of the table, then made my way to the open chair. My arm brushed against the light-gray floor-to-ceiling curtains, nervousness putting a distance between myself and the table.

I sat and smiled at Noah on my left, then turned the other direction to face Declan, who looked around the table, silent. Everyone chattered and filled the misty-colored room with noise and laughter.

"I hope you like spaghetti," I said to my right as a bowl of cooked angel hair noodles came my way. Using the tongs, I loaded my plate. Declan reached to grab the bowl from me, his fingers skimming the back of my hand. I could feel the calluses on his fingertips which matched mine. I refused to even acknowledge the jump of my pulse his touch elicited.

"It's one of my favorites, and this smells delicious." He smiled and dished himself a helping of pasta.

Once all the dishes had made their way around, Noah broke his conversation with Phillip and turned to me. "So, Pippa, you and Declan sounded pretty great. When is your competition?"

I swallowed my mouthful. "Oh, um, Solo and Ensemble is in February, but it's not really a competition. Although, there is a big one in March that I think we should enter." I hadn't talked to Declan about it yet, and I could see him eyeing me from the corner of my vision.

"Which one?" Declan asked.

"The National Competition of Young Musicians."

Wiping his mouth with his napkin, he cleared his throat. "You seriously interested in doing that?"

I nodded. "I think we sound great. With a few more months to practice, who knows how amazing we'll be? If I ever stand a chance of doing it and doing it well, it's with you."

"Isn't it in New York this year?" He took a sip from his water glass.

"Yeah, at Carnegie Hall."

"We could stay at my dad's place." His eyes glinted as he watched me. "This would be awesome. I've always wanted to enter the NCYM."

I nodded and grinned. "Me too."

Yes, he was my competition and enemy, but knowing we'd both wanted to do this made me feel almost . . . connected to him.

"Is there like a trophy or some sort of prize?" Noah asked, reclaiming my attention from Declan.

"Sorta. There's a pretty decent cash prize for the top performance, but people mostly go because of the scouts."

Noah's brow furrowed. "Scouts?"

"Yeah. People from Goddards, NYU Tisch, Juilliard, and several other prestigious music schools will be there." It'd be a collection of all the people who held my dreams in the palm of their hands, gathered in one room. They all already had my applications, and I'd finished their auditions just before school started last fall. "This would put us in front of them and get us on their radar. And if we won, well . . ."

"But won't they already be set for the incoming fall students by then?" Noah took a bite, sucking a long noodle into his mouth.

I shook my head and said, "These schools usually hold a few spots open specifically for the NCYM winners and finalists. If they don't snatch them up, they dip into their bank of waitlisted kids."

"If you're serious about doing this, you can count on me. It'd be awesome." Declan's dark eyes searched my face as he gave me a grin that sent a shiver through me down to my toes.

"Great." I returned his smile and glanced down at my plate, moving the noodles around with my fork, suddenly unable to meet his eyes.

"I'm sure you guys will be fantastic. They'll probably scoop you up in a heartbeat, and you'll leave us all behind." Noah draped his arm around my shoulder, startling me with the added weight.

"Thanks, Noah." I pulled myself upright in my chair. The weirdness of having him affectionate with me was too much. Yes, I'd liked him forever. And yes, I would've thought this would thrill me . . . but it didn't. Instead, I got the impression he was trying to place his own personal stamp on me. Property of Noah Foss.

Declan cleared his throat and diverted his attention back to his plate, not looking at us. It was the height of awkward. The three of us sat there, saying nothing as the adults and

Phillip talked about the possibility of Marshland High making it to the state basketball finals.

My brother's voice was loud and clear. "It'll happen if Coach doesn't . . ."

I tried to focus on the conversation, I really did, but the goings on under the table were making it a challenge. On my left, Noah's knee pressed against mine. On my right was Declan's. Squished, claustrophobic, and a bit anxiety-inducing was the best way to describe it.

Thankfully, Noah removed his arm from around me and continued his dinner, jumping into the conversation the rest of the table was having.

The meal blurred by. I picked at my food and didn't eat much. How could I with Declan's leg pressed up against mine? What's worse, I kind of liked it. What the hell was wrong with me? Enemy city rat, remember that?

I couldn't like this guy. Not even a little. I absolutely refused to. It would complicate things way too much.

"Pippa, can you help me carry things to the kitchen?" Mom asked, standing.

Nodding, I stood in a flash, my chair nearly falling over in my haste. Declan's hand shot out and caught it before it could clatter to the floor.

"Thanks." I grabbed my nearly full plate along with the bowl of meatballs and sauce, then followed Mom to the kitchen, relieved to be out of my Noah-Declan sandwich.

At the sink, Mom turned on me and beamed like she knew a secret.

"What?" I asked, setting the bowl down.

Raising her eyebrows, she grabbed the dishtowel and wiped away some sauce she'd gotten on her hand. In a voice she reserved for secrets, she asked, "What's going on with you and that Declan boy?"

My head recoiled, and I wrinkled my nose. "Nothing."

Mom stared like she was waiting for me to give her another answer.

Pressured by the suffocating silence, my mouth went on autopilot. "We're just doing a duet together. Nothing else, I swear. Well, okay, we're chemistry partners too, but that's it. Why? What's wrong? Why are you asking me this?"

Her upturned lips looked like an archer's bow, the tips pulling taut as she watched me. "I think he might be interested in you. *And* . . ." She drew out the word as if she wanted me to finish the sentence for her.

"*And* what?" I didn't like where she was taking this.

"I suspect with his talents and the way you two complement each other . . . well, I think you might be developing a soft spot for him." She crossed her arms over her chest. The look on her face suggested that she was pleased by her deductive skills.

"No." I slashed my hand through the air and took a step closer. Our words still barely above a whisper, I added, "I don't want to like him, so I don't. Period."

I turned to leave when Mom answered, this time in her normal voice. "You can't just stop the feelings you have for someone. Not when your heart knows the truth."

Stopped at the doorway, I turned to face her.

"I should know. Lord knows how I tried not to like your father." With that, she turned to the dishwasher and began loading.

Unsure what she was talking about, I lifted my arms up in the air and went to retrieve more dishes. Declan's eyes met mine across the table as I cleared the plates from the adults. He didn't smile, but his gaze was soft and warm. It made me tingle. I liked it. Bad, Pippa, bad!

Returning to the kitchen, I heard plates and dishes clatter and clank from behind me. Handing off my stack to Mom, I turned, nearly running into Declan.

"Oh!" I jumped and took a step back.

A shocked smile filled his face. "Sorry, I just thought I'd help." He sat the dishes on the counter, beside my pile. "Why don't you let me load the dishes, Mrs. Wyndham? That way you can get back to your guests. I mean, I barely know anyone in there anyways, so no one will miss me."

Mom's mouth popped open in surprise. "I couldn't possibly do that, you're a guest."

"Then to thank you for dinner. Plus, I normally do the dishes at home, so I really don't mind."

Mom looked to me. It was a rare occasion when my decisive and self-assured mother didn't know what to do.

"I'll stay and help. Don't worry, we got this." I went to stand beside Declan.

"You're sure?" She dried off her hands.

"Yup," I answered as Declan nodded.

"Well . . . thanks." Smoothing her hair, she handed over the striped dishrag and went back to the dining room.

Declan reached for the towel in my hands and flipped it over his shoulder. "Okay, I'll load, you put away the leftovers?"

I bent down to the Tupperware drawer and smiled as I remembered Mom's face. She was going to seriously love him now. I stood and scooped the meatballs and sauce into a large glass container. "You don't realize this, but you just scored major brownie points with my mom. She hates doing the dishes."

"She seems very nice. And I really don't mind. I actually like doing the dishes. It gives me time to think." He dutifully rinsed off a plate before slipping it into the bottom rack.

Lips pursed, I nodded. Snapping the lid on the sauce, I moved to the noodles. "Yeah, I don't see it. Then again, when I do the dishes, someone always comes in and starts talking."

I put all the containers in the tall stainless fridge and tossed the remaining garlic bread into a Ziploc. Returning to the sink, I rinsed off the dishes and handed them to Declan.

When the dishwasher was full, I washed my hands and hopped up to sit on the white-and-gray flecked granite counter. "I should probably be getting you home. It's late."

Outside the window over the sink, the sky was dark and a dense fog had settled in.

Declan leaned back on his heels and then popped his toes down with a tap on the wood floor. "I'll go pack up . . . Clarence? What do you think of that name?" One side of his mouth twitched and he took a step toward me, our eyes now level thanks to my perch.

Wrinkling my nose, I shook my head. "Nah, it needs to be something sexier."

"Sexier? Why? Let me guess." He straightened his shoulders, came even closer, completely invading my space, and cocked his head to the side. "To match me?"

My stomach exploded, like fireworks had shot off inside me. Exactly.

I sucked in a breath, stiffly laughed, then jumped down, pushing him back as I did so. "Not quite, hot stuff. Come on." I motioned for him to follow me.

Declan veered toward the music room as I grabbed my keys and coat before poking my head into the dining room. "I'm gonna run Declan home. I'll be right back."

Mom looked up. "Okay, Sweetie, drive careful."

Noah stood. "Want me to come with?"

I didn't. "I'm fine. He doesn't live that far away. I'll be back in a jiff."

Noah sat, his smile faltering. Not that long ago I would've done anything to be alone with Noah in a car. But now, something was just . . . different. I still liked him, a lot, but it wasn't the same.

Standing behind me, Declan held onto his cello case. "I'm all packed. Thanks again for dinner, Mr. and Mrs.

Wyndham. It was nice meeting everyone."

Mom stood and came over to walk us out. "It was our pleasure, Declan. I hope we'll see a lot more of you." She patted his shoulder as we walked out the front door, closing it behind us once we were down the front steps.

"Yup, you do the dishes and my mom will love you forever." I went down the misty path, a little bounce in my step.

Hands tucked in his pockets, he caught up with me. "If only *you* were so easy to figure out."

I looked over at him. "Are you trying to figure me out?"

He shrugged. "Maybe."

"I'm not that difficult."

"No?" He looked at me with an arched eyebrow.

I nodded. "Yup, pretty simple. Music and the cello are my life. That's about it."

And *you*, you obnoxiously cute boy, are a huge threat to everything I love.

"I think there's a lot more to you than that."

A flurry of energy unfurled inside me. I looked away and aimed my fob to unlock the car. Declan stowed his cello and hopped in. I went around to my side, pondering his words. Why would he want to figure me out?

We rode in silence down my tree-lined road. Fog made the streetlamps look like they were wearing halos. As we passed Quinn's yellow craftsman, I pointed it out to him. I figured since he was her date, he might need to know.

"Cool." He nodded and watched it roll past his window.

"So are you excited for the dance?" Something inside my stomach tightened. I wanted him to say he wasn't. How terrible of a friend am I?

I really didn't want it to bother me.

But it did.

"Sure, I guess. It was nice of Quinn to ask me." He

turned to look at me. "How about you?"

"Yeah, it should be fun. It'll actually be my first Winter Formal."

"Really? You seem pretty popular."

A breathy laugh left my lips. "Uh, no. My brother's the popular one . . . not me. I'm just his orch-dork sister."

He smiled and ran a hand through his messy dark hair. "You going to the basketball game the night before?"

"Probably. Quinn usually drags me."

"I'm sure Wonder Jock will appreciate that."

I spared a glance his way and asked, "Why do you dislike Noah so much?"

"I don't." His shoulders raised in a shrug. "He's just not someone I'd ever be friends with."

Pulling into the underground parking lot of his high-rise building, I slowed to a stop and looked at Declan. "Noah's a nice guy. You might be surprised."

"Jocks are the same everywhere you go. Cocky and self-absorbed."

"This coming from the guy who wants to steal my chair from me because he's so sure he's better than me."

A slow smile spread across his lips, and he leaned toward me, putting our faces mere inches apart. "Oh, I'm definitely gonna get your chair before the year is up."

I leaned even closer, my brows raising in a challenge. "Dream on."

Reaching toward me, Declan brushed my hair over my shoulder. His fingertips grazed my neck and sent a shiver over my skin in a trail of goosebumps. "Oh, I'm dreaming, Princess."

♪

Mom sat on the edge of my bed and played with the hair tie looped around her wrist. She hadn't said much since I got home, but her silent questions were deafening. I held out my hand for the elastic, and she placed it in my palm. Downstairs, Dad was strumming a tune on his guitar. It was actually the first song he'd ever taught me to play, "Tonight You Belong to Me."

"You've been awfully quiet this evening," Mom said, folding her hands in her lap and shooting me a knowing glance.

I shrugged. "Is there something I should be talking about?"

"Um, how about this competition in New York for one, and two, this very nice Declan boy. I like him, Pippa."

"The competition isn't until March. I figure I have time to work you and Dad up to letting me go." My over-protective parents were no doubt going to have trouble letting me fly to the other side of the country. "And you shouldn't like Declan. He's a threat."

A slow smile traveled across her lips as she shook her head. "You can go to New York."

My eyes narrowed and met her matching green ones. "What? What's the catch? That was way too easy."

"It's an excellent opportunity for you. Plus, Declan said you could stay at his father's place, which I feel mostly comfortable with. Depending on which week in March it is, I might be able to go with you. My piano students wouldn't mind a week off, I'm sure. I do have one big concert that month though."

"Really? Why are you suddenly being so cool?"

Grabbing one of my hands, she reached out with the other and cupped my cheek. "You are an extremely talented girl. Your father and I know that only too well. We want what's best for you. Of course you can go. Now, if you were asking us to send you to Cancun for spring break, the answer would be decidedly different. But this is your future we're talking about. Now, don't get mad at me, but I do like knowing that Declan will be there with you, on the off chance I can't make it."

"What does that even mean?" I chuckled. "He did the dishes, Mom. He didn't save a life or cure cancer."

"I'm not saying he did, you little toad." She laughed and let go of my hand. "Seriously, how many teenage boys do you know that would willingly offer to do the dishes? None. He's a nice boy. That's all I'm saying."

"Or there's a possibility that you're entirely too trusting, and he's just trying to worm his way into your and Quinn's affections so I'll let my guard down, and then he'll be able to overthrow me." I flipped the covers back and climbed between the sheets with a smug look on my face.

Mom shook her head. "Wow, you've really thought about this. Maybe I'm wrong, but I get a good feeling about him."

"Declan might be nice. But he *wants* to take away the very things I care the most about."

"Ah, well, a little competition is good for everyone. It keeps you on your toes."

That sounded like something Declan had said about me.

Dad popped his head in the doorway, guitar in hand, and turned what he wanted to ask us into the new lyrics of his song, "You girls ready for bed?"

A glance at my alarm clock told me it was nearing eleven, and I had to be up early for school. Thank goodness I'd had a light load of homework tonight and got it done moments before Mom arrived at my door.

"Yup." Mom leaned over and gave me a quick peck. "Night, love you."

"Love you guys." I looked into the faces of my parents, and a surge of contentment flowed through me like a wave of warm fuzzies.

Mom stood and went to kiss Dad on his stubbly cheek.

He leaned down so it was easier for her to reach, never stopping his melody. One day, I wanted a love like that. Something easy and light and all-consuming.

Before I turned out my light, Dad stopped his soft song and came over and planted a kiss on my cheek. "See you in the morning, Love."

With a yank on the chain, my lamp flickered out. In the darkness, a blue light blinked from my nightstand where my phone was charging. Once I was alone, I reached over and grabbed it. I had a text message from Noah.

Noah: Do you like Declan?

CHAPTER *Eleven*

*Music replays the past memories, awaken our forgotten
worlds and make our minds travel.*

—*Michael Bassey Johnson*

Quinn stood beside me in front of my full-length mirror.
Her wide eyes, minus her usual glasses, stared at our formal
bedecked reflections, a happy grin filling her features. Declan
was waiting downstairs. He'd rung the doorbell moments
earlier, and Mom had hollered his arrival up to us. My brain
conjured up images of what he might look like in his tux.
With his dark hair, height, and broad shoulders, he'd look
amazing. Like a young James Bond.

Noah would be here any minute, which made my nerves
coil into a tight ball. I'd managed to evade flat out answering
his text asking if I liked a certain cello player. Friday, I spent
all day just avoiding him period. I didn't want to face it. Now
I wasn't left with a choice, I couldn't exactly hide from my
date. Not knowing how to label my feelings for Declan was
a serious problem. I didn't *want* to like him, but that was
proving to be a bit of a challenge.

Phillip did a little knock on my doorframe, then peeked

in and unzipped his maroon hoodie. "Well, don't you ladies look fabulous?"

I smiled and did a quick twirl, then noticed my brother watching my best friend. For a moment, I wondered if he was regretting spending all his money on his car instead of coming with us tonight.

"It's a shame you aren't going." Quinn tilted her head toward her shoulder and clasped her hands coyly together in front of her. Demure was not a word I'd normally use to describe her, but right now it was spot on. Her eyes blinked more than normal thanks to the contacts, which she hated with a passion. I was surprised she was even willing to put up with them for the night.

The bell rang again, snatching my attention and making my pulse jump erratically. I inhaled a shaky breath. Excitement and dread coursed through me. This was Noah. The boy I'd been crushing on for years. And I really did like him, but I was terrified he'd start questioning me about my feelings again.

Because I didn't have an answer to give him.

"Pips, Noah's here," Mom called up the stairs.

"We'll be down in a minute," I shouted back.

I glanced back at Quinn only to realize she and Phillip were standing close and chatting in hushed voices. He reached up and twirled a nut-brown curl around his pointer finger, smiling at her. My mouth popped open. Was he flirting? With my best friend?

"Um, I'm gonna head down." I grabbed my clutch and smoothed the front of my black chiffon skirt.

"Okay, I'll be right there." Quinn met my eyes, looking completely over the moon.

My gaze darted to the mirror one last time, making sure my makeup looked okay and that there were no snags in my hair. I'd styled it in an intricate braid that swooped along the bottom of my hairline, then swirled back onto itself. Each section of the braid had been pulled slightly so it was fluffier and thicker than normal. It felt elegant and I loved how it looked as it ran along in scallops against the pale skin of my neck.

Leaving them alone in my room, I went to the top of the stairs and looked down. Noah wasn't there, but Declan was, hands tucked in his pockets, looking into the living room. He hadn't noticed me. My eyebrows rose as I took in his still messy dark hair paired with the sleek black tux that hugged him in all the right places.

He was better than James Bond.

Way better.

Wow.

Stepping down onto the top step, I glanced back to see if Quinn was coming. Feeling nervous, I suddenly didn't want to go down alone, but she was still in my room. I turned forward, startled to see Declan staring up at me. Definitely no going back now. I met his wide eyes with a slight smile. His lips parted, a corner hitching up. He ran a hand through his hair and watched as I made my way down.

When I got to his side, he shook his head and gave me a once over, swallowing hard. "You . . . you look incredible. Wow."

I averted my eyes, tingly sensations flooding my body. "You look great too. I like the Chucks."

With a laugh, he lifted a Converse-clad foot and gave it a little shake. "Had to add a bit of me to this monkey suit."

"Indeed."

Our eyes met and we both grinned.

"Pips, you look awesome!" Noah's voice registered from the living room.

I turned and saw him in a white tuxedo jacket with black pants. His hair perfectly coiffed, he looked incredibly handsome. How I always pictured he'd look.

Arms outstretched he walked to me and engulfed me in a hug. The scent of his spicy aftershave clung to him. "I knew you'd be even more gorgeous than you already are."

I smiled at his compliment and leaned back, still in his embrace, to look up into his eyes. "Thanks, I like the tux."

Knowing Declan was beside me, watching this exchange, made me uncomfortable.

Mom rushed in, camera in hand. "Let me get a picture." She looked between the three of us. "Where's Quinn?"

"She's just finishing up." I glanced up the stairs again, wondering what on Earth they could still be talking about.

"Well, let me get a shot of the three of you while I'm waiting." She gestured for us to all get closer.

Noah lifted both his hands making the rock-on gesture for the picture. Declan took a step closer to me and put his arm around my waist, his left palm resting on the bare skin of my lower back. I heard him intake a sharp breath just before his fingertips came to rest over the lace edging. The warmth from his hand sent a streak of heat through me.

"Say cheese." Mom hefted her large camera to her face and looked through the viewfinder.

I leaned my head toward Declan, trying to be seen around Noah's raised hands, and we all obediently said cheese and grinned.

"Wait for me!" Quinn rushed down the stairs and sidled up to Declan's right side.

He kept his arm around me as Quinn leaned into him, a huge grin on her face. Mom snapped a few more shots before Phillip photobombed us and used my shoulders to jump up from behind me.

Dad came and stood beside Mom as she lowered the camera and watched us.

"You guys better get moving. The limo out front just

honked." Dad draped an arm around Mom's shoulders.

Declan's hand dropped away, taking all my warmth with it. Noah put his arm around me as Declan turned to his date, smiling. A pang of jealousy hit me in the chest, and I struggled to brush it off. Corsages and boutonnières exchanged, we headed out the door as Mom told us to be safe.

Leaning in, Dad kissed my cheek. "You look lovely."

"Thanks." I smiled.

Phillip sat on the stairs, watching us leave. Too bad he wasn't coming with us. "Hey, Pips, come here a second."

"Yeah?"

"I know Noah is my best friend, but if he hurts you or does anything stupid, you'd still tell me, right? You know I'm not really a fan of you dating him, but I'm trying to be cool with it for you. But if he does anything to upset you . . ."

I nodded and glanced quickly to Noah waiting on the front porch before looking back to Phillip. "I'll be fine. You don't need to worry."

Spinning away, I walked to the door, my skirt swishing. The early winter air hit my skin and I shivered. Wishing my dress had more coverage on the bodice as the breeze cut through the lace and whipped behind me, I hastened my stride.

Noah opened the door of the limo and Quinn slid in, then Declan. Before I entered, Noah's hand clasped onto my shoulder to stop me.

"You know, I'm really glad you said yes." His blue eyes glinted.

I smiled and looked away before my cheeks burst into flames. Never did I expect to be in this situation. I'd always assumed I'd be a spectator in his life, and now here I was, Noah Foss's date.

And feeling so unbelievably confused.

Other guys from the team and their dates filled up the

seats of the long car. I waved to Lucy, my ex-stand-partner, and she returned the gesture. Quinn and Declan leaned together in conversation, and I sat between Declan and Noah . . . again.

"So, who's the guy with Pippa's friend?" a guy near the back named Chad asked, his hand resting on Lucy's knee, who was eyeing Declan appreciatively.

Noah leaned around me, his gaze darting to Quinn. "That's Declan. He's from New York. He's Pip's cello . . . person."

Cello person? I snickered. Way to pay attention.

"Hey." Declan's arm raised in a wave as he addressed the car.

"So do you play any sports?" Sydney, a girl in a short yellow dress, asked. She was on the cheer squad with Lucy. They were both actually pretty nice. Most of the cheer squad was, honestly. I just felt so out of place next to them.

Sitting up straight, Declan cleared his throat and shook his head. "Um, not really."

"Pity, you're cute," Sydney answered, coyly batting her lashes. "But I only date athletes."

"Uh, and you also have a boyfriend." The buzz-haired guy from my English class leaned out from behind her, shooting a glare at Declan and looking pissed.

She giggled before sitting back in her seat. "Relax, Tom—doesn't mean I can't look. Certainly doesn't stop you."

I turned to Noah as the couple started to bicker, but he didn't say anything.

Sydney patted Tom's leg and leaned in to kiss him, effectively putting an end to their argument.

When he resurfaced from Sydney's lips, Tom turned to Declan with a sneer on his face. "There is something to be said for being an athlete. I mean, we're practically gods: we're talented, we know how to win, and we always get the girls.

Nothing an orchestra dweeb like you could even begin to understand." One of the teammates beside him gave him a high-five.

Next to me, Noah leaned forward and got a high-five of his own. Declan didn't say anything, but I could feel his leg stiffen next to mine. I shot a look at Noah, because possibly he didn't realize it, but jerk-wad Tom had essentially insulted me as well. Noah looked at me and shrugged, at least attempting to wipe the grin off his face, but clearly he wasn't going to disagree. Disappointment filled my very core. I couldn't remember ever seeing Noah as anything but kind to others. It was one of the things I liked most about him. Yet here he was helping to belittle Declan.

Turning my focus to the back of the limo, I nodded as they continued to laugh and pasted a tight smile on my lips. Loud enough to ensure they'd hear me, I said, "And yet, isn't it sad to think that this, right now, this is your peak. Declan and I, well, *we* orch-dorks still have our best years ahead of us. You guys will most likely end up spending your days asking, 'would you like fries with that?'"

Beside me Declan snorted and Quinn raised a hand, which I leaned over and high-fived.

I met Tom's glare and caught the word "bitch" leaving his lips. Noah adjusted beside me and I glanced to him, meeting his blue stare.

He raised an eyebrow. "Wow, such high hopes for me. Thanks."

My head tilted to the side. His future was something Noah worried about, and I knew it. He didn't know what he wanted to do after graduation. He didn't really want to do the college thing. My insult to Tom suddenly felt a little harsh. "You know I don't think that about you. Tom back there, definitely. He's a jerk. But not you."

Noah nodded and looked out the window. Hurting his

feelings had been the last thing I wanted to do.

I put my hand on his arm, wanting to make things right. "You do realize he insulted me as well as Declan, right?"

"Tom was joking around, just giving Declan a hard time."

Angling myself in my seat toward Noah, I shook my head. "No, he was being an ass. I'm not gonna let some creep pick on any of my friends or me like that. If I embarrassed you, hurt your feelings, or ticked you off, that certainly wasn't my goal. But I'm not going to just let it slide."

The limo pulled up outside a fancy restaurant and Noah met my eyes. "Look, I don't want to argue, not tonight. Let's just forget this and have fun."

I nodded and followed him out of the car, not wanting to ruin our Winter Formal. Declan and Quinn clambered out right behind us.

"Thank you for that," Quinn whispered in my ear.

Smiling, I grabbed her hand and gave it a squeeze, then laced my arm with Noah's as we walked through a lane of twinkle-light-wrapped trees and went inside. I glanced back at Declan, who was smiling down at Quinn.

One shocking thought permeated my senses: I wanted him to look at me like that.

And that wasn't okay.

♪

After we took our photographs, we came down the long marble stairs that descended onto the dance floor. I held tight to Noah for fear I might trip. The students on the dance floor pulsated in time to the heavily thumping bass. I spied Lexi and her date, a tall dark-haired guy I recognized from the lacrosse team. The smile on her face told me she was having fun. Noah's hand clasped mine as we stepped off the last step and wound our way to join in the fray. I lost sight of Declan and Quinn in seconds. Noah's hands grabbed my waist as a slow song came on and we shuffled along in a circle, keeping some distance between us. It was nice. Exactly what I'd always dreamed about. But I wasn't as over the moon as I would've thought I'd be.

Jenna and her date were with their group. She spotted me and waved her hand above her head, a huge grin on her face. I waved back, wishing I knew her date a bit better. Apparently, they'd gotten friendly this past summer when they were both counselors at a horseback riding camp. He was tall, blond, and seriously cute. They made an adorable couple.

"Are we okay?" Noah asked, pulling my attention back to him, a curious smile on his lips.

I nodded. "I'm sorry about the limo. You know me, sometimes I let my temper get the better of me."

"I know." He tweaked my chin. "It's okay. Tom knows how to push buttons."

"Clearly." I caught sight of Declan over Noah's shoulder. He stood taller than most of the people in the room and towered over petite Quinn. Her arms were wound around his neck and she rested her head on his chest. They looked cozy. And super comfortable. And too damn close.

It's the first freaking song! What was this?

My breathing hitched as I realized how annoyed I was with my best friend. I'd almost prefer Lexi had asked him.

Declan scanned the crowd, looking for something, then his eyes settled on me. Our gazes locked until Noah pulled my attention back to him.

"Everything all right?" he asked.

"Yeah, just taking it all in. It looks so beautiful." It really did. We were under a large domed marble rotunda. When the spotlights hit it, flecks of the gold veining shimmered.

As he glanced around I looked back at Declan, who was

talking to Quinn, a big smile on his face.

"It is beautiful, but nowhere near as beautiful as you tonight."

I smiled and looked away. "You know, never in a million years did I ever think we'd be here together."

"Is this a bad thing?" A slight frown marred his lips.

"No. I just . . . I never expected you'd ask me." In my peripheral vision, Declan caught my eye—he was watching me. "I am kind of curious about something."

"What's that?"

"Why did you really asked me out?"

Noah glanced to the ceiling and shrugged, then met my eyes. "Truth?" He continued at my head bob. "I've wanted to ask you out for a long time, like since we started high school."

My mouth popped open in shock. Seriously? "Well, why didn't you?"

A soft laugh escaped him. "Your brother."

"Phillip?"

He nodded. "He felt weird about me asking you out. You remember that time, a few years ago, when we came in the house, him with a bloody lip and me a black eye?"

"Yeah?"

"Well, that was the first time I talked to him about you. And he flat out told me not to go there. You were *very* off-limits."

"So what, did he have a change of heart?" I could totally picture Phillip getting all protective on Noah—even though it seriously annoyed me. I was perfectly capable of making my own decisions, and I didn't need my big brother rushing to my rescue. When it came down to it though, even I had to admit it was a little odd to be with Noah when my brother wasn't around.

Noah shrugged. "Not really, I just told him I was gonna

ask you out whether he liked it or not. I was tired of doing what he wanted. Although . . . I'm thinking I might be too late."

Declan.

My eyes darted to where I'd last seen him; he was there, his eyes now latched onto mine.

I had to wonder what would have happened if Noah had asked me out sooner. Before Declan ever arrived. I'd probably happily be with Noah. And I definitely wouldn't be so damn confused. I met Noah's gaze, unsure how to reply.

"I'm pretty sure at one time you liked me." His blue eyes never left mine. "Do you think there's a chance you might again?"

"I do like you, Noah." I did. He was seriously hot and sweet and everything I ever wanted in a guy. It's just now there were two guys, and somehow this had blasted so far past complicated it wasn't funny.

He shook his head. "No, I've seen the way you look at him—and the way he looks at you. It's the way you used to look at me. Now . . . everything's changed. It's all different."

The music accelerated into a frenetic beat. Couples split apart. Noah took a step back and ran a hand over his face.

We stood there looking at each other, not dancing. Of course I wasn't certain since I wasn't looking at him, but I swear I could feel Declan's eyes on me. "I don't know what to say. I don't think I look at Declan any different than I do you."

He reached up and cupped my cheek, bringing his face a breath away from mine. "Just tell me I'm not too late."

CHAPTER *Twelve*

*Music is the literature of the heart; it
commences where speech ends.*

—*Alphonse de Lamartine*

Noah and I had the limo to ourselves after dropping the others off. Quinn was our last stop. Declan had been our first. In the silence, Noah's hand grasped mine. His thumb rubbed the back of it as we pulled the short distance to stop outside my house.

"I'm just sorry I waited so long to tell you how much I like you." Noah stared at our joined hands. "No idea how sorry. I really hope you'll give me a chance."

This all seemed like a surreal dream. Who'd have thought I'd even be considering turning him down? Quinn would never in a million years believe this.

"Noah . . ."

He shook his head, his blond hair now messy from repeatedly running his hands through it. "It's okay, Pips. I get it. I think you like us both. You should know, I'm not giving up."

A slight smile curled my lips, and I pulled my hand from

his and opened the car door. We both climbed out onto the sidewalk, then Noah leaned into the car and told the driver he'd walk home from here.

"Um, well, I guess I'll see you later." I raised my hand in a small wave and turned toward the house. Every fiber of my being wanted to avoid an uncomfortable good night. Heck, the whole last part of the evening had been pretty high on the awkward scale.

"Pippa, wait."

I spun back to face him, shivering from the cold night. "Yeah?"

Taking a step closer, he didn't say anything, but in a swift movement, he cupped his hand on the nape of my neck and brought his lips to mine.

This was very different from the first time we kissed ten years ago. But his lips were still just as soft, and he was still very much all Noah. The first time we'd been playing hide-and-seek with Quinn and Phillip. We hid in the cupboard under the kitchen stairs, and, curious how it all worked, he'd smooshed his face against mine. We both came to the same conclusion: gross.

What can I say? We were eight.

But this . . . this made my heart rate rise, and I had to admit it was the very opposite of gross. It was actually quite nice. It wasn't a long kiss, but it was enjoyable. Leaning back, he watched me with a slight smile, waiting for my reaction.

Stunned and a little starry-eyed, I looked up into his handsome face. "You definitely learned a few more skills since the last time you kissed me."

That got a blast of laughter from him, which made me laugh too.

"Well, I would hope I'd have learned some things since then." His hands slid down my back to rest on my hips. "Did you know you were my very first kiss?"

Chuckling, I looked down at the buttons on his jacket. "You were definitely mine."

"I kinda like that."

I looked up and met his eyes, wondering if he could really be *my* Noah? Did I even want him to be mine?

My thoughts took a sudden sharp turn to Declan. Had he kissed Quinn tonight?

"So . . . think you might give me a chance?" Noah's voice interrupted my thoughts, bringing me back to the moment.

My eyes widened, and I could clearly see the hope and worry etched on his face. This kiss had done nothing to ease my confusion. In fact, it'd tripled it. I opened my mouth, not sure what to say, and shrugged my shoulders.

Noah took a step back and looked down, scuffing the tip of his shoe against the sidewalk. "He better realize how lucky he is."

Popping up on my tiptoes, I pressed a kiss against his cheek. "Noah, I may not know what I want, but I do know that I had a great time tonight. I'm really glad you asked me."

With a brief bob of his head, he tucked a hand in his pocket. "Me too. Night, Pips."

He turned from me, gave a little wave, and headed home. I watched him only a moment then bounded up the front steps and let myself in the door, ready for some warmth.

Mom and Dad were in their pajamas on the couch, watching a movie, an empty bowl of popcorn perched between them. Dad's guitar leaned against the side of the armrest. His head was lolled back against the cushions, mouth agape, sound asleep.

"How was it?" Mom stood and came over to me.

I shrugged. "It was fun. I'm tired though."

"Why don't you go get changed and get to bed? You father's out cold. We're getting too old to stay up this late." She laughed. "I'm going to get him into bed too."

Dad grumbled something unintelligible.

Glad she hadn't peppered me with questions, I leaned in and kissed her cheek. "Night, Mom."

Popping upstairs and into my room, I sighed as I grabbed my pajamas from my drawer. The dress and makeup came off and the jammies went on. Once I crawled into bed, I stared at the ceiling, unable to sleep. I don't know how long I laid there. My mind just kept running through the events of the evening. Over and over. Noah had kissed me. Did I want him to do it again? Did I want him? A clicking sound hit my ears, but I ignored it. Noah's kiss had definitely been nice. Not earthquakes and church choirs, but I enjoyed it. A lot.

Restless energy coursed through me. I couldn't stop wondering what had happened between Declan and Quinn. Every time I looked at him at the dance he'd been looking at me. Yet because Quinn had walked him to his door, I couldn't stop the mental image of them kissing. The smile on Quinn's face as she ran back hadn't helped at all. *Click.* Maybe it'd be better if they did end up together, and I stayed single. It'd give me more time to focus on my cello and long-term goals. Hell, maybe she'd keep the enemy side-tracked long enough for me to kick his butt. *Clickity click.* Lord knows I didn't want any of this boy drama. They were distractions. A couple cute ones, but distractions nonetheless.

Another light ping and I rolled toward the sound, wondering what it could be. A succession of three fast taps. What the . . . ? I climbed out of bed to investigate. At the window, I pulled back the curtain.

Declan? He stood on the lawn illuminated by the streetlamp, carrying a handful of pebbles, his arm poised to lob another one. When he saw me, he stopped, dropping what he had in his hand and waved.

I slid my window up; the music note window clings

must've given away which one was mine. "Declan? What are you doing here?"

"I wanted to talk to you," he whisper-yelled.

"Okay." I watched him and waited for him to continue.

Reaching up, he rubbed the back of his neck and looked behind him. "Can you come down for a couple minutes?"

The clock on my nightstand read a little after two in the morning. Mom and Dad were definitely fast asleep by now. I glanced back to Declan and held up one finger before sliding my window shut.

My feet slid into my fuzzy unicorn slippers, a gift from my grandma, and I grabbed the hoodie hanging at the bottom of my white metal bed frame and threw it over my tank top. For a moment I thought about slipping into my jeans, but I decided not to. Flamingo pajama pants were fine, right? Quietly, I opened my door and crept down the hallway, avoiding the spots I knew creaked. Breath caught, I snuck past my sleeping parents' room and down the stairs. Pausing at the door, I put a hand to my messy ponytail and quickly tried to straighten it.

Why was he here? What could he possibly have to say that couldn't wait until morning? My fingers curled around the knob as I pushed it open. Declan stood on our covered front porch in his black leather jacket, hands tucked in the pockets of his jeans, rocking back on his heels.

"What are you doing here?" I asked as I slipped outside and closed the door behind me. Zipping my hoodie, I stepped closer to him, shivering with the chill on the air.

He pointed to my feet and smiled. "Nice slippers."

"Thanks, but I doubt you came here at two in the morning to compliment my footwear. What's up?"

"I had to talk to you." He looked me up and down like he was enjoying the funny picture I made.

It annoyed me.

My sleeves fell over my fingers so I clutched onto them, irritation sparking in my stomach. "Why?"

Declan looked down to the wood-planked floor of the porch. "I . . . um, I wanted to make sure you got home safely."

I quickly turned and looked back at the house, then back at him. "Uh, yeah, I did."

He nodded, a sudden nervous look in his brown eyes.

"You know, you could've just texted me."

One hand slid from his pocket to run through his hair and scratch the back of his head. With a grin, he took a step forward and said, "Well, I also wanted to thank you for what you said in the limo."

"Oh." I shook my head and looked away, grateful it was dark out. "That was nothing."

"It wasn't nothing to me."

He was close. My previous feelings of annoyance vanished, and I was left with a tingling low in my tummy. If I wanted, I could reach out and brush my fingers through his dark hair. And boy, did I want to. I looked to my unicorn-covered toes, then out to the street. I didn't see any unusual cars. "How did you get here?"

Clearing his throat, he said, "I walked."

"At two in the morning? Declan, really, you could have just texted." A nervous laugh was on the tip of my tongue, but I held it in. Why would he walk all that way just for this?

He took another step toward me. We were now close enough that I could feel his rapid breath on my cheek. My heart stumbled, faltering in its steady beat, and my knees went all flubbery and weak.

Whispering, He leaned in: "But if I'd texted, I wouldn't've been able to do this."

His hands cupped my face and, as if in slow-motion, his warm lips met mine. Heat seared my insides and my heart beat a prestissimo tempo. Frissons of electricity sparked though my entire body.

I'd never felt anything like this. Holy shit.

My hands rose to his chest as a shocked squeak escaped my throat. Declan held me with a nervous stiffness until I relaxed into him. I closed my eyes and slid my palms over the soft t-shirt he wore under his open leather jacket and up to twine around his neck. My fingers played with the hair at his nape as I pulled him closer. A low noise escaped him, making my toes curl and sending a shiver that scattered a wave of goosebumps over my skin.

Noah's kiss couldn't even begin to compare to the feelings Declan was stirring inside me. Not even close.

This was church choirs, earthquakes, and fireworks all rolled into one.

Declan leaned back a smidgen, just long enough to catch his breath. A smile curved his lips as he lowered his mouth to mine again. This time one arm snaked behind me, pressing me flush against his chest. The other came up and cradled the back of my neck. His tongue touched my bottom lip, and I instinctively opened my mouth to his. My heart thundered as a soft moan left my throat.

He seriously knew how to kiss.

Breathing heavily, he pulled back and rested his forehead against mine.

I smiled, a shaky sigh escaping my lips.

"You okay, Princess?" he asked and took a step back.

Nodding, I giggled. For the first time, his nickname for me didn't trigger that prickle of irritation that usually went through me. No, this time all that coursed through me was warm fuzzies. "You definitely couldn't do that over a text."

He laughed softly as he rubbed his thumb against my cheek. "You have no idea how long I've wanted to kiss you."

A shiver went down my spine, and I wasn't sure if it was

from the chill in the air or his words. I didn't protest as he bent down again to kiss me. In fact, I went up on tiptoes and met him halfway, wanting his kiss. It didn't last nearly long enough to please me. As he pulled away, he cupped my face in his hands again and kissed my nose.

"Um, I should probably get back inside." My voice sounded higher than normal.

"Yeah." He took a step back, his breath curling in misty tendrils. "I guess I'll see you Monday then."

I nodded and he turned, stepping down onto the top step. "Declan?"

"Mmm?" He spun back to me, and I was right behind him. Now we were eye-to-eye. Before I could change my mind and chicken out, I leaned in and gave him another toe-curling kiss.

"Night." Biting my bottom lip and trying to suppress a giddy grin, I turned and went inside, locking the door behind me. As quietly and quickly as possible, I hurried up the steps, hoping to catch one last glimpse of him from my window. In my room, I threw back the curtain and watched as he stepped off our grass onto the sidewalk, he jumped up and hit a low hanging tree branch before he disappeared.

This night turned out so much better than I ever could have hoped.

♪

Monday after school, Declan and I were in the band room, settling in to work on our duet. My eyes met his as he sat the music on our shared stand and grinned. A flush crept into my cheeks as I remembered our kisses. This is pretty much how the whole day had played out. Long looks, flirtatious grins, and a lot of blushing—okay, the blushing was solely done by me.

It also hadn't escaped my notice the way Quinn now

looked at him. At the very least, she was seriously interested. Even Lexi had acknowledged Quinn's interest. Not that she'd turn him down if he asked her out—she didn't work that way—it was more that she was aware of what was going on.

But now I was struggling with the guilt. I'd kissed him back, so I was at fault.

"You ready for this?" His lips tilted in a grin as he lifted his bow.

"Let's do it." Nodding, I silently counted us in.

The room filled with the perfect harmony of our instruments. My fingertips ran over the fingerboard with the aggressive melody of the beginning. Grace notes tripped from our bows as we tossed the main melodic strain back and forth, echoing each other in a flirty dance.

I glanced up to see Mr. Woods leaning out from his doorway, a smile on his face, confirming what I suspected. We sounded awesome.

We hit the slow melancholy part, and I loved the way Declan played it with such emotion and longing. His instrument sang under his skillful hands. A thrum of happiness rushed through me as we played. The pace picked up again, and we took turns plucking the melody. The race to the end was upon us. I glanced over as Declan started the fast section, his hair swishing back and forth as he bowed like mad. I quickly joined in, and we brought the piece to its completion.

Declan immediately looked over at me, his brown eyes sparkling. He's good. Really good. Too good?

Even knowing he might steal my seat away from me, I still wanted to lean over and kiss him. It's practically the only thing I'd thought about all day. Heck, ever since we'd kissed. Maybe that'd been his plan all along.

"You guys, that was incredible!" Mr. Woods clapped from

the doorway and came toward us. "Have you turned in the application for the National Competition of Young Musicians?"

I shook my head. "I was just finishing it up. I need a little more info from Declan before I can hit send. And we need to make a submission video."

"Well, get on that. You two have a really solid shot." Turning, Mr. Woods went back to his office. "I'm only gonna be here about another fifteen minutes, so start wrapping up."

Declan nodded and met my eyes. "You want to run through anything else, or are you ready to pack up?"

The look he gave me wasn't anything out of the ordinary, but it still made my insides tremble with a nervous energy. This was so bad. The way Quinn now ogled him and the sheer distraction he was to me, I couldn't do this. I couldn't go down this path. I should be with Noah. Or really no one. I didn't want to travel down this road anymore. Was it too late to do a u-turn and run like hell?

"Let's go ahead and pack up. We can work on it again later this week." I stood and rushed to the storage room, needing some space to clear my mind.

This couldn't go any further. I had to stop it before it turned into a runaway freight train and destroyed my whole life in its inevitable crash. My future and Quinn were too much to risk. As if that wasn't enough, there was still the Noah issue. I had these two guys who were both amazing, yet incredibly different, and I liked them both.

Only one of them made me see stars.

It worried me how much I wanted to see where things with Declan and I could go. I feared just how easily he might tempt me to veer off course. I couldn't let that happen.

I laid Francesca in her case and secured the bow as Declan knelt beside me to do the same.

"Everything okay?" he asked without looking at me.

"Fine. Why?"

Declan shrugged. "You just seem to be . . . in a hurry."

"No, not really. It's just been a long day." I couldn't admit that I was in a rush to get away from him. The more time I spent with him, the more I liked him.

A lot.

The more he made me forget Noah, which I thought would've been impossible.

Standing, I tossed my case over my shoulder and headed for the door. "See you tomorrow, Declan."

"Pippa, wait up. I'll walk out with you."

My feet reluctantly slowed, and I waited for him to pull up next to me. Heat flashed over my body as his arm brushed against me, staining my face crimson.

We didn't say anything as we walked out to the parking lot, the cold air making our breath visible. In the distance I saw Quinn leaning against my SUV. She pushed off and approached us, a smile on her face.

"Hey, you two! How was practice?" She slid herself between Declan and me, putting an end to the awkwardly stretching silence. The way she looked up at him made my stomach drop.

"Good. Woods was leaving so we couldn't practice long," Declan answered. "What are you still doing here?"

"Oh, I was just waiting for Pippa. I wanted to talk to her."

I adjusted my messenger bag so I could fish my keys from the flap. Once I found them, I pushed the button and my taillights flashed.

"Well, um, I'll see you two later," Declan said as he looked to Quinn with a smile and nod then walked away.

My mind raced with things I wanted to say to him, but I couldn't get any words past my lips. And next to Quinn was the last place I wanted to say them.

"We need to talk." Quinn motioned to my car and proceeded to walk over and jump in the passenger side.

Sighing, I opened the hatch and stowed my cello before hopping behind the wheel. "What's up?"

"I'm so confused."

Join the club.

I looked at her as I slid the keys in the ignition to get the heat going. Her brown hair was in a low ponytail that she'd draped over her shoulder. She pushed her glasses back up her nose as she watched Declan arrive at the bus stop.

"What about?"

"Phillip and Declan."

I shook my head. "Want to elaborate?"

She exhaled heavily. "This is going to sound crazy, I know. But I swear Phillip and I had a . . . a moment. It was when we were in your room. It was like he *finally* saw me. He looked at me like a guy looks at a girl he likes."

"That's great! So what's the problem?"

"Declan."

Apparently, he was a lot of people's problem at the moment. My brows scrunched together. "Declan? Why?"

Part of me wanted to come clean, tell her I'd kissed him and that there was definitely something happening, but I knew how she could be. Stubborn and territorial. In seventh grade, we both had a crush on the same guy a year above us. She made absolutely sure she won him, even if it meant pointing out all my flaws. She'd flirted like mad and got asked to the dance. I stayed home. Honestly, after seeing how far she was willing to go, our friendship had never quite been the same afterward. Well, that and I always knew she had a ready replacement for me in Lexi, which didn't make me feel that great. But I wanted to be her friend, and for the sake of our friendship, I tried to overlook all this.

"I think I might actually like Declan. He was so sweet at

the dance, and he's really cute and funny."

I nodded, not wanting to say anything and agree with her for fear she'd think he was even better. "Yeah, but you've liked Phillip for years. If you have a chance with him are you saying you wouldn't take it?"

"I don't know. It seemed like Declan and I had a kind of connection. I think he likes me, which would be such a nice change from Phillip and never being sure how he feels."

"W-what makes you think Declan likes you?" I ran my thumb against the calluses on my fingertips, their familiar roughness calming, despite feeling like I'd been punched in the gut.

She shrugged. "He's a good listener, he laughed at all my jokes—even the lame ones. Heck, he agreed to go to the dance with me in the first place. And when I dropped him off he . . ." She paused and glanced my way, her lashes momentarily resting against her pale cheeks. "He did this thing with my hair. God, it was so sexy."

They kissed. They had to have. There was no way I was about to ask her what he'd done. I didn't want to know.

Maybe he really did like her.

"Do you think he'll ask me out?"

My mouth opened to speak, but I couldn't find the words. Instead I looked like a guppy, mouth opening and closing.

"Pips?"

"Um . . ." I shrugged. "I couldn't say, but I'm sure if he likes you he'll ask you out." It pained me to say the words, but it was true.

It's just . . . if he liked her so much, what the hell was he doing kissing me?

CHAPTER *Thirteen*

Music is the divine way to tell
beautiful, poetic things to the heart.

—*Pablo Casals*

Laying on my bed, I stared at the ceiling with my headphones blasting a sappy brokenhearted song. The sound of a basketball bouncing and banging against the garage gave Phillip and Noah away. Practice must've gotten out early, which surprised me because they had an away game tomorrow night. Mom had already informed me that Noah was staying for dinner again. It was the second time this week. His mom was working late, and his dad was on a business trip. He seriously needed his own room here.

"Pips." Mom smacked my bent knee. "Hey, I want to talk to you."

I slid my headphones off, sat up, and drew my legs to my chest. "What's up?"

"I was curious how things were going with you and Noah since the dance."

My nose scrunched as I launched into a quick, but probably confusing, synopsis of where we stood. Conveniently leaving out anything about our kiss or my jumbled feelings for Declan—the very ones she'd picked up on earlier.

"So now that he's interested in you, are you saying you're not that interested in him?"

"Not necessarily. I mean, I like him, but I just don't know how much anymore. I don't know if I can see him as my boyfriend. It was just . . . strange."

She shook her head, a smile spreading her glossy lips at my shrug. "I never thought I'd live to see you willingly wean off of Noah."

"Neither did I," I said with a sullen sigh.

Her arm rested on my knee as she leaned forward, brushing my hair over my shoulder. "Think it might be because of a certain handsome cello player?"

My face flushed and I pinched the fabric of my bedspread, separating the top layer from the batting inside. "Declan may have a small role in why my feelings are changing."

"Well, your crush on Noah has gone on way too long without him doing anything about it."

"He said it was because of Phillip that he didn't do anything sooner. That he'd actually liked me for a long time."

Mom tilted her head up and brushed her hair out of her face. "And what about things with Declan? What's going on there?"

"Oh, um." I picked up my headphones and busied myself untangling the white strands. "Quinn's crushing on him now."

"Really? How does he feel about that?"

My brows furrowed in confusion, and I shook my head, not sure how to answer.

"Does he like her too?" she clarified.

I made a noncommittal sound to suggest I had no idea.

"Hmm, well, I've seen you two around each other and

heard you play together. I still say that boy likes you."

He *had* kissed me—*really* kissed me. He'd walked all that way at two in the morning to do it. Just thinking about it sent a flutter straight to my stomach.

"Even if I did *maybe* sorta like him, I couldn't go for a guy that Quinn wants. Or, more importantly, let down my guard to someone who could take first chair away from me."

Mom's shoulders sagged with a sigh. "Pips, I think if you'd be honest with yourself, you'd admit you've liked him long before Quinn's little crush started. Have you even told her you like him? Given her a chance to take a step back? I mean, they've gone on one date. He's not her property. And I'm sure even she has to see how well the two of you complement each other."

"She actually noticed it first. She thought he liked me. But I gave her permission to ask him out. She was worried I'd be upset by it and I assured her I wasn't."

Mom nodded. "And yet here you are, upset."

I scowled at her. "It doesn't really matter though. He's a distraction that I don't need. And okay, I'll admit he's cute . . . really cute. But I *have* to stay focused. If I let myself relax, even a little, Goddards could slip through my fingers. Declan could get my spot. And when I add that onto Quinn and her new feelings, that's the girl code right there, and I . . . I don't even want to touch that."

"Your cello is important, that's true." Mom's voice was calm, the complete opposite of mine. "But if you don't get into Goddards, there are other great schools out there. It's not the end of the world, I promise."

I shook my head and opened my mouth to speak, but she stopped me with a raised hand.

"I know how you feel about Goddards. Just do me a favor—don't forget living a full life is also important. Of course your father and I want you to reach for your dreams and continue to be amazing with your cello. However, I don't want you to grow up and look back on this time and have regrets. You're too young for that. You've got to take time to relax and have a little fun, Pips. You're always so hard on yourself. Take a risk or two. How else are you going to know you're alive?"

"I'll know I'm alive once I've gotten into Goddards."

She nodded and stood. "If you say so. Dinner's ready. I'll go call the boys in."

She left my room, and her words ran through my mind on loop. Would I regret this? Would I always wonder what could've been?

Without a doubt, I knew one thing I'd regret. Coming in second to Declan. Him stealing my place at Goddards. Him taking my focus away from my goal. And okay, yes, maybe even him. But a love life just wasn't important right now.

♪

Hands tucked in the pockets of my jacket, I stood on the front porch. Noah had whispered in my ear to meet him out here moments earlier. Now I was waiting for him to say his goodbyes. I sat on the top step, my mind swirled back to Declan standing right here and me stopping him from leaving and leaning in to kiss him.

I remembered how his lips felt, how warm he'd been under my fingertips, and the sensations he'd created that had my insides on the brink of overflowing. It made me wonder things I shouldn't even be thinking. Could we be more than duet partners? Could I do it without sacrificing my dreams? Without losing Quinn? Was anything with him even remotely possible?

"Hey, Pips, thanks for meeting me out here." The door closed behind Noah with a soft click.

I looked up to him as he lowered himself beside me,

grateful for the interruption from the dangerous direction my thoughts were traveling. "Of course. What's up?"

He picked at his fingernails and sighed. "I owe you an apology."

My brows lowered in confusion, and I ran my thumb against the callus on my pointer finger. "What for?"

"The limo at Winter Formal. The more I think about it, the more I realize I should've told Tom to shut it. Declan is your friend . . . even if he is my competition." A small grin formed on his lips. "I should've stuck up for him . . . and you."

"Oh." I nodded. "Thanks."

Reaching over, Noah grasped my hand. "What would you say to seeing a movie this weekend? If you're not busy."

With a squeeze, I glanced at him. "We could get a group together and go see something Saturday evening. I've got a make-up cello lesson in the morning."

A slow sigh left his lips. "Yeah, we could do that. Or . . ." he gave me an intense look, as if willing me to fill in the words for him, "we could go see something, just the two of us."

My teeth worried my bottom lip as I tried to find the right words. "Noah . . . it'd probably be better if we went as a group."

"Well, I was kind of hoping we could spend some time together. Just the two of us. See where this might go." He looked hopeful.

His kiss hadn't made me feel the way Declan's had. And he certainly wasn't the one I couldn't stop thinking about. But I still liked him. Good Lord, I wasn't even making sense to myself anymore. Right now the best thing would be to avoid both boys and just stay single and focus on anything but romance.

Sighing, I shook my head. "Noah, I can't. I need to keep

my focus on practicing and being the best so I get accepted into Goddards. I don't have time for dating."

"Right." He sniffed, giving me the impression he didn't believe me.

I gave a tiny shake of my head. "What was that for?"

He angled himself to face me. "You mean to tell me if Declan asked you out you wouldn't jump at the chance to go with him?"

"No, I wouldn't." Okay, *probably* not. God, I hated these waffling emotions.

"I find that hard to believe."

Irritation surged through my veins. "You know, despite what you may think, having a boyfriend isn't high on my list of things to do. I get that it's a common stereotype for girls, but I think if you actually paid attention, you'd find far fewer of us actually care about it as much as you think we do. And I, for one, have much more on my mind than getting a guy." I stood and stepped onto the porch. "Important things to worry about, like college and scholarships and competitions. Sorry to disappoint you." Marching to the door, I went inside, ignoring Noah repeatedly calling my name.

Stupid boys.

Pulling out my phone, I shot Jenna a text.

Me: Boys suck.

Jenna'd been the only one I'd even hinted to about my confused feelings for Noah and Declan. We'd been bored in health and had spent the time texting back and forth. I wasn't the only one worried about how Quinn would take it. Her newfound crush put a major wrinkle in things.

I went upstairs, wanting to get into my homework and forget all about Noah and Declan and all the thoughts of them that swirled around my brain.

My phone pinged, and I pulled it from my back pocket

as I closed my bedroom door behind me, expecting it to be Jenna. Instead it was a message from Janey, my cello teacher.

> Janey: Bring your duet partner on Saturday and we'll work on some fine tuning.

I sighed and ran my hand through my hair. Clearly the universe wouldn't let me forget about Declan.

> Me: Okay, I'll see if he's available.

Janey was the principle cellist with the Portland Symphony. She was one of my favorite people in the whole world. She'd been with the New York Philharmonic for years, but then she moved home to Portland to be near family.

I sent Declan a quick text to see if he'd be able to make it. As I cleaned off my cluttered desk and sat down to work, my phone alerted me to a new message.

> Jenna: What happened?

I quickly recapped my conversation with Noah.

> Me: I don't know what I want anymore.

> Jenna: Well, Noah's hot. You can totally send him my way if you want. ;) Or Declan. Whichever. I'm not afraid of Quinn.

> Me: Lol, I'll keep that in mind.

I went back to reading, but moments later, my phone pinged again.

> Declan: Wouldn't miss it. Can you give me a ride?

> Me: Sure, I'll pick you up around 9.

> Declan: We can finish up the NCYM application after.

I sat my phone aside and opened my history book. I was about halfway through the chapter when Phillip popped his head in my door.

"Hey, Pippy, you got a second?"

I blew out a long breath and scrunched my nose at the hated nickname. "Don't call me that, Phil." I threw his right back at him. "And sure, come on in. What's up?"

Phillip sat on the edge of my bed and leaned his elbows on his knees. "What's the deal with Quinn?"

"What do you mean?" I turned to face him.

"The other night, I don't know, I kind of got the vibe that she might . . ." He paused, his green eyes darting away from mine before adding, "be into me."

I snorted a laugh. Hello, Mr. Oblivious. "And why would you think that?"

"She was a little, well, almost flirty."

"What would you do if she *did* like you?"

He shrugged. "I don't know."

Spinning back around in my chair, I grabbed my highlighter off the desk to continue my reading. No way would I give up Quinn's secret so easily. "Well, figure out what you'd do, then come talk to me again."

"Pips." He groaned and flopped onto my bed.

"What? Why does it matter so much?"

"'Cause I can't stand for you to know something I don't."

I laughed. "Tough."

"Fine, you pain in the ass." He pulled himself up and tossed a heart shaped pillow at me, sending my highlighter careening off the text I was marking in a bright pink wound across the page.

As he opened my door, I threw the pillow back and hit him in the back of the head. I laughed and put my hands up to protect myself as he lobbed it back at me then quickly shut the door.

Glancing back to where he'd just stood, a thought popped in my mind: what if I could make something happen between Quinn and Phillip? If I could swing it, she'd forget about Declan in a heartbeat.

♫

Declan sat beside me at my desk as we worked on my computer to fill out our entry form to the National Competition of Young Musicians. We'd just gotten back from Janey's studio. She'd helped us refine the small stuff, like crescendos and decrescendos, basically the loud and soft parts, and really attacking the accented notes. All the little things that really made the piece shine.

She'd been impressed with Declan—offered to take him on for lessons right there. Considering how long her wait-list of prospective students was, all who would jump at the chance to audition for her, it was a big deal. He not only bypassed the wait-list but the grueling audition process. I wasn't about to tell Declan this. He'd happily accepted her offer.

"You know, Princess, this isn't how I pictured your room at all." He looked around at my white shelves packed with picture frames, books, and stacks of sheet music and song books.

"Oh? What's so surprising?" I glanced up at him as he took it all in.

"Probably that." With a smirk he pointed a finger to my poster of Douglas Booth. Hair mussed. Sexy grin on his lips.

I chuckled. "If you were a girl, you'd get it."

"Oh, is that so?" He laughed. "I think I just found what I should name my cello. Booth. I like it." His eyes glinted in mirth. "It kinda sounds like a mysterious detective." He laughed. "A sexy, mysterious detective."

Smiling, I shook my head and asked, "Um, this application wants your middle name?"

"Matthew. What's yours?" He leaned closer.

My hair fell around my face and I did nothing to move it, preferring to hide behind it as I typed. "Hope."

"Hmm, Phillippa Hope, pretty." Reaching over, he pushed my hair back.

My eyes stayed glued to the screen. I didn't want to see the look on his face. "How about birthday?"

"July fifteenth. What about you?"

"November eighteenth." I grinned, enjoying getting to know him a tiny bit more.

He fell silent as I typed in the address that he'd written down on a piece of paper for me.

"You know, somehow I didn't picture Douglas Booth as quite your type." He brought us back to our earlier discussion.

"What, tall, muscular, talented, and insanely hot? I can see your point. Poor guy, it's a wonder any girls like him."

Scrunching his nose up, he made a *bite me* face. "I just pictured your type being more . . . musical."

"Well, I'll tell you what, you can get me a shirtless Adam Levine poster for Christmas if it'll make you feel better."

"Fine, I guess I'll take the Yo-Yo Ma one back." He leaned back in his chair and propped his feet up on my desk. I shoved them off and snickered as he landed with a thud.

"A fabulous cellist he may be, but he's no Adam Levine."

"If you say so." Declan leaned forward to peer at the screen.

I glanced at him. "Application's done. Now we make a video, and then we're ready to send this in."

"Let's do it."

Declan went to the chairs we'd set up and grabbed his cello. I leaned my cell phone up against a stack of books and hit record, hoping the first time would be perfect. Francesca in hand, I sat next to Declan.

We'd decided earlier that he'd introduce us as I got settled. "I'm Declan Brogan, and this is Phillippa Wyndham. Our piece is 'Passacaglia' by Händel-Halvorsen. We thank you for your consideration."

Through minute bow movements, I counted us in. We moved through the piece like we'd been playing together forever. It was easy and effortless to play with him. I'd never particularly enjoyed doing duets. I always thought I thrived on solo performances. But now, after having him as a partner . . . well, let's just say I had a newfound appreciation.

When we finished, I stood and hit the stop button. We'd done it perfectly the first time. With a few clicks, I sent it to my email, then attached it to our application. "You want to watch it before I hit send?"

He nodded. I tapped on the attachment and we filled the screen. Watching us play was strange. For the first time, I noticed how often Declan glanced at me. It was a lot. Warmth spread over my skin, staining my cheeks and neck.

"We sound amazing."

"We do." I grinned. With a tap on my touchpad, I hit send. It was official, we were entered. Now we had to wait to see if we got in. Hopefully come March, we'd be New York bound.

Declan scratched the back of his head. "Have you ever been to New York?"

"Nope."

"Not even for college auditions?"

I shook my head. "I did either video auditions, live chat auditions, or when they held open auditions anywhere near here, we went there."

He nodded and moved closer to me. "It's such a cool city. I'll have to take you sightseeing."

"That'd be fun. Maybe we can catch a show on

Broadway. I've always wanted to go to one."

"Definitely." His lips tilted in a lopsided grin. Lifting his hand, he brushed my hair away from my face and tucked it behind my ear. "Do you have any idea how badly I want to kiss you right now?"

A thrill of anticipation had my tummy flipping. I wanted him to kiss me. Just how much I wanted it was startling. Words encouraging him were perched at the tip of my tongue.

Instead, as he leaned closer, I whispered, "We can't, Declan."

He stopped and looked up at me, brow furrowed with confusion. "Why not?"

I sighed and closed my eyes. My best friend might kill me for this, but he had to know why. "Because Quinn likes you."

Shaking his head, he met my gaze and, in a soft, sincere voice, asked, "What about who I like?"

CHAPTER *Fourteen*

But without music, life would be a blank to me.

—*Jane Austen*

Friday evening and I found myself in the Pearl District in downtown Portland, just leaving Janey's studio from my normal lesson. Cello strapped to my back, I stopped and looked around. The sun was almost completely down, just the pink glow on the horizon was left. Closing my eyes, I inhaled the crisp winter scent on the air. It smelled like the cold and firewood.

"A Princess in the Pearl. How proper."

Smiling, I turned toward the voice. Declan was sauntering toward me, his jacket zipped, a shopping bag in his hand.

My fingers curled around my keys in my pocket, and I stepped to the side as a group of hipster-looking guys walked around me. "What are you doing down here?"

"Getting my mom's Christmas present." With a grin, he lifted the brown bag. "Are you just getting out or going in?"

"Out." Just seeing him made me smile. Memories of our kiss hit me and I shivered.

He glanced at his watch. "You want to grab some dinner?"

I lifted my phone to check the time and nodded. "Sure."

"Where's good?" he asked.

"Um." Quinn's mom had just hired Phillip and it was his first night waiting tables. It'd be fun to see him in action. "Want to go to The Live Oak? It's Quinn's mom's diner."

He nodded. "Sure. Can I catch a ride with you?"

"Yeah, my car's just around the corner." We walked down the street of cute little shops and restaurants, their fronts decorated in holiday finery. I looked in the windows of one low-key grill and saw a college-aged guy in a beanie nursing a beer. He looked up and gave me a friendly smile and wink. I returned the grin and walked on. The Pearl was one of my favorite areas in Portland. The only downside was everything was more expensive.

Declan cleared his throat beside me. "So, have you lived in Portland all your life?"

"Pretty much. We moved from Tigard into the actual city of Portland when I was seven."

"And Tigard is just down south, right?" His eyebrows rose in question.

My head bobbed. "Yeah, it's really not all that separate of a city anymore, it's just on the outskirts now."

We stopped at the intersection, waiting for the MAX light rail to zip by. I was parked across the street. "What about you, did you always live in New York before here?"

"Yeah, but my mom gets shuffled around a lot with her job. Before my parents divorced it wasn't a big deal; Dad and I'd stay home when she'd go. Now she wants something more stable. Mostly 'cause she knows I don't like staying with my dad and his new wife. Which is why we're here. She's hoping this Portland job will allow her to stay in one place."

"That had to be hard." I adjusted my cello strap and

looked at him. "My dad works a lot and often late hours, but it'd be strange to have him be away for so long."

"I guess you just get used to it."

Once the MAX passed, we crossed the street. At my car, I clicked the fob and the lights flashed. Declan hopped in the passenger side as I loaded Francesca into the back. I climbed into the front seat and started her up, getting the heat going. I rubbed my hands together and tucked my fingers into the sleeves of my jacket before placing them on the cold steering wheel. Looking over at him, I was curious to learn more about him. "So what about your old school and your friends? Do you miss them?"

He raised a shoulder. "Some days. The conservatory I went to was pretty cool, and I miss that, but I still keep in touch with the people I want to, so it's not too terrible."

"A conservatory sounds so fancy." I threw a smile his way. "You must have had some crazy competition there. I must seem like nothing compared to them." I checked the traffic and signaled before pulling out onto the street and navigating toward the Oak.

"Actually you're more competition than they ever were. *I* was always the section leader for all the groups I was in. There was only one girl who was insanely competitive. Kara. I actually once caught her trying to tamper with my cello."

My head turned to him, my mouth open. "Seriously? Why would someone do that?"

"She wanted my place. And she was willing to do whatever to get it."

"What happened to her?"

He reached back and rubbed the back of his neck. "Um, not much, since she didn't do any damage. I just got a locked storage cubby for my instrument from then on."

I pulled off the road into the parking lot and killed the engine. I could see Phillip through the windows standing at a table, pad in hand, Quinn's mom next to him smiling.

Declan and I went to the door, which he held open for me. I wanted to pry and ask if he'd had a girlfriend at the conservatory, but I also didn't want to give away just how interested I was.

"Pippa." Quinn's mom Sarah came over and wrapped me in a quick hug. Looking to Declan, she raised one eyebrow and asked, "Who's your friend?"

"Oh, this is Declan. He was Quinn's date for Winter Formal." My cheeks reddened at the mere mention of the night, but I carried on. "We just ran into each other outside our cello teacher's studio."

She held out a hand, which he accepted. She grinned. "Well, it's lovely to finally meet you. Quinn's told me all about you. And so has this one here." She motioned her thumb toward me. "But last I heard you were giving her quite a run for her money."

A shocked laugh escaped my lips and my brows rose as I looked at her. She was almost worse than my own parents.

Declan grinned and looked at me. "Oh? And what did you hear?"

Quinn's mom looked at me, the edges of her mouth twitching. "That's for me to know, young man." She turned to me. "And I'm guessing you'd like to be seated in Phillip's section."

I nodded, wicked smile on my face. "Is there any other section?" Laughing, I added, "How's he doing?"

"Phillip's working here?" Declan looked around, a slow grin forming on his lips.

My best friend's mom craned her head to look into the dining room. "Yup, tonight's his first night. He's doing pretty well. Let's get you seated."

We followed her to a two-person table. Declan took the offered menu, then looked around and up at the ceiling.

"This place is so cool."

"Thanks, I try." Sarah smiled. "I'll send Phillip over to get your order."

As she walked away I leaned onto the table, closer to Declan. "In the summer, she opens the roof, and it's the coolest thing. The breeze comes in, ruffles the leaves on the tree, you can see the moon and the stars peeking through the branches and . . . it's just the best."

Declan's eyes sparkled as he looked at me. He matched my pose, bringing his face closer to mine. "Then we'll have to come back here in the summer."

"Don't let me interrupt your make-out session. I just need to take your order."

I leaned back and turned my head to Phillip, who was smirking, pleased with himself.

"Seriously?" I rolled my eyes at him.

My brother just laughed. "What can I get you guys?"

Once we ordered, Phillip went off to the kitchen. He looked comfortable in his new role. But this place was like a second home to us, so I guess that made sense. I noticed Quinn's mom checking up on him and talking with his customers and hovering just a smidge, but she looked pleased.

"What's that about?" He gestured to the picture of Quinn's dad with its candlelight vigil.

I took a moment and looked at the photo. I could only conjure up vague memories of him now. "That's Quinn's dad. He was a firefighter. He and another fireman died in a fire ten years ago." I recapped the story and looked away.

"That's rough. Quinn mentioned something about him dying, but I assumed he'd gotten sick, and I didn't want to ask."

"Yeah. It's still pretty hard on her."

We fell silent. I watched Phillip load a tray of food and

make his way to a table of young teen girls. They giggled and blushed as he got closer.

"So I'm curious. What's it like being a twin?" Declan asked as he fiddled with the salt and pepper shakers at the side of the table.

"Annoying."

He smiled. "Who's older?"

"Phillip, by three minutes."

"Does that mean he gets to be a protective older brother?"

Nodding, I said, "He sure thinks it does. He also believes that his opinion carries more weight than mine because he's older." I shook my head at my brother's stupidity. "Did you say you were an only?"

Our drinks were placed in front of us as Declan answered, "No. I have a half sister, but I rarely see her."

I took a sip of my soda and looked around the room. My brother was flirting with the girls, and a thought hit me—this time next year everything would be so different. We'd all be away at college. I, if I was really lucky, would be in New York at Goddards. Phillip in Eugene, preferably with Quinn, as they both had their hearts set on going to the University of Oregon. Jenna at OSU. And Noah, he'd be . . . well, he didn't know where he wanted to be. And I knew he worried about that. Heck, we were all stressing and worrying about where we'd be next fall. It'd be weird to not see them every day. My focus shifted to Declan. Where would he be? Wherever he ended up, I hoped it wouldn't be my seat at Goddards.

♪

Outside Declan's condo I rapped lightly on the door, making the Christmas wreath jingle. Judging by the poshness of the exterior and the well-appointed lobby, this condo was going to be super nice. I took a deep breath, nervous and excited to see him.

I survived term finals and finished all my concerts—in fact, last week was my last performance with the Portland Youth Symphony until after the new year. I was blissfully free. This winter break meant nothing but freedom, which meant Declan and I were getting in practice sessions whenever we could. Solo and Ensemble was just around the corner. So was the NCYM. Well, it would be if we got accepted, but I couldn't imagine us not.

The door swung open and Declan's mom greeted me with a smile. "Pippa, welcome, come on in."

"Thanks." I stepped inside and slipped my rain-spattered cello case from my shoulder, then handed her my coat. With her dark slacks and button-down top, she looked like she'd just gotten off work.

"Dec's just around the corner in his room. First door on your left."

With a nod, I followed her directions and passed through their swanky apartment. The windows were floor-to-ceiling and made up most of the walls. The dreary, rainy Portland skyline and Willamette River view was spectacular. Their Christmas tree was set up in a prominent spot, reflecting off the glass panes. It looked like the pages of a Pottery Barn catalog.

I came to a closed door, and as I raised my hand to knock it swung open. Declan's brows shot up, as though he were surprised to see me. My hand dropped, and I matched his shocked stare. "Hi."

"You're here. I didn't hear you arrive. Sorry."

"No worries, your mom gave me good directions." I shifted my case and looked at him with a grin.

Clearing his throat, he said, "Come on in."

The white walls of his room had very few adornments.

No posters or decorations like mine. He had two smaller cellos hung on the wall. My guess was they were the ones he'd played when he was younger before moving up to his current one. Shelves of books filled the space above his bed, like a headboard. In the corner, near another tall window overlooking the same view as the living room, he'd set up two chairs next to his music stand. His cello was out and waiting.

"I'm surprised you wanted to come over here this time." He closed the door, his low voice pulling my attention.

I laughed and sat on the floor to pull out Francesca. "It's Christmas break, so my family and Noah are constantly around. They're driving me insane."

"Noah is, really?" His eyebrows rose in surprise.

"He's always at our house hanging with Phillip. They're loud and obnoxious, and I'm just so done with everyone."

"Really? I'd have thought you'd like Noah being around." Declan turned and grabbed his cello.

My shoulders rose in a shrug, and I shook my head. "He's Phillip's friend, so I don't really get a say. I'm stuck with him."

"But . . . I thought you guys were kind of . . . dating?" His eyes darted to mine as I sat down, then quickly away.

I shook my head, wondering how he'd gotten that impression when Noah and I hadn't done anything together since Winter Formal. "No, not dating. We just went to that one dance together and now things are . . . complicated."

He silently sat, played a couple notes, then adjusted the tension on the hairs of his bow. I joined him. He stared out the window as I got ready to tune.

"I was pretty sure you *like* liked him." His head angled toward me again, his forehead furrowed as if he were trying to sort out a complicated puzzle.

I opened my mouth and closed it, overanalyzing my

words. Part of me wanted to lay it all out on the line and admit to my confused feelings for Noah, but I couldn't. Not when I also liked Declan far more than was smart. "Um, growing up I liked him, and I do still, I guess. But now . . ." I shook my head and paused, intending to finish my thought, but I found I couldn't—not with the way Declan was looking at me.

"And now?"

I looked to my bow and copied his earlier movements, adjusting the tension on the hairs and avoiding his eyes. "Now, I don't know. Things are . . . *different*."

"How so?"

Because of you. But I wasn't about to come right out and say that. Just thinking it made me flush. Clearing my throat, I kept my gaze averted and mumbled, "Well, our competitions are just around the corner, and I need to focus my time and energy on that. I don't have time for a relationship right now."

Declan nodded, pulled out new rosin, lightly scraped the top with a quarter from his pocket, then ran his bow through it before offering it to me. I took it, my fingers brushing against his, which sent sparks flying. With a couple slides over my bow to coat the horsehairs, I handed it back, careful not to touch him again. He played a tuning note, and it didn't take much to get our instruments in sync.

My back straight, I adjusted my cello against my frame. I'd forgotten a hair-tie, so I flipped my hair over the shoulder opposite my instrument, then glanced to Declan to make sure he was ready. His eyes were glued to the music, so I didn't even have to ask. With my bow, I indicated to him we were starting. We jumped into our flawless dance of moving bows and vibrating strings.

Every time we practiced, it sent chills up my spine that radiated out to the tips of my fingers and toes. I glanced his way, my brain flashing our kiss to the forefront of my thoughts. My distraction made me flub the notes of an easy passage, and I turned my focus back to the music, trying to ignore the heat building in my face.

We finished and Declan cleared his throat. "Should we run that section again?"

The tip of his bow tapped the section I'd messed up on. The part where I'd gotten distracted thinking about his perfect lips and how warm and amazing they'd felt kissing mine.

"Sure." We ran it again, this time with no mistakes.

"So I'm thinking we should start working on doing it by memory." He stretched his neck from side to side, which made a soft popping sound.

Sighing, I stuck my tongue out. "Ugh, I hate memorizing. I suck at it."

"We'll just have to practice more then." His brown eyes caught the light as he smiled.

With a deep breath in, I closed my eyes and tried to remember the start of the piece. My bow slid across the strings in the correct arrangement. Declan's cello joined and sang out in harmony with mine. I cracked an eyelid and saw his eyes closed as well. And that's when I lost the music.

He continued on a few more measures then stopped. "Not bad at all. You've got almost the whole first page."

"I'm pretty sure it was because of you. Once you joined in, it's like my fingers just knew where to go."

Leaning closer, he ran his thumb over my cheek. "You've got something on your face."

I didn't move. I couldn't. His touch took my breath away. My cheek was cool compared to his skin. My brain went fuzzy, and I felt as though an invisible tether was pulling me to him. I leaned closer, and our faces were almost touching. I held my cello and bow in one hand and shifted them to the side. Closing the distance between us, I placed my lips on his and kissed him.

Declan's free hand slid from my cheek to curl around the nape of my neck.

His lips were soft, and hot damn, he made me feel incredible.

My fingers knotted in the soft fabric of his t-shirt before sliding up his chest to twine in his hair, nails scraping against his scalp. With a groan, he pulled me closer. If only we didn't have our cellos in hand.

"Declan, I—" His mom stood in the doorway, hand on the knob, mouth agape. We split apart and looked at her.

My stomach churned with mortification, and I knew I was beet red from my hair all the way to my toes.

Declan cleared his throat. "What's up?"

"Uh . . ." One side of her lips hitched up, something I'd seen on Declan too many times to count. "I was going to run to the store, but I think I'll save it for later. Do you guys still have some practicing to do?"

His head bobbed. "Yeah, we're working on memorization."

"Huh, interesting technique." She turned with a nod and left the door wide open.

I covered my eyes with my hand. "I can't believe that just happened."

He chuckled. "Don't worry about it."

"It's embarrassing." I dropped my hand and briefly met his eyes.

"With how much I talk about you, I don't think my mom is all that shocked."

My gaze dropped to the floor, and I asked, "You talk about me?"

"Does that surprise you?"

Nodding, I smiled. "A little."

"You know, I thought you said we couldn't kiss." His mouth twisted into a slight smile.

I sucked in a heavy breath. "You're right. I shouldn't have, I'm sorry. I just—"

He grabbed my hand. "No, no, no. That's not what I'm saying. I definitely wanted you to. Trust me. I'm just having trouble navigating your signals."

Meeting his eyes, I cringed. "I know. It's just that I don't want to hurt Quinn. She likes you. But . . . I can't deny that I *really* like kissing you."

"Well, at least that's good to hear." He leaned his face toward mine. "I *really* like it too. You do it incredibly well." With a soft laugh, he leaned the rest of the way, and this time *he* kissed me.

♪

Declan stood beside me as I opened my locker and pulled out my books for our new history class. New term meant new classes. Now we only had history and orchestra together. Leaning in, he smiled at me. With the red door open, it partially hid us from view. In a swift move, Declan placed a peck on my cheek.

"I'm sorry, I couldn't resist." His happy grin stretched from ear to ear.

I shook my head, unable to stop my own smile. Damn it, I liked him. As much as I wanted not to like him or to deny the feelings churning inside me, I couldn't.

"Come on, let's get to history, Princess." His nickname now made my heart flutter.

The door shut with a rattle and I turned, Declan right behind me as I went toward our class. In the distance, I saw Quinn. We'd only hung out once over break. It was weird not seeing her much. But then again, Lexi had been popping up with her more often than not lately. Quinn stood, brown hair falling on her shoulders, chatting with Phillip and laughing. My brother reached out and put his arm around her shoulder, giving her a quick and playful squeeze. She looked as if she might melt from his touch.

"You know, if I had to guess, I'd say Quinn's interested in your brother." Declan nodded to where they stood, a slight smile on his lips. "Not me."

I sighed. "She likes you both. Phillip's a little slow on the uptake, and I don't think he knows what he wants anyway."

"Well, maybe someone needs to help him catch on a little quicker. Then you wouldn't have to feel guilty for . . . anything."

I looked up at him, then dropped my gaze. "I don't."

That was a lie. Knowing Quinn liked him, that they'd already been on one date, added to her being my bestie, made it super complicated. Starting something with Declan was playing with fire—in more ways than one. I couldn't lose focus on what he stood to take away from me.

His head tilted to the side, he looked at me as if to say, *really?*

"Okay. So . . . maybe I do feel guilty. I can't help it. She's my best friend, and I feel like I'm doing something behind her back."

He nodded, an I-told-you-so look on his face.

We walked past the pair, Phillip's eyes met mine, then quickly looked back to Quinn. She didn't notice us. Her eyes were firmly locked on my brother.

How could he seriously not be sure if Quinn liked him? She really couldn't be more obvious.

I glanced back before I stepped through the classroom door and went to a desk on the side of the room, past Jenna sitting in the front row. She smiled when she saw Declan and me. Mr. Ferngren was setting up the Smartboard for something. He was by far my favorite history teacher ever.

He made it fun and exciting.

A loud buzz signaling the start of class rang through the halls. "Good morning, class. Today you're lucky—we'll be taking it easy and watching a video. Get comfortable and make sure you take notes."

A round of whoops filled the room as students settled into their chairs. Mr. Ferngren flicked off the lights and hit play. Desks squeaked as people moved them so they had a better view. The two guys in front of Declan and me both put their feet up. Mr. Ferngren didn't notice, as he was standing in the doorway whispering with Principal Nacer.

In the darkness, Declan slid his desk closer to mine. After waiting a few moments, he reached over and covertly grabbed my hand, his fingers lacing with mine. He glanced at me, his lips a lopsided slash, and I was so thankful the lights weren't on. My breath hitched as his thumb lightly ran over the top of my knuckles. Eyelids fluttering closed, I no longer paid attention to the video we were supposed to be watching.

Opening my eyes, I saw Jenna glancing back at us. She raised a brow at our nearness, but I didn't care. Jenna wouldn't tell anyone. She'd always been there for me when Quinn wasn't, heck, even when she was. The biggest difference between her and Lexi was Jenna was my friend too.

When the lights flicked on, we separated. Declan slid his desk back into its line and I sat up straighter, quickly jotting down the couple things I remembered in my notebook. Despite our distance, the fluttery sensation low in my stomach refused to dissipate.

My phone let off a string of chimes from my bag and I cringed. I'd forgotten to silence it this morning. I rushed to quiet it, glancing at the teacher to see if he'd noticed.

Phone now safely shushed, I noticed I had new texts and an email. I pulled up the texts first.

Jenna: I totally saw that.

Jenna: You LIKE him!

I suppressed my grin and didn't reply. Instead, I went to my email. It was from the National Competition of Young Musicians, regarding our application. My fingers ached to open it, but class was almost over, so I'd wait.

Declan's eyes were on me, and I shifted the screen so he could see the email notification box on my screen. With a nod, he turned to face the front.

"I hope you paid attention, because there will be a quiz tomorrow, first thing." Ferngren waved a stack of papers as the bell buzzed. "Class dismissed."

I stood and bolted to the hallway, phone in hand, following behind Jenna. She stopped and spun, looking between us, then pointed to my raised phone. "Okay, what's going on?"

"I think we're about to find out if we're headed to New York or not."

"Seriously? What are you waiting for?" She pushed my hands up, signaling I should read.

My eyes darted to Declan. After this, I wouldn't see him again until orchestra. He leaned into me, looking over my shoulder and peering on as I tapped the email.

"Dear Ms. Wyndham and Mr. Brogan, after reviewing your application materials and submission video, we . . . regretfully inform you that we cannot offer you a spot in the National Competition of Young Musicians . . ." My voice faded in disappointment. I was so sure we had this in the bag. "Damn it." Turning to Declan, he sighed and wrapped his arms around me in a reassuring hug.

When he leaned back, he said, "It's their loss. We would've rocked it."

I smiled up at him and laughed. "We so would have."

"I'm sorry, guys." Jenna looked genuinely disappointed for us.

"What's happening?" Noah's voice came from behind me as Declan stepped away from me.

"We didn't get into the NCYM." That meant there'd be no trip to New York with Declan. I blew out a heavy breath, feeling as if a million pounds had settled on my shoulders.

"I'm sorry to hear that, Pips." Noah put an arm around me and gave me a quick squeeze. "You guys were really sounding great. They don't know what they passed up on."

Nodding, I looked up into his blue eyes. "Thanks, Noah."

Declan smiled tightly and looked between us.

"Um, I'm gonna head to class. See you later." Jenna gave a little wave and shyly looked between the guys. "Bye, Noah."

"Later, Jen." Noah barely looked to her.

Her eyes rolled heavenward—she wasn't a fan of being called Jen. Shaking her head, she fell into step with another group of senior girls.

"At least you can ease up on the practicing, right? Maybe we can do that date now." Noah acted as though Declan wasn't standing right beside us.

My mouth popped open, and I glanced at Declan, who had a curious expression on his face, then looked back at Noah. "I've still got a lot of practicing to do. That's pretty much the story of my life. Sorry, Noah."

He shrugged. "That won't stop me." Reaching up, he tweaked my chin then walked away, calling to one of his friends in the distance.

I spun to face Declan again, taking in his furrowed brow and intense look of dislike as he stared at Noah's retreating back. The warning bell rang and I groaned, so done with the day. "I've gotta get to geometry. Mr. Adams will kill me if I'm late again."

"See you in orchestra." He pulled out his phone and

started tapping away at the screen, not seeming to be in any hurry and clearly not caring if he was late.

CHAPTER *Fifteen*

The cello is the most perfect instrument aside from the human voice.

—*Zuill Bailey*

The tiers of the music room were full of students, instruments in hand, standing and ready to go home. Class was over, but Mr. Woods stopped us from leaving.

"Just a reminder, Solo and Ensemble is now less than a month away. Get your practicing in, ladies and gentlemen. We are down to the wire. Oh, and we'll be doing our seat testing on Monday and Tuesday. Come in and be prepared should anyone challenge you."

From the back of the room groans and sighs met Woods's reminder. The challenge piece would be pulled the day of, from the music we'd been working on for the last few weeks. I felt ready. At least for Solo and Ensemble, heck, even for the NCYM that we weren't going to now. Janey had been drilling me on memorizing both my solo and our duet, and now they were seared into my brain. My biggest worry was getting them confused and slipping into one while I was supposed to be playing the other.

This chair challenge, though . . . That had me a bit worried. I knew Declan had been practicing just as much as I had.

Glancing over at him, my mind continuously circled around one thought: is he going to challenge me?

"Want to run through our duet quick before we leave?" Declan asked.

"I can't." I shook my head. "I promised my mom I'd run into Vancouver with her." She had a friend from college, Caleb, who owned a music store up there who always gave her a discount on her students' materials. Personally, I thought he had a crush on her since he always flirted with her. But they'd known each other longer than she'd known my dad, so maybe they were just super good friends.

He shrugged. "I could come over later."

I nodded. "Sure. How about five-ish? We should be home by then."

Meeting his gaze, I sighed. It seriously sucked that we wouldn't be able to go to New York. I hadn't realized just how much I'd been looking forward to it until it was taken away. I'd wanted him to show me a little bit of his world. Maybe get some insight into what made him tick.

"I'll be there." He stood and waited for me to lead the way into the storage room. Once inside, we put our instruments away. Two other cellists and a few of the violinists were finishing up.

"Later, Pips." Celeste waved at me. I waved back. She left her cello in its storage slot and left the room. I was surprised she wasn't taking it home to practice. Then again, she was last cello. If she wasn't planning to challenge anyone, no one would be challenging her. And this far into the year, Declan and I were still the exception. Most people didn't lug their cellos home unless they absolutely had to.

Declan stood and swung his case over his shoulder as my clasps snapped shut. Standing, I faced him, a smile playing on my lips.

Threatening gray clouds covered the sky as we made our way to my SUV. Declan waited for me to put my cello in the back then walked to my car door and opened it for me. I was surprised he hadn't taken off for the bus.

"If you don't hurry, you're gonna miss your bus," I said as I slid behind the steering wheel.

"I don't care," he said with a shrug and leaned inside the car. The tip of his nose touched mine, and I had trouble focusing on his face he was so close. "I really need to do this."

I put my hand on his chest and gently stopped him. "Just so you know," I leaned back a fraction of an inch, "just because I like your kisses doesn't mean I'm gonna let you take my seat."

Tilting his head, our lips now barely a breath apart, he said, "I'd be upset if you didn't fight me for it."

His mouth descended on mine, and for a moment, I panicked. What if Quinn saw us? But the way his lips felt and with his hand cupping my cheek, my ability to think clearly vanished. Declan was kissing me. What more could I ask for? I twined my arms around his neck and threaded my fingers in his dark hair. We had an insane chemistry even without our instruments.

The hiss of the bus's brakes stopping on the street pulled us apart. Declan's lips curled and he came back for another.

I pushed at his chest. With a laugh and my lips partially pressed to his, I said, "Go, you don't want to miss it."

The muscles in his chest flexed under my fingertips as he raised his shoulders. "It's a city bus; there'll be another."

We kissed again, the cool late winter air brushing past him and bringing his scent of rosin and laundry detergent to my nose. The combination did something to me that made my head spin. He was just so damn wonderful.

My phone vibrated in my bag. Pulling back, I looked into his chocolatey eyes. "I've gotta get that. It's probably my mom wondering where I'm at."

Declan leaned away and watched me answer the call, bracing himself with his arm against the roof of my SUV.

"Hey, Mom. I'm on my way. I got hung up on my way out. I'll be home in a minute or two."

I shivered as Declan reached out and tucked my hair behind my ear to stop the wind from blowing it in my face.

Hanging up with Mom, I smiled up at him. "I've got to go. I'll see you tonight."

He nodded and leaned down for one last quick peck. "See you later."

As I pulled out onto the road, he was walking across the parking lot to the bus stop, confidence in his every step. I liked the way his body moved under his black leather jacket. And Lord, did he have a seriously cute butt.

Rain spattered against my windshield, and I flicked on the wipers. My thoughts went to orchestra. With the only chance to move up a chair—or down—a weekend away, my nerves were wound tight. It didn't help that I was still upset about the whole NCYM thing on top of it. I wondered, if Declan were to challenge me, how would I feel about him afterward? Would it change anything? It'd certainly confirm my suspicions that he was after everything I'd fought for. And it definitely wouldn't matter how cute his butt was if it was sitting in my seat. Then again, if he didn't challenge me, it'd be like he was *letting* me keep it. I didn't like that scenario any better.

As I pulled into the driveway, I couldn't decide which option was worse. Only one thing was certain: there's no way I'd go down without a fight. My future at Goddards, the New York Philharmonic, *everything* was at stake here.

♪

Mom and I walked through the back door of the house, each carrying a small box filled with various piano books.

My mind kept circling around my problems. Declan. Noah. First chair challenge. Competition. Declan. Quinn.

Declan.

I wasn't denying any longer that I liked him. A lot. At least not to myself. Quinn . . . well, I still had to figure out how to come clean with her, and that wouldn't be easy. Telling her scared me. But that did nothing to stop my feelings. Neither did the vulnerability Declan made me feel. I was trusting him not to crush all my hopes and dreams, which was terrifying. Especially since I knew his hopes and dreams matched mine. A part of me worried that he really was my enemy, and his attention toward me was nothing more than a ploy to distract me. But it definitely didn't feel that way when he kissed me.

Goodness, when he kissed me . . .

Noah and Phillip were crashed on the couches, bags of chips opened on the coffee table, TV blaring. They had a late game tonight. I had no plans for going. Quinn had asked me to go with her, but I didn't want to. I'd seen Noah play often enough, and Declan was coming over to practice. We had more important things than basketball.

"Hey, let me get that." Noah popped up when he saw me and smiled, grabbing the box from my hands to follow Mom into the music room.

"Thanks." I handed it over and looked down to my brother.

Mom laughed. "Thanks, Phillip. Don't rush."

Phillip pulled himself up and sauntered over to Mom. "Sorry. Let me help."

Shaking her head with a laugh, she nodded to the music room door. "Just get the door, would you?"

Boxes set down, Mom kissed Phillip on the cheek and smiled before heading into the kitchen to start on dinner.

"You staying, Noah?"

"I wouldn't miss it, Mrs. W." He stopped at my side and tucked his hands into his jeans.

"We've got to leave in a couple hours," Phillip added.

Mom pushed up the sleeves of her sweater. "Why aren't you guys practicing before the game?"

"We did a practice before school this morning—Coach had something this afternoon he couldn't reschedule."

"Hey, can I talk to you for a second?" Noah looked to me and used his head to gesture to the front porch.

I nodded and followed after him. "What's up?" I asked, shutting the door behind us and wrapping my arms around my middle to hold in my warmth. Just off the porch, the wind tossed the leaf-bare trees and the rain came down in torrents, splashing up off the puddles on the ground from the non-stop storm.

His eyes narrowed as he looked me over. "Okay, I kinda need a favor from you."

"A favor? What kind?"

"The guys on the team are going out tonight after the game. I was hoping you'd be my date, so I wouldn't have to be the only single guy there."

A soft laugh left my lips. "Noah, you could ask any girl to go out with you and they'd jump at the chance. I'm definitely not your only option tonight."

His shoulders rolled forward, and he cleared his throat. "Maybe not, but you're the only one I really want to take."

His words should've made my heart soar. But they didn't. They were nice to hear, don't get me wrong, but they just didn't make my insides melt like they would've a year ago.

"I'm really flattered, Noah, but I can't tonight. I've got homework to finish up, and I've got to practice."

He ran a hand through his blond hair. It was getting longer and shaggier than he normally kept it. "Okay. Got it. So, how are *things* with Declan?"

There was a definite pissy undercurrent in his voice. I could easily read between the lines and figure out the subtext of his words.

"Declan and I aren't together, if that's what you're thinking." Yes, we'd kissed, but we'd never even gone on a date. He definitely wasn't my boyfriend. Besides, it's not like it was any of Noah's business.

He looked at me, not saying a word, then shook his head. "I've seen the two of you together. I'm not that stupid, Pips."

"Noah, I'm not dating anyone. Declan is my duet partner and my friend." My eyes widened as I looked at him, trying to get him to understand. "I'll admit, I do really . . . like Declan." I looked down at my hands, uncomfortable telling him that. "But we're not dating. Can we go inside now?"

Declan was due to show up in half an hour, and I wanted to get some practicing in before he arrived.

Noah nodded and tucked his hands in his pockets, rolling his shoulders forward. "So you like him, I already knew that. Where does this leave me?"

"I don't know where it leaves you, but it leaves me unsure about what I want. I like you both, Noah."

"If you like me, why won't you let me take you out on a date? It feels like you're avoiding me."

That was a really good question. Why didn't I want to go out with him? I suddenly realized how close he'd gotten and took a step back. "I just . . . I don't know what to say. I don't know why. I just . . . I've got a lot going on and . . ." I trailed off, unable to get out a coherent thought.

"Pips, just give me a chance. I might surprise you." Reaching around me and putting his body closer to mine, he opened the door, and we walked in.

With a nod, I said, "I'm sure you would. I've got to go practice."

I didn't know how to feel about our talk. Admittedly, there'd been a slight disturbance to my stomach at his nearness, but nothing like I felt when Declan was around. He made fireworks shoot off inside me and got my normally overwrought brain to slow down and just take in the moment. Did that mean I'd made up my mind? Did I want Declan? It was a choice between the guy who might possibly be my enemy or the boy I'd been crushing on since we were kids.

Before I could veer into the music room, Noah's hand lightly clasped my arm, stopping me.

"Are you coming to the game tonight with Quinn?"

I shook my head. Quinn and I hadn't been hanging out much lately. We were drifting, and I hated it. Lexi had happily seized the opportunity to squeeze her way back in. Truthfully, our separation was mostly my fault. I couldn't listen to Quinn gush over Declan, knowing what I was doing. I couldn't handle the guilt. Her crushing on him while I was the one kissing him made me certain I was the world's worst friend. But I was afraid to tell her. I knew exactly how she'd react. "Um, I wasn't planning on going. I've just got so much to do tonight."

He pressed his lips together in a thin line and nodded, then turned to join Phillip back at the TV.

In the music room, I sat in my chair, gathered my bow and Francesca, pulled my hair up, then slipped in my earbuds, exhaling a leaden breath. I needed to take a step back, unwind, and definitely not think about Noah, my music pieces, not getting into the NCYM, or even Declan. A mind breather. "Welcome to the Jungle" by Guns N' Roses blasted and I closed my eyes and quickly joined in with the melody. I'd always been good at playing by ear; most string players were. And playing rock music was just plain fun.

The cello was peculiar in that one moment it could

sound like the sweet song of a violin and another like a guitar. But one thing you might not expect: it could rock out like no other. Pure perfection in one instrument.

I bowed with aggression, letting out my frustration and worry. Then I realized something was different. I wasn't alone.

My eyes flicked open and Declan sat beside me, cello out, playing along in harmony doing the driving back beat like it was nothing. Like we'd played this oodles of times before.

When the hell had he gotten here?

A smile hit my face and I kept playing, enjoying our impromptu duet. A chill went over my body and goose-bumps peppered my skin. This was awesome.

He looked up at me, huge grin on his face, as we wrapped the song.

I yanked out my earbuds and laughed. "That was incredible!"

"That's what we should've done for the NCYM audition. Something totally different and unique." He scratched his jaw and said, "I didn't know you had that in you."

One brow raised. "If it's music, I've got it in me."

"That was amazing." Noah stood in the entry, watching us and looking less than thrilled.

Grinning at him, I brushed the tendrils of hair that'd escaped away from my face. "Thanks."

Declan's only reply was a curt dude nod of acknowledgment that Noah had even spoken.

"Sorry to interrupt. It's been a long time since I've heard you play like that. I was curious. I'll let you get back to it."

The stand with our duet piece sat on the side of the room. I reached over and grabbed it, sliding it in front of us just in case we needed it. My phone and earbuds slid from my hand to the floor. My bow now had some scraggly broken hairs, so I leaned over and grabbed my small pair of scissors off the console table and snipped them off.

Declan stood and closed the music room off after Noah walked away. "So, what's the deal with Wonder Jock?"

Shrugging, I shook my head. "What do you mean?"

"When he answered the door, he said, 'I should've known it was you.' I get the impression he doesn't like me much."

I wrinkled my nose as I fought back a chuckle. "He's definitely not your biggest fan."

A bark of laughter left his throat. "Thanks for sparing my feelings there, Princess."

Warmth curled inside me and settled low in my stomach. Oh how very different I felt about that nickname now. "Oh please, I never pegged you for someone who overly cares what other people's opinions of him are. You're a New Yorker."

With a nod, he plucked a single string, making it hum. "True."

I watched the muscles in his back flex under his dark sweater as he reached over to open our music and unfold it to one long stream of paper. He may have been on the slim side, but he was definitely fit.

A knock on the door drew our attention, and Noah poked his head in again, smiling at me but totally ignoring Declan this time. "Phillip and I are heading over early. I still hope we'll see you tonight."

He winked.

In my peripheral vision, I saw Declan glancing between us.

Weirdness inched its way down my spine and settled in my stomach. "I thought you guys were getting dinner here?"

"Nah, we decided to grab something on the way instead. So . . . maybe we'll see you there."

Shaking my head, I said, "Um, still not going. Sorry, Noah."

"Later then." He closed the door behind him and I could hear the front door open, my brother chuckling about something.

"So, you ready?" I turned to Declan, who was now watching me intently.

His eyes flicked up to mine and he nodded. "Let's get to work."

We made our way through the duet from memory, bit by bit. As long as he was playing his part, it was like my fingers just knew where to go. I was proud of us.

We reached the point where most of it was memorized. There were only a couple spots where I had to glance at the music. But it wouldn't be much longer that I'd need that. Once we finished working through it, we glanced at each other and grinned. Every time I looked him in the eye, the thought of how much I wanted him to kiss me paraded through my mind. I couldn't help it. It forced me to acknowledge that I didn't feel that way about Noah. It wasn't even remotely the same. God, it'd be so much easier if Noah made me feel the way Declan did.

"I want to work on the plucking section near the beginning, let's run it again." I looked to make sure he agreed. "Let's start at the top."

He put his bow in position, and we took it from the first measure. We ran it several more times, took a quick break for dinner at Mom's insistence, then came back and had a little fun playing some rock music before we played our solo pieces for each other.

Hearing him play reminded me how good he really was. It brought to mind our chair challenge.

"You sound amazing." I laid my cello on its side on the floor and turned away from him, studying the music on my stand, nervous to talk to him. "So . . . are you planning on challenging me for my chair?" My stomach clenched with the words now out in the open.

Declan's free hand ran through his hair. "I've been trying to decide if I should."

"Oh? Why is it a decision?" When I looked up at him, one corner of his lips had curled up.

"Why?" His eyebrows rose in shock. "Because I *really* like kissing you. And I'm absolutely positive that if I challenge you, you'd never let me do it again."

I laughed. "No. Well . . . only if you beat me."

He chuckled. "Oh, I see how it is."

"I'm just kidding. But I do want to be prepared. So . . . are you?"

"You wouldn't be mad if I did?"

I pulled my hair from its tie and ran my fingers through it, struggling to be honest with myself. "I don't think so. Or if I was, I'd probably get over it. I know this stuff is important to you too, it's just . . . this is my life, Declan. My cello is who I am."

He set his cello aside and leaned forward to cup my cheek. "Pippa, you are so much more than your cello."

The way he said my name in his low voice made a tingle spark to life deep inside me that quickly ignited and spread like wildfire.

"I am?" The words squeaked from my throat as he guided my face toward his.

"You're smart." He leaned in closer. "Kind, a good student, and a wonderful friend." His head tilted toward me, our lips almost touching. "You make me better. You're . . . you're pretty amazing."

My eyes widened and I grinned.

"And you're insanely hot." He closed the small space between us, his lips just grazing mine.

I pulled back for a moment. "You really think I'm hot?"

A soft puff of air left his lips. "Oh, yeah, Princess."

His hands curled in my hair and he pulled me back to his lips. This time his kiss was way more than a graze. My heart thundered in my chest, and I melted into him. I wound my arms around his neck, wanting more. *Craving* more.

A loud ringing filled the room making Declan groan and pull away from me. My hands slid down his chest as he reached for his phone that he'd tossed into his case.

"It's my mom." He answered his cell and talked to her a moment. "Okay, I'll head out in a couple minutes. Yeah, me too. Bye." Standing, he tucked his phone in his back pocket. "Come on, Booth, let's get you in your case." He shot me a cheeky grin and kneeled down.

Sighing, I stood and flipped my long hair back over my shoulder. Disappointment surged in my chest; I didn't want him to leave. I was enjoying kissing him far too much. I watched as he loosened the hair of his bow and ran a soft cloth over it to remove any residual rosin, then after setting it aside, he wiped the strings of his cello as well.

When he finished putting it away, he stood and pulled his cello case over his shoulder. "Walk me out?"

"Of course. Do you need a ride?"

"No, my mom let me use her car."

I nodded and smiled up at him, hoping we'd continue what we started once we got outside.

He followed me out the double French doors and onto the illuminated front porch. The earlier storm had passed, leaving the dark night sky still spotty with clouds. How late was it? As I turned to face Declan, he caught me by the waist and pulled me to him, his lips finding mine in a soft, sexy kiss. My hands involuntarily pressed against his chest and curled into his t-shirt. I didn't want it to end, but I knew he had to go.

Pulling back, he rested his forehead against mine. "I should get going."

"Okay," I said, wishing he could stay.

"Well, maybe in just another minute." His hand twined in my hair and he brought my face to his. Our lips met again, and as his tongue brushed against my mouth, I opened to him. With a moan, he held me tighter and deepened the kiss. I caught a slight hint of his familiar scent and my knees went wobbly.

"You aren't together? Right." Noah's sarcastic voice cut into our moment.

Declan and I split apart, meeting each others' eyes before we turned to see Noah, my brother, and Quinn, all watching us. The look on my best friend's face was like a dagger being tossed straight through my heart.

"Game's over. Um, we won." Phillip cleared his throat, looking beyond uncomfortable. "We were just stopping by quick to make sure you really didn't want to come out with the rest of the team tonight."

Quinn snorted a derisive laugh. "Clearly she *really* doesn't. Looks like she's far too busy backstabbing her friends."

Shit. I'd just made a huge mistake.

CHAPTER *Sixteen*

Music, once admitted to the soul, becomes a sort of spirit,
and never dies.

—Edward Bulwer-Lytton

All weekend long I'd tried to talk to Quinn. I'd called. Texted. Walked over to her house. Nothing. She refused to see me. She'd even refused to talk to Jenna when she'd tried to intervene on my behalf. But today at school, she didn't have a choice. I rushed across the parking lot, got inside and stowed my cello, then went off to find my probably now ex-best friend. My worry about Quinn pushed my probable chair challenge to the back of my mind. It was still there, I just didn't have the energy to stress over it.

In the distance I spotted her, talking to a guy near our lockers. As he walked away, I arrived at mine and twisted the combo lock. "Hey, Quinn, how was your weekend?"

She glared at me. "Like you care."

"Of course I care. Want to let me explain?"

"She doesn't want your explanation." Lexi popped up from behind me, glaring at me when I glanced her way.

Quinn shook her head, her glasses slipping down her

nose. "You don't need to explain, it was perfectly clear as I watched you sucking Declan's face. You weaseled your way between me and the guy I really liked and who liked me. I hope you're happy with your conquest. Was he worth it?"

"What? That's not—"

Her face contorted in disgust. "God, you even said you didn't want him. You told me it was fine to ask him out. You're such a liar."

I shook my head, not really sure how to respond. "It *was* fine. I didn't feel—"

"Whatever, Pippa, I don't care," she spat the words.

"Yeah, whatever, Pippa," Lexi parroted as she crossed her arms over her chest, looking pleased with the situation.

"Lexi, stay out of it." I turned back to Quinn as Lexi feigned being offended. "That's not how it happened. We didn't—" Before I could finish, she scoffed, rolled her eyes, and walked away, taking her backup best friend with her. Although, from the looks of things, Lexi wasn't her backup anymore.

A warmth radiated into my back from behind me, and I had a hunch whom it might be. Declan.

"Any luck?" His familiar deep voice was somehow soothing. He'd texted me all weekend, just to make sure I was doing okay.

I shook my head. "Nope. She's gonna hold onto this one for a good long while, I just know it."

Hands came up and rubbed my shoulders; I felt myself relaxing into him, despite knowing I shouldn't let him touch me. That's what'd gotten us in this trouble in the first place.

"For what it's worth, I'm sorry."

Turning to face him, I weakly smiled. "Thanks, but it's not all your fault. I was very willingly on the other end of that kiss."

The bell rang, signaling us to hurry to class. With a

squeeze, Declan said, "I'll see you later. You sure you're okay?"

Nodding, I could feel my eyes start to water so I turned and rushed off to class. With a shake of my head, I tried to stop the waterworks before they got started. Quinn hadn't even given me a chance to talk, to try and set things right. Lexi certainly hadn't helped any. It upset me that my best friend could so easily brush me aside. And honestly it ticked me off. Both at her and myself. This was Quinn's MO. Anytime she got pissed at me, she froze me out as she paraded Lexi around. I shouldn't be surprised at her reaction. But I still was. And it still hurt. I just wanted a minute to try to explain things, but she clearly wasn't ready to give me that.

I took a deep breath before entering my first class. Dwelling on this right now wouldn't help. I had to get through the day and survive the chair challenge this after-noon, which meant I needed to focus and not let my emotions get in the way.

♫

I sat in the practice room with Declan where no one could see us, waiting for Mr. Woods to give us the go ahead. We were the last two in the cello section to challenge, and the last pair of the day.

How the chair challenge worked was we'd anonymously take turns, each playing the same passage Wood had selected from one of the pieces the orchestra was working on. The class would then vote on which person had performed it best.

A tangle of knots filled my stomach and my heart thumped in my chest. I'd done this before—it'd been a while—but really, I should've been calmer than this. Somehow this one felt like an *actual* challenge. I didn't have my normal confidence because I was going up against such a strong player. It also didn't help that I'd seen Quinn before class. I'd ventured a smile and she'd turned her head up and ignored me, talking to Lexi like I didn't exist. No, I didn't expect her to be happy about this or forgive me instantaneously, but I at least wanted a chance to try and make it up to her.

Damn it. I was so mad at myself. I should've plucked up the courage and told her the truth when all this started. It wouldn't have been pretty, but it would've probably been better than this.

"Whenever you guys are ready." Woods popped his head in and smiled, pulling me from my thoughts.

Declan had offered not to challenge me at all, but I couldn't accept that. I knew he wanted to and anyway, if he didn't challenge me I'd feel like I was getting the seat by default. And I'm not going to lie, there was a pretty big part of me that wanted to know which one of us would ultimately come out on top.

"You want me to go first?" His eyes searched mine and when I nodded, he gave me a small smile. Picking up his bow, he took a deep breath and launched into our challenge piece.

Closing my eyes, I listened. The notes bounced from his instrument and I could only hope I'd keep it together and play it better than he had.

Worried thoughts tumbled through my mind. What would I seriously do if he took my chair? Could I still like him if he did? Had this all been just a ploy to distract me? My stomach lurched as I tried to imagine him sitting in my spot. The chair I'd been in since I started playing. This could affect my getting into Goddards. I realized I was holding my breath and blew it out.

I watched as his eyes followed the page in deep concentration. He was focused and played the notes to perfection, but he didn't do any of the dynamics, and it fell a little flat.

Was he doing it on purpose?

Once he finished, the class clapped and I waited a moment for them to finish, then I took my turn. I started out bright and bouncy, attacking the accented notes and trying to make it perfect. I crescendoed into the loud part and then took the decrescendo into the light plucking part. I managed to lose myself in the piece and stopped worrying about all the other external crap. It was just me and Francesca, kicking some serious ass.

Wrapping the passage, I held the final note with a soft vibrato and lifted my bow from the strings. When I looked to Declan, he bowed his head as if he already knew I'd won. Which raised my suspicions further.

"Alright, come on out," Mr. Woods called.

We stepped from the room and stood just outside the practice room door, waiting to see where we'd be sitting.

"Raise your hand for player one." Woods did a quick count. "And player two." He did another count. "Okay, who was player one?"

Declan nodded. "I was."

"Please take your spot in the second chair."

Relief washed over me, and my knees went weak.

"That means, Pippa, you'll be staying section leader. Congratulations."

I went to my seat and settled back into my comfy spot. Glancing over at Declan, he avoided looking at me. He reached and gathered his music, waiting to be dismissed. This wouldn't mean anything if he threw the challenge.

"Alright, we'll finish off with the violins tomorrow. Well done, violas and cellos." The basses could've challenged, but the three we had decided not to.

The class packed up and quickly thinned out. I followed Declan into the practice room to our cases and knelt beside him as we went through our routine to put our instruments away.

"Congratulations, you really did play it better." He looked at me, and offered me a small grin.

"Did you let me win?" I flipped the clasps shut and stood.

He shook his head and flinched back. "What?"

"Did you throw it so I'd keep my seat?"

"Are you serious?" He laughed. "Of course not. If you hadn't wanted me to challenge you with everything going on with Quinn, I wouldn't have. But if we're going to go through with it, you can count on me showing up and fighting. I had the chance to take your seat, and I messed it up."

"Really?"

He stood and grabbed my hands. "Pippa, you're a great player, and you played better than me today. You deserved it this time. I lost my focus and, well . . . it showed."

A slow smile spread over my lips and a giddiness hit me. "So I actually beat the amazing Declan Brogan."

"Don't rub it in." He smiled and released one of my hands so he could push my hair back over my shoulder, his fingers trailed through the long strands and sent a shiver down to my toes.

"Are you going to be okay with this?" My fingers gripped tight to my cello strap, nervous for his answer. Now I'd find out if it was really just a game to him.

"Of course I'm fine. Disappointed, but fine. You deserved it." He bent down again and secured his case before standing and looping it over his shoulder.

So worried how I'd feel, I never stopped to consider how he'd take it if I came out on top. From the very beginning, his over-confident attitude had put me on edge. Had me doubting my abilities. But now here we were, him probably feeling everything I'd been expecting to feel.

"You ready to go?" Declan asked and motioned for the door.

With a nod, I veered around a viola player and out of the room. Declan walked me to my car. I was torn; I wanted him to kiss me, but for the sake of my friendship with Quinn, it'd be better if we didn't. Just then Quinn's little car drove past us. As she looked through the window she spotted us and glared. Lexi sat in the passenger seat with an identical expression on her sourpuss face.

"I don't know how to make this up to her. She's so angry with me." My eyes followed her out of the parking lot.

"She'll come 'round." Declan adjusted his cello strap and looked at me, his brows lowering. "I'm probably going to regret asking this, but what does this Quinn situation mean for you and me?"

I slid my cello in the back and went around to my door. My breath left me in a whoosh as I sat down on the driver's seat. "I don't know. With her so upset, it wouldn't feel right to keep this up. Maybe it'd be better if we just take a step back and cool things off, at least until I can sort this mess out with her."

"So that means no more kissing then, right?" He scrunched up his face in disappointment.

"Yeah . . . that'd probably be best."

He groaned and ran a hand through his messy hair. A suggestive look crossed his face and he gave me a sexy grin. "What about a goodbye—for now—kiss?"

My eyes darted to my lap, contemplating his request. I wanted to kiss him. Oh, how I wanted to kiss him. But with everything that had happened, getting some space was probably the best thing for both of us.

"Do you really think that's a good idea?"

Declan leaned closer to me, his lips looking extra kissable. "I think it's an excellent idea. My best ever."

Meeting his gaze, I couldn't stifle my smile, but I managed to keep it small. "We can't. It'll just make me want you more when I know I can't have you."

He cupped my face and ran his thumb along my cheekbone. "But you *can* have me." He rested his forehead against mine.

My breath caught in my throat and I fought the urge to tilt my lips up to his. He was so close, it'd be so easy. Instead, I inhaled his scent, wanting to memorize it for the distance that was about to come between us. With a whisper, I said, "I should go."

Taking a step back, he nodded and ran a frustrated hand over his face. "See you tomorrow."

As he walked away, my heart clenched. I worried that no matter what I did, I'd wind up losing one of them. Declan or Quinn, I couldn't choose, and I wouldn't. This was going to suck.

♪

Five days later and there was still no change on the Quinn front. Saturday morning arrived and, as I laid in bed, I decided to try one more time. Throwing the covers off, I hopped into jeans and a sweater. My sneaker-clad feet hit the stairs, and I rushed to the entry and grabbed my coat.

Dad's guitar sang from the living room. He stopped playing and looked up at me. "Where you off to?"

"Quinn's."

"You guys finally talking?"

I shook my head. "That's why I'm going. I have to try again."

He nodded and played a sassy little tune. "Good luck."

Spinning, I headed out the door and hopped down the front steps. I walked quickly past the two houses between us. It was still technically winter, but spring was starting to surface in the small green shoots popping out. On her porch, I pasted all my courage together and hit the doorbell.

Shuffling sounded inside and I could hear Quinn tell her mom she'd get it. The door opened and I saw a smiling Quinn. Then she realized it was me, the smile faded, and the door slammed shut.

"Quinn, open up." I knocked on the door.

"Just go away, Pippa."

"Five minutes, that's all I want. Then I'll go away and leave you alone."

Silence. I rang the bell again. Nothing. I knocked and Quinn's mom answered. "Hey, Pippa."

"Can I please talk to her?"

She shook her head, a sad look in her hazel eyes. "She's not ready to talk to you. Is there anything you want me to tell her?"

I paused and thought. What could I say? I couldn't very well tell her it wasn't my fault; I'd kissed him back and very much enjoyed it. No, I didn't pursue him with the intent to hurt her, but I also didn't put a stop to where we kept taking it. "Um, can you just tell her that hurting her was the last thing I ever wanted to do?"

Quinn's mom nodded. "I'll tell her."

My shoulders slumped, and I stood there as the door closed again. I'd lost her. And that broke my heart.

Stepping off the porch and onto the sidewalk, I walked home. I turned back and looked up to her bedroom window. Quinn's pale face was wreathed by her blue striped curtains as she looked down on me. Her eyes narrowed, and I could feel her anger drilling into my bones.

Would we ever recover from this? Right now, it didn't feel like it.

CHAPTER *Seventeen*

*When I hear music, I fear no danger. I
am invulnerable. I see no foe. I am related to
the earliest times, and to the latest.*

—*Henry David Thoreau*

Quinn hadn't spoken to me for two weeks. And Noah had been avoiding me like the plague. I'd made an effort to distance myself from Declan. Well, as much as I could. We now only practiced at the school. I didn't trust us alone together. If left to our own devices, I had no doubt we'd end up lip-to-lip in no time. Especially since that's exactly where I wanted to be.

Solo and Ensemble was this weekend and the only emotion spiraling around inside me was dread. It meant an awkward day spent waiting around between performances with Declan. At least both my pieces were ready. I'd spent my lesson with Janey practicing with my accompanist and it'd gone perfectly. At least the musical sphere of my life was going right. For the most part.

The final bell of the school day sounded and without even looking at Declan, I stood and made my way to the storage room. I knelt down to pack Francesca away and tried to hurry. Declan followed suit next to me.

"How long are we going to do this?"

Not looking at him, I asked, "Do what?"

"Pretend there's nothing between us just to please Quinn." Frustration tinged his voice and I knew he wasn't enjoying this any more than I was. He'd even dialed back how often he texted me, which I hated.

My gaze snapped to his as his eyes searched mine. A part of me curled up and died knowing he was off-limits. Would I ever get to kiss him again?

I was seriously missing the kissing. Hell, I missed just being close to him.

"Quinn is my best friend and I . . . I screwed up. I let my feelings for you, a guy I *knew* she liked, override my better judgment. I don't know how, but I have to fix things with her." I quickly snapped my case and stood; Declan did the same.

Leaning closer to me, his breath grazed my lips. "Pippa, come on, it's not as if you were intentionally chasing me. We've spent so much time together, and it just kind of . . . happened. I'm not interested in anything more than friendship with Quinn. Ever."

A rustling behind me drew my attention and I turned to see quite an audience of fellow orchestra students, quietly listening as they packed up, moving as if they were slogging through a largo movement.

"I want to be with *you*. I like *you*. A lot. And we have a hell of a lot more in common than Quinn and I ever will."

"I've known Quinn since I was seven." I spoke softly, matching his level. "I committed one of the cardinal girl sins. You don't go after a guy your friend likes. Period."

He shook his head. "The night of the dance I didn't want to be there with Quinn. I wanted to ask you, but Wonder

Jock asked first. I only said yes to Quinn 'cause it meant I'd get to be near you. Jesus, Pippa," his voice was no longer quiet, "instead of kissing my *actual* date that night, I came to your house and kissed you. *I want you.* So, if you want to blame someone then technically it's all my fault, because I started this with that kiss."

They didn't kiss? It'd been driving me mad thinking Quinn might know what it felt like to kiss him. I closed my eyes and tried to refocus on the problem instead of my relief.

"But I didn't stop you from kissing me, and I should have." My fingers latched onto the strap of my case, and I hauled it over my shoulder.

Declan's hands curled around my shoulders, pulling me closer. When he spoke, his words were soft, pleading. "We have something. Something I've never experienced before. I don't want to lose this."

"I can't hurt Quinn any more than I already have." My eyes held his, hoping he could see how much this was killing me. "You should probably ask her out and give it a real try with her." I pulled away from him and turned to see a large number of people who were now standing still, just watching us like we were their own personal soap opera.

Before I could walk away Declan grabbed my hand. "Is that really what you want? You want me to date her? Be with her?"

I dropped my gaze to the carpet, my face flushed due to the audience we'd acquired. "It doesn't matter what I want. Not anymore."

He released my hand, and I quickly left. Him dating Quinn was far and away the last thing I wanted. But Quinn wanted it. And if that'd magically make things right . . . oh, who was I kidding? It'd epically suck.

Tears burned my eyes as I climbed the stairs and pushed through the double doors that led to the parking lot. I had to get away before anyone saw me crying. My feet smacked against the pavement as I broke into a jog, my cello jarring itself against my back. Eyes watering, my composure was almost completely gone. I sniffed back snot and wiped at my damp cheeks.

As I got to my car, I saw Jenna waiting for her school bus with her younger sister. I quickly looked away. I didn't want her to see me upset. If she did, she'd hightail it over here, and I just didn't want to deal with anyone right now. I didn't need any attention when I was on the cusp of falling apart.

Desperate, I used my sleeve on my nose, then dug into my bag in search of my keys. I looked up as Quinn drove through the lot. She slowed as she got close to me. Our eyes met and I swear I saw a flash of concern in them before she looked away and hit the gas.

That did it. Tears overflowed and streamed down my cheeks in a steady, silent current. I wiped away the evidence with my sleeve as I frantically resumed the searched for my keys.

Fob finally in hand, I clicked the button, pulled up the back, shoved my cello in, then rushed to jump in the front seat. My vision far too blurry to drive, I sat there, my tear-streaked face laid on my arms, hunching over the steering wheel. I'd lost my best friend and the guy I'd completely fallen for. Misery clawed at my heart, and a sob burst from my throat.

A knock on the window made me jump. I looked up to see Declan standing there, looking at me, concern etched in his eyes and the set of his jaw. I wiped at my cheeks again as he opened the door and leaned in.

"Slide over. I'm driving you home."

I shook my head and sniffled. "I'm fine. Go, you don't want to miss your bus."

"Pippa, slide over. You can't drive like this."

Nodding, I hoisted myself over the center console and pushed my bag to the floor. Declan went and put his stuff in the back and climbed in.

"Buckle up." He turned the key in the ignition and we pulled from the lot. "Was that Quinn I just saw?"

"Yeah." My voice sounded strangled and strained.

"And she didn't even stop to make sure you were okay?"

I shook my head.

He sighed, his mouth in a tight line. "Friends forgive friends. It's not like we were trying to hurt her. She has to know that." After a couple miles, he flicked the blinker on to turn onto my street. "She can't make someone want her. It doesn't work like that. Maybe I should talk to her."

"No, it wouldn't help." I wiped at my cheeks. "She's the most stubborn person I know, and a master of holding grudges." Inhaling deeply, I shook my head and ran a finger under my eyes to remove any smudged mascara, trying to get myself together before I had to see my mom. The car slowed and turned into my driveway, then came to a stop.

"Are you gonna be okay?" He pulled the keys out and handed them to me. Our fingers touched and a ripple of electricity raced up my arm.

I squeezed my eyes shut tight, wishing I could ignore it. "I will be. Thanks for driving me."

"It's the least I could do."

Reaching for the handle, I pushed the door open. But his words stopped me from climbing out. "I know you feel guilty, and I know I'm a huge part of that, but, Pippa, I . . ." He paused and sighed. "You know how I feel. I want you to be happy. Just let me know what you want and I'll do it."

Turning back, I looked into his warm, brown eyes. "Give me time to sort this out."

"I'll be here whenever you're ready. But I'm not . . ." He

held my hand between both of his. "I'm not going to ask Quinn out. And I'm not going to be able to turn off my feelings for you."

His words made a warm glow radiate inside me.

My teeth sank into my bottom lip, then slowly released it. I so badly wanted him to kiss me. But that would be counterproductive. I had to stop wanting that. With a nod, I pulled my hand back and got out of the SUV. We met at the back hatch where he popped it open and handed me my cello before pulling his things out. He looked sad. As I looped my cello over my shoulder, he raised his hand and trailed his knuckles over my cheek. His touch sent a tremble though me. He wasn't making this easy.

He cleared his throat. "I'll meet you at Solo and Ensemble tomorrow morning."

It was at a local high school across town, so we didn't have to go too far.

"Are you sure? I can give you a ride."

He shook his head. "I don't think that'd be a good idea."

My chest tightened as I watched him walk away. I hated this. Quinn went on one date with him and now she felt she had full claim to him. That was messed up. And yes, I know I should've admitted to liking him, but this still felt silly and childish. I just didn't know what else to do, aside from staying away from him, to save our friendship. Especially if I couldn't talk to her.

I didn't move from my spot behind my car until I couldn't see him anymore. Pulling my phone from my pocket, I sent Quinn a text.

Me: We really should talk. Can we meet?

I didn't expect an answer. She hadn't replied to any of the dozens of texts I'd sent her to say hi and see how she was doing—why would she this time? I knew firsthand how she shut people out.

When we were ten, Quinn had been livid at me because I'd agreed to go to a slumber party that she hadn't been invited to. It was a girl who I'd met at a summer music camp. Quinn didn't even know the girl, but still, she was angry. She went a month and a half without talking to me. That was one of the first times Lexi came into the picture, and I was pushed out. Back then I'd been devastated. Now, as much as I loved Quinn, I was moving up the path from guilty to irritated.

Clomping up the back steps, I opened the door and Mom was in there working on dinner. It involved a delicious-smelling marinade and chicken. "Mmm, smells good."

Smiling at me, she gestured toward the window. "What was all that about?"

"Declan drove me home."

"Why? What happened?" Her brows pulled together and she quickly did a head-to-toe once over on me. Presumably checking for any injuries I might have. The only ones I had were emotional and invisible.

"'Cause I was upset."

Her head tilted to the side. "Yeah, your puffy eyes and red face gave you away. Quinn still not talking to you?"

Shaking my head, I sat my cello down and put my bag on the hook by the door. "Nope."

"What about Noah?"

"Nope."

"Looked pretty intense between you two out there. Is everything okay?"

"Not really." I plunked myself down at the table and laid my head on my arms. "I can't . . . I can't . . . ." I'd never really had boy problems to talk about before. Not like this anyways. I'd always been so gone over Noah, and Mom already knew everything about that. This just felt different. Weirder. More personal. "I can't like Declan anymore."

"And why is that? Quinn?" At my head bob, she continued, "She may like him, but that doesn't have to stop you from liking him. Plus, I thought she was crushing on someone else."

Mom turned to me, looking like she was waiting for something. When I didn't say anything she prompted me, "Well, am I right? Does Quinn like someone else in addition to Declan?"

"How did you know?"

"Please, I'm a mom. I've watched you kids grow up and I notice all sorts of things. The two of you will make up. You always do. I doubt a guy will come between you for long." She put down the potato and peeler she was holding and came to sit by me, giving me a hug. "Things will sort themselves out; they always do. You know Quinn gets like this sometimes."

The problem was, it wasn't just any guy. It was Declan. He challenged me and pushed me and made me work harder. He made me better at something I loved. Just being near him made me ridiculously happy.

I laid my head on her shoulder and sighed. "I feel like everything's crashing down around me, and I'm losing the things that really matter."

She kissed my forehead. "It may seem like it now, but I promise, it's not the end of the world. I remember right after I graduated from college, I met your father. I was doing grunt work for the big auditorium downtown, and I'd been asked to deliver something to the ad agency where your dad had just started as a copywriter. When I first met him, I was instantly gone over him. Which was bad, since I had a serious boyfriend at the time."

"Really? Who?" I met her sparkling eyes, curiosity spilling over inside me.

"Caleb."

"Wait, Caleb? The guy who owns that music store in Vancouver? The one who always flirts with you and gives you a discount?" I'd never be able to look at him the same way again.

She nodded, her auburn hair falling around her face. "Yup, we started dating my senior year of college and after graduation things were getting serious. Then your father came into the picture. We started hanging out as friends, and I loved how he played the guitar, and, oh man, did he catch me off guard. I tried so hard not to like your dad, but . . . it didn't work. So, I broke things off with Caleb only to find out your father had started seeing this very pretty girl at his office."

My eyebrows rose as she stood and went to check on dinner. I'd never heard this story before. Obviously I knew the ending, but I was still on pins and needles waiting for her to continue. I followed her into the kitchen and asked, "Then what happened?"

A soft sigh escaped her lips. "Well, I had to pluck up the courage to fight for what I wanted and tell him how I felt. Turns out he felt the same, and well, you can guess the rest."

"Why are you telling me this?"

"Because, you can tell yourself you don't like Declan, or that you can't like him, but no matter what you've decided, your heart is going to want what it wants. Not your head. And the same goes with him. Quinn can *want* him to like her, but she can't force it. Why don't you go relax and grab a snack? Read a book. I'll holler when dinner's ready."

Weak smile on my lips, I grabbed a couple Oreos from the pantry, snatched up my book bag, and headed upstairs.

I laid on my bed, my mind dancing with images of Declan. The way he played his cello, and how his fingers moved over the instrument, making it sing. The way he'd look over at me while playing and smile with his crooked grin. The way he'd kiss me, and I'd forget everything but him. I didn't want to lose him. I couldn't.

Ugh, when did I become this girl? My focus used to be so solid. I knew what I wanted. Lately my mind was everywhere it didn't need to be.

This whole debacle had made me certain of one thing: Noah definitely wasn't the guy for me. I wasn't feeling his absence. And now I needed to talk to him, make things right, and let him down gently. I didn't want to do it, but I had to. Dread didn't even begin to encompass how I felt.

CHAPTER *Eighteen*

*To play a wrong note is insignificant. To play without
passion is inexcusable.*

—*Beethoven*

The spring breeze fluttered the skirt of my long black dress. All my performance dresses were long. It was either that or give the audience a peep show. So *not* what I was going for. I brushed a puff of lint off the skirt, then closed my eyes and took a deep breath of the cool early spring air. I'd come outside to center myself before performing my solo. I held my cello in my hand and mentally rehearsed my piece. My accompanist waited in the room for me, but I still hadn't seen Declan. We'd promised to be there for each other's solos. It surprised me just how much I wanted him there. He had a strange, and very unexpected, calming effect on me.

I couldn't let this get into my head.

My phone rang, and, grateful for the distraction, I slid my thumb across it to answer Jenna's call. "Hello?"

"Hey, I just wanted to call and wish you good luck today!" Her voice was perky and chipper.

"Thanks. What are your plans?"

She was apparently headed to her grandparents up north. Jenna had a huge family, and she was always busy with them. Including her sister, who was a couple years below us, she had two little brothers still in early elementary school, and her mom had just given birth about six months ago. Her family was incredibly nice and always welcomed me.

"Any improvement on the Quinn front?"

I shook my head then realized she couldn't see me. "Nope. Still ignoring me."

She sighed. "I'm sorry, Pips. She'll come around."

"I hope so."

"And Noah, have you talked to him?"

"Not yet."

"Shoot, my dad's signaling me to wrap it up. I gotta run. Text me when it's over and let me know how you did."

We said our goodbyes, and I closed my eyes and inhaled deeply again. I was grateful to have her as a friend.

A hand clasped my shoulder, startling my eyes open. Marshland High's last chair cellist, Celeste, stood in front of me. She had her case strap on her shoulder and was getting ready to leave. Smiling at me, she leaned in and said, "I can't believe this is our last Solo and Ensemble, can you? Holy cow! But you're gonna do great, though. You always do."

"Thanks, I hope I do okay. And I know, it's crazy. I can't believe we're here already. How do you think you did?"

"Okay." She waved her hand back and forth. "I didn't practice as much as I should've."

With a sympathetic nod, I said, "I'm sure you did great."

"Well, I'll see you later. Good luck." She hopped down the steps and turned to wave at me before walking away.

It had to be getting close to my performance time. Sighing, I went back inside, up the stairs, and to the class-room I'd been assigned at check-in. I waited until the performer inside finished then went in and sat down. A short guy with wire-rimmed glasses and a viola stood to do his solo. I was next.

I couldn't focus on the music being played. Instead, I kept glancing at the door, wondering where Declan was. Maybe he'd decided to put *a lot* of space between us and just be around me when only absolutely necessary. Maybe I was asking too much of him to wait for me to figure out this Quinn situation. Maybe he just didn't like me as much as I liked him.

I didn't like thinking that.

"Miss Wyndham?"

I zoned back in to see the short guy had left the room and it was now my turn. Standing, my accompanist went over to the piano, and I took the center of the classroom, placing my rockstop on the floor in front of the chair.

My heart thundered in my chest and I tried to disguise my shaky breath. "Hi, I'm Phillippa Wyndham, and I'll be playing David Popper's 'Tarantella Cello.'"

Sitting, I situated myself then looked over at the pianist and gave her our signal. She played a tuning note. I made the necessary adjustments to Francesca then nodded to her again when I was satisfied.

The piano started in a pretty dance through the notes. When it was my time to join in, I closed my eyes and let the music take me away. I didn't worry about Quinn or Noah. I didn't even think about Declan as I played. The music washed over me and a smile found my lips. I was doing great. The notes flowed from me and I knew I was killing it. When I hit the melancholy part toward the middle, I put all my sadness and emotional baggage—I certainly had enough of it right now—into the notes. I didn't open my eyes again until I'd finished my piece.

Declan was sitting off to the side, in the seat next to the

door. He must've snuck in before I'd started. I'm sure my face positively radiated the happiness inside me at the sight of him.

"That was lovely, Miss Wyndham. Give me just a moment." The judge in the back was a man about my father's age. He had dark black hair that matched his suit. I watched as he scribbled on my score sheet. Setting his pencil down he smiled. "You have an incredible gift, young lady. I really have nothing to say. You play as if the cello were a part of you. I felt your emotions throughout your song, really wonderful. I hope you'll always play."

I smiled. "Thank you." Inhaling a deep breath, I turned and stepped toward the door, making way for the next performer.

My accompanist joined me in the hallway, followed by Declan, whose cello was still in its case on his back.

"Thank you so much, Connie." I shook her hand.

"Always my pleasure. I've got to get to my next room." She tucked her music for my piece back in her bag as she scurried off.

Declan cleared his throat from behind me. "Sorry I was late. I missed my bus."

Spinning around, I met his gaze, feeling super pleased with myself. In the background I could hear a flute running through scales and a clarinet somewhere nearby practicing the same section over and over again. I hoped it wasn't Lexi. I didn't want to run into her today. "It's okay. I'm just glad you made it."

"I wouldn't have missed it. I promised you." He slipped a hand in the pocket of his black slacks and tucked his thumb under the strap of his case.

"When do you play?"

"Not until after our piece."

I walked toward where I'd parked my case. "You still

want me to be there?"

"I always want you there."

My stomach was full of butterflies at his words, and I bit my lip, looking away. "Then I wouldn't dream of missing it."

"Let me get Booth out, and we can find a quiet corner to run through a few things."

He knelt down, and I admired his backside in his black pants. He flipped the clasps up, then opened the top. I sucked in a deep breath as his white shirt stretched across his broad shoulders. Closing my eyes, I spun away. My mind was so not in the right place right now.

"You ready?"

With a quick turn, I faced him again. Shy smile on my lips, I nodded my head in agreement. "Let's go."

We managed to find a small spot where not many other musicians were practicing. We tuned, did a couple scale warm ups together, then ran through our duet a couple times.

"We should head in there." Declan looked up from his watch and nodded in the direction we needed to go.

Clinging tightly to my cello, I stood and followed him. This school was new and ultramodern. It was a stark contrast to our ancient, but newly renovated, brick behemoth.

"I think this is our stop." He gestured to the white printed page under the blue placard that read 115. I leaned down and checked the sheet, making sure our names were on it. There we were, in the two o'clock slot.

We peeked through the window on the door and saw a violin trio listening to the judge, grins on their faces. They must've done well. Quietly, we opened the door and took a seat on the chairs lining the perimeter of the class. A violin and flute duo took the stage, well, if you could call the front of the classroom a stage. We were next.

Declan's arm rested against mine and I could feel the

heat coursing through his thin button down into my bare skin. A tremor ran up my spine.

"You cold?" Declan leaned and whispered in my ear, which elicited the same response.

"Just nervous." I turned and smiled.

Reaching over, he grabbed my hand and gave it a reassuring squeeze. His eyes alone told me that he thought I could do anything.

The duo finished and we listened to the judge. She was tough and picked on tiny things in their performance. Nervous adrenaline made my hands shake—better for the vibrato, I told myself.

"Declan Brogan and Phillippa Wyndham," the judge announced once the room had settled back down and people were seated.

We stood, took the stage, and quickly double-checked that our instruments were still in tune. Then Declan stood and in his rich baritone said, "Good afternoon. I'm Declan Brogan, and this is Phillippa Wyndham. We'll be playing Händel-Halvorsen's 'Passacaglia.'"

My eyes clapped onto his, and he gave me a shining smile as he sat down. I waited for him to get settled, then I lifted my bow, gave the cue, and we launched into our duet. I closed my eyes, focusing on Declan and hearing how my part fit perfectly with his. The music sent goosebumps down my arms and legs. We poured ourselves into the song.

Once we finished, the grumpy judge from earlier had disappeared. She now had a smile on her face. Standing, she clapped. "I've never seen two cellos perform this piece, and I must say, it was marvelous."

I turned to Declan, and he looked beyond thrilled. I wanted to throw myself into his arms.

"I can tell you've practiced extensively together, and it definitely shows. My only comment would be not to rush the ending. I was disappointed it was over. Absolutely beautiful."

We stood and thanked the judge, left the room, and rushed to our cases. Cellos down, Declan grabbed me and wrapped me in a tight hug. He lifted my feet off the ground and spun around.

"You were amazing!"

"So were you." I gave him a happy squeeze before he released me.

He took a step back. "I still can't believe we didn't get in to the NCYM."

"Me, neither." I looked away and bent down beside my case, packing Francesca up. Declan knelt beside me and brushed my hair over my shoulder. Turning, I met his gaze and froze. Everything about him was delectable. One side of his mouth quirked up and I sucked in an unsteady breath.

"I wish we were going. I really wanted to show you New York. God, I can't believe this is it. It's all over."

My voice wouldn't work with his proximity, so I nodded my agreement. We were still kneeling, my ankles screamed in protest, but I couldn't move. Declan grabbed my chin between his forefinger and thumb, then pulled me closer. My breath caught in my throat as my heart raced. Pausing just before our lips met, he veered off course and kissed my nose.

"I should practice." He cleared his throat and stood, glancing around. I stayed crouched down, looking up at him. "I'll be right over there." He pointed toward the end of the hallway.

He walked away and I sighed. I'd wanted that kiss so bad. I could still feel where his lips had briefly touched my skin. I finished securing the clasps on my case and went to keep him company.

Strains of Declan's music hit my ears. He was a wonderful player. And strangely, it no longer felt like a competition between us. If he found success as a musician, I'd be thrilled for him. That sudden realization startled me. I stopped walking. My eyes ran over his long frame, my thoughts all twisted in a tangled snarl.

Would I be okay if he got in to Goddards and I didn't? Yes . . . probably. The mere idea threw me for a loop. Sure, it would suck, and I'd be extremely disappointed, but I couldn't hate him for it. I didn't think I could hate him, period.

My heart did an accelerando in my chest, and I took a step back. I set my cello case down and leaned against the cold gray metal lockers, just hidden from his view.

I leaned my head back and listened to the melody. Declan stopped playing, and his head popped out from around the corner. "You alright?"

Turning, I nodded, my mind still swirling. "Yeah, just listening. Sounds amazing."

He studied me before continuing to practice. Squeezing my eyes shut, I took a deep breath. Just because he might be successful didn't mean I couldn't be, too. It wasn't an either/or situation . . . necessarily.

Somehow, I had to navigate this thing with Quinn, keep Declan at my side, and not hurt Noah. All while hopefully getting into the school of my dreams and setting off on the path toward my future career. No biggie.

Determination hit me like a lightning bolt, and I smiled. I wasn't going to give either one of them up. I could keep both Quinn and Declan in my life. I *would* keep them both. I just had to keep telling myself that.

Moments later Declan appeared. "I should get in there. My time's in just a few minutes."

I pushed off the lockers and mutely followed. He walked to the same room I'd been in earlier. The same judge would be critiquing us. I was curious what he'd say.

We waited until we heard the muffled melody stop, then

we went in. The previous performer was listening intently to the judge. I saw an older woman sitting to the side. Declan gave her a smile and nod. She must be his accompanist. I was surprised we didn't have the same one, since we had the same cello teacher. I took my seat as the guy who'd just performed grabbed his stuff and left the room.

Declan stepped to the front of the classroom and the woman sat at the piano. As they tuned, I looked around the empty room. It was the end of the day, which explained my being the only other person.

"Hello, I'm Declan Brogan, and today I'll be playing 'Gypsy Airs' by Pablo de Sarasate." He nodded to the pianist, and they jumped right in.

My gaze darted between Declan and the judge. Despite how beautiful the music sounded, the judge showed no sign of emotion. I smiled, watching Declan's brown hair swish around his forehead as he got into the loud, fast section.

Once the music ended the only sound in the room was the scratching of a pencil coming from the judge's table. When he stopped writing, he looked up at Declan.

"That was wonderful. You're a very talented young man. I'd suggest you watch the slower sections. They felt a little rushed and almost devoid of emotion. You really need to let your pain and happiness sing through your instrument and into the room."

Declan's brow furrowed as if he were pondering what he'd just heard. "Okay. Thank you."

"Really, very lovely job."

Standing with a small bow, Declan went toward the door. I stood and followed, looking back at the judge. He added Declan's paper to the stack and stuffed his pencil inside his blazer's internal pocket. I stepped into the hallway as Declan knelt at his nearby case to pack up.

"You sounded fabulous."

He just grunted.

"You okay?"

He clipped the last clasp and stood. "Yup. I've got to catch the bus. I'll see you Monday."

"I can give you a ride." I pulled my keys from the pocket of the black fleece jacket I'd just slipped on.

"It's okay. I'll see you Monday." He turned and headed down the hallway. An air of anger or disappointment, I couldn't pin down which one, crackled around him.

He was upset and clearly wanted to be alone. I'd have probably been upset too if the judge had told me my music was devoid of emotion. Still, a tiny part of me worried that maybe he just wanted to be away from me.

My phone pinged, and I grabbed it. A new email scrawled across the top of my screen. My eyes widened as I realized whom it was from. The National Competition for Young Musicians. What on Earth could they want?

CHAPTER *Nineteen*

Music must be emotional first and intellectual second.

—*Maurice Ravel*

I'd tried to run after Declan, but by the time I got outside, the bus stop was empty. Now home, I tossed my phone on my bed, frustration coiling in my muscles. Calling him wasn't working either. He wasn't even responding to texts. At least Jenna had, and she was beyond thrilled for us. She really was a great friend. But Declan was the one I seriously needed to talk to. This was big. Humongous. Something he'd definitely want to know. Snatching my phone up again, I pulled on a UO Ducks sweatshirt and ran down the stairs.

"Mom, I'm going over to Declan's. I can't reach him, and I have to tell him the news."

"Drive careful, Sweetie." She looked up from her perch on the couch, pausing as she folded the laundry. Dad was around here somewhere, but I hadn't seen him. "Oh, and remind your brother to come in and do the dishes if you see him. I'm tired of nagging him."

"Will do." I spun out the front door and jogged to my

car. I smiled and waved at Noah, who was shooting hoops with my brother. He inclined his head, a tiny smile on his lips. He still looked mad at me. Or maybe the look was more disappointment. I needed to make time for a conversation with him. But right this very moment, I didn't care. Big things were happening.

I relayed Mom's message to Phillip, and he groaned and tossed the ball to Noah. "Fine, I'm on it."

On the road, I made my way through the neighborhood, glancing at Quinn's house as I drove by. When I pulled into the parking lot under Declan's condo, I realized I didn't have the access code to the elevators. Backing out, I ended up circling the block what felt like a million times until a parking spot on the street opened up.

At the building's front door I punched in the number for Declan's condo in the intercom.

"Yes?" His mom's voice startled me as it came through the speaker louder than I remembered it from last time.

"Hi, um, this is Pippa, Declan's cello partner."

"Oh yes, hello, Pippa."

My breathing sounded labored, and I tried my best to disguise it, but I didn't think it was working. "Is there any way I can see Declan? I have some news for him."

"Of course, I'll buzz you in, come on up."

A mechanical hum sounded and I pushed on the metal bar, swinging the large panel of glass inward. The lobby was mostly grays, whites, and shiny silvers. Clean, lush, and *very* nice. I rushed to the elevator and repeatedly pressed the up button, impatient to get upstairs. Once on the empty elevator, I was able to catch my breath a bit on the ride up to the twenty-seventh floor.

The doors opened and I stepped out into the hallway. In the distance, Declan was waiting for me just outside their condo, still in his black trousers, his white shirt unbuttoned, his hands tucked in his pockets. He looked appealing as hell.

"Pips, what's going on?" His brow was furrowed, and the dark circles under his eyes gave a small clue to his exhaustion.

"It's not over. We're not done."

He shook his head. "What are you talking about?"

I passed over my phone, screen lit up, the email already displayed. He took it from me, and as he read, I said, "We got in. We're going to New York."

He began to read aloud, his brown eyes gleaming. "A disqualification due to the competition's age requirements leaves us with an opening that we are pleased to offer you. Please let us know your decision as soon as possible." He looked up, his eyes bright and excitement rolling off him. "We got in."

Nodding, I couldn't stop from smiling. "We did. This is it."

His arms wrapped around me, and he held me tight to him, burying his face in my neck. I felt him inhale and I squeezed my eyes shut in pure happiness. My arms wound around his waist and I splayed my hands over his muscular back. He held me tight then leaned away and met my gaze.

"So we're going to New York," he stated, a smile from ear to ear.

His mom stood in the doorway just behind us, her expression matching his. "In two weeks, no less."

A nervous chuckle left my lips. "Looks like it."

"Well, we better keep practicing,   then." He gave me another big hug, this time lifting me off the ground and making me squeak.

"Pippa, come inside, and I'll write down some information for your mom." She looked to Declan. "And I'll call your dad tonight and get things set up."

Declan took a step back, and, with a hand on the small

of my back, he guided me to their door and inside. We went to the brown leather couches and sat down.

He angled himself to face me. His voice soft and hesitant, he said, "I miss you, Pippa."

That so wasn't what I'd been expecting him to say. I opened my mouth, but no sound came out. Sucking in a breath, I watched as his eyes seemed to search my face. "I'm right here."

"It's not the same, and you know it." His head tilted and his brows lifted.

There was no point denying it, I knew exactly what he meant. He missed us, the way we used to be. So did I. Nodding, I looked down to my jeans and pulled off a stray string. I balled it up between my thumb and forefinger, still not looking at him. "I do know. And I miss you too." I chanced a glance up at him. "A lot."

"Pippa . . ." His hand came up and with his knuckles, he caressed my jaw. "I don't want to bring all this drama with us to New York. I want to take you there and show you my city. Have fun."

His hand curled around the side of my neck and I reached up, putting my hand over his. I'd tried to convince myself he wasn't meant to be mine. That he was either my enemy or that he belonged to Quinn. There was just one gigantic, insurmountable hurdle that I kept getting tripped up on. If he wasn't meant for me, why did he have to complement me so perfectly? And why the hell did I want him so badly?

♫

Staring out at the dreary day, the thunder rumbled outside my window and the rain pelted against the glass. Tomorrow was Monday, and I still hadn't a clue what to do about Quinn. I flopped onto my bed and stared at the ceiling, blowing out a long deep breath. Homework sat beside me unopened and untouched.

"Okay, it's all settled." Mom popped through my open doorway. "I've spoken with Mr. Brogan, and all your travel plans are made. You're all set for New York. I wish I could be there with you." Mom had one of her biggest piano performances in LA the same weekend as the NCYM. It'd been on the calendar long before Declan and I even considered applying for the competition.

"I wish you could come too. Thanks for getting everything set up on such short notice." I gave her a small smile, but my heart just wasn't in it. The funk I was wading through apparently couldn't be downplayed.

"I thought you'd be thrilled about this. Why do you look so miserable?"

I sat up and grabbed my pillow, clutching it to my stomach. "I'm thrilled about getting into the competition, but everything else is just . . . ugh. It's this whole stupid thing with Quinn. And I'm kinda dreading staying at Declan's dad's place. It just feels too . . . weird. Especially with what's going on between us."

"Well, I spoke to his stepmom as well, and she seems very nice. Plus it's only for three days. And Mr. Brogan is trying to get tickets to a Broadway show for you guys."

"That'd be cool." I tried to look happier. Something told me I wasn't all that successful.

Mom came to my side and sat beside me, leaning up against my headboard. "You're not fooling me. What happened now?"

I shrugged. "I like him. And . . . I'm afraid of losing Quinn because of it. But if I stay away from him to make her happy, I lose him and I'm miserable. Then there's always the old trusty issue of what if he kicks my ass musically. We're up for all the same schools, and he could easily take a spot that should've been mine. I mean, yes, I'd be happy for him, but if he got into Goddards and I didn't . . ." I couldn't finish the thought.

She brushed my hair over my shoulder then put her arm around me and gave me a squeeze. "Well, it definitely can't be easy on him either. He's probably feeling all the same things you are."

Tossing my pillow aside, I drew my knees to my chest and bit my lower lip, a heavy weight of confusion settling on my chest.

"I know you haven't told Quinn anything, but have you at least told Declan that you like him?"

I shook my head and scrunched my nose. "Kind of, but not really." I'd told him I liked kissing him, but that was about it. I couldn't bring myself to tell him I liked *him*. All of him. He had to know though, right?

"Why not?" Mom brushed my hair off my face, tucking it behind my ear.

"Because if I tell him, it's essentially me choosing him over Quinn. She'd never forgive me."

Mom pursed her lips and thought a moment. "If he was her boyfriend, then I could see her getting this upset. But as it is, he's just someone she's crushing on. He's not even the only one, for Pete's sake. And, to me, it's *very* clear that boy likes *you*. Now you may not like what I have to say, but this isn't exactly the first time she's done something like this. She's chosen other things and people over you more than once. What kind of friendship is that? Is it the kind you really want to have?"

Reaching over, I grabbed the book I had to read for my English class. "I don't know, I'll figure it out."

She patted my knee and stood. "Dinner will be ready in just a bit."

"Thanks, Mom."

The door closed with a soft snick behind her and I turned my focus to the page, trying to immerse myself in the story. My brain kept skipping through thoughts, and I had to keep re-reading the same sentences over and over.

A knock sounded on my door, and I sighed. My book landed on my coverlet with a puff of air. Clearly, I wasn't meant to read right now. "Come in."

Phillip came in and looked down at me. "Hey, can I talk to you a sec?"

"Of course."

He hopped on my bed and grabbed my book, strumming his thumb along the edge of the pages.

"So what's the deal with Noah?"

My brow furrowed. "There is no deal with Noah."

"I know he likes you, and you used to like him, too, or so I thought. What happened?"

I shrugged. "You know when you build something up in your head and you think it's going to be amazing, then when you actually get to do it, it isn't that awesome and it just doesn't feel right?"

"Not really, no." He shook his head.

With a scoff, I said, "I did like Noah. For a long time I was so certain he was everything I wanted and more. He's still a great guy, it's just . . . he feels more like a brother now."

"He blames everything on Declan."

My head bobbed in agreement. "Declan's a huge part of it."

"Noah doesn't like him."

"I already gathered that." I chuckled. "Declan doesn't seem to be his biggest fan either."

Phillip tossed my book aside and met my eyes. "Noah's pretty miserable. But . . ." His eyes darted away and he looked nervous. "But I'm kind of glad it didn't work out. Not that I don't want either of you to be happy, but you two together, it was just . . . weird."

"Well, you're in the clear. I don't think we're meant to be together. I am sorry that he's miserable, though. It's not what I wanted. I'm going to talk to him about it, I promise."

He nodded and started to get up.

"Wait. I need to ask you about something."

"Shoot." He settled onto the foot of my bed.

I cleared my throat and looked to my tall white bookshelf behind him. On it was a picture of Quinn and I when we were twelve. Our silly brace-faces made me smile. "Quinn. Do you *like* like her?"

"Quinn?"

"Yeah, you guys seemed to have a moment before Winter Formal. And, I don't know, I just kinda sensed there might be something there."

He looked away. "Wouldn't it be super weird if I liked your friend?"

I shook my head and scrunched my face. "Please, I liked yours for years."

"And that *was* weird." His eyes widened, silently saying, *see, I told you so.*

Quinn would kill me if I told him the truth.

I chewed at the inside of my lower lip, making a bump that I'd undoubtedly keep biting. She already wasn't speaking to me and maybe never would. It's not like it could get any worse. There was also the possibility that my telling him could jumpstart something between them. This was one possible way that both Quinn and I could be happy. Mind made up, the words blurted from my lips. "It's not weird when she already likes you."

Phillip didn't say anything. He leaned his elbows on his knees and clasped his hands together, staring at my fluffy rug.

Silence filled the room. Why wasn't he saying anything?

Did I just monumentally screw things up? Shit. "Phillip?"

His head tilted to the side, and he looked me in the eye, sober expression on his face. "Are you serious? Quinn really *likes* me? Like, she's actually into me?"

Nodding, I raised my brows. Normally I could get a good read on his feelings, but his face was blank, like a well-seasoned poker player.

He stood and headed for my door.

"Phillip, wait."

Not stopping, he said, "I've got think about this."

That wasn't the reaction I'd hoped for.

I sat in my history class, quietly working on the pop quiz Mr. Ferngren had surprised us with. It'd been a week since I'd told Phillip about Quinn's crush. He'd done nothing. Which meant it'd now been one more week of Quinn still not talking to me. I'd tried to get Noah alone, but he'd turned to the avoidance tactic. And Declan was still distant and now more guarded than ever before. At least our getting into the NCYM had helped him get over his moodiness after Solo and Ensemble, but now he was going above and beyond in giving me my requested space.

To sum it up, the past week freaking sucked. The only person who seemed not to hate me was Jenna. At least that was something.

Declan and I continued to practice together after school. But now the innocent brushes of his hand against mine were few and far between. There were no more instances of him tucking my hair behind my ear or using any other little reason to touch me. And he'd only been close enough that I could smell his rosin and clean soap scent once.

God, I missed him.

It was like being trapped in a nightmarish in-between.

This was by far the longest Quinn and I'd ever gone without talking. And Phillip, he was just being plain weird. He'd now taken to avoiding Quinn, but watching her whenever she wasn't looking. I wanted to hit him and tell him to suck it up and just ask her out because clearly he felt *something* for her.

"Alright, class, put your pencils down and pass your papers up the aisle."

I reached behind me for Declan's pile, and when our fingers brushed, that familiar rush of excitement coursed through me. I met his gaze and bit my bottom lip before I quickly turned back, continuing the paper chain to the front of the room.

"Go ahead and pack it up. The bell's about to ring." Mr. Ferngren walked along the front row gathering the stacks. Tapping them on his desk to even the edges, he sat down and began prepping for his next class.

The bell rang. I grabbed my bag and made a beeline for the door. No one walked with me anymore anyway, so there was no reason to hang around. Straight to Mr. Adams's geometry class, I waved to Celeste as we passed each other. She gave me a look that said she felt bad for me. It seemed everyone knew the drama surrounding my life right now. And everyone was falling into either Team Pippa or Team Quinn. Jenna was emphatically on my side. Not that I'd had much time for her with all the practicing and homework I'd been doing. Another thing to add to list of stuff I already felt crappy about.

I was about to step into my class when a hand on my arm stopped me. I turned to find Declan, his face serious. "I know you don't agree with me and you don't think it'd be a good idea, but I'm going to talk to Quinn. I've stayed away long enough, I can't do this anymore. I don't want to."

My mouth popped open to speak, but the bell rang and Mr. Adams's voice stopped me.

"Pippa, time to step *inside* the classroom. Say goodbye to your friend."

Declan left without another word.

Maybe him talking to Quinn wouldn't be the worst thing.

Who was I kidding? It'd be catastrophic.

CHAPTER *Twenty*

I think music in itself is healing. It's an explosive expres-
sion of humanity. It's something we are touched by. No
matter what culture we're from, everyone loves music.

—*Billy Joel*

Mom stood beside me, waiting in line at the airline counter to check in. I'd been looking around for Declan, but he hadn't shown up yet. We'd made no plans for where to meet. We hadn't really talked outside of our shared classrooms and practice sessions. I didn't even know if he'd actually talked to Quinn. If he had, it hadn't made a bit of difference. She was still ignoring me. But right now, I couldn't dwell on that. I had the flight looming ahead of me to concentrate on.

"You got everything?" Mom asked, giving me a once-over.

I nodded. "I think so."

My cello was draped over one shoulder. I was going to have to check Francesca and I was jumpy at the thought of letting her out of my sight. I'd already put luggage tags on the case. Three of them. Just in case any fell off.

"You look nervous," Mom leaned in and whispered in my ear.

"I am. I hate flying."

"You'll do fine." She stopped and looked around. "I wonder where Declan's at? Is he meeting you at the terminal?"

My shoulders lifted in a shrug. "We didn't make any plans. I'm guessing I'll see him on the plane."

Mom's brow furrowed. "Why didn't you make plans?"

"It's kinda hard to when you're trying to stay away from each other and barely talking."

Her head shook. "You know, this is getting ridiculous. You and Quinn have to sort this out."

My eyes widened. "It's stupid is what it is. Clearly our friendship doesn't mean as much to her as I'd assumed. I've continued to call and text. I've even gone by the Oak and talked to her mom, and nothing. I thought my steering clear of Declan would've shown her that I'm trying to make her happy, but it's like she doesn't give a crap. I don't know what to do." My voice rose at the end of my rant.

At a throat clearing behind me, I slowly turned, knowing exactly who it was. Declan. Of course.

"I found Declan." Mom smiled wryly.

He raised a hand. "Hey."

"Hey." Nerves made my stomach twirl like a top. He did that to me. Constantly. I just hoped this trip wouldn't be as awkward as the past few weeks had been.

"You ready for this?" His eyes sparkled, and on his lips was the first real smile I'd seen in a long time. It was as if being away from school and our friends had him feeling lighter. I know that's how I felt.

I sucked in a breath and nodded as warmth hit me square in the chest and spread throughout my entire body, flushing my cheeks. I both hated and loved how he had such an effect on me.

"Let's do it then." He gestured to the counter, it was my turn.

I spun. Mom gave me a knowing motherly look with one of those mom smiles that told you she was pleased with what she was seeing. I stepped up to the clerk and proceeded to hand over Francesca and the suitcase I was checking. All I had for the plane was my carry-on filled with a change of clothes and my iPad—stocked with books and movies, and our sheet music—just in case.

All checked in, I stood to the side with Mom, waiting on Declan. I wondered how he'd gotten here since his mom wasn't with him.

Leaning into me, Mom whispered in my ear, "Quinn's shown you what's more important to her than your friend-ship. And I'm getting tired of her treating you this way. If you want Declan, fight for him." She kissed my cheek before straightening.

I met her gaze, and she reached out, flipping my hair over my shoulders. Declan finished up and headed toward us, clutching his boarding pass and carry-on in one hand.

"I love you, sweet girl."

"I love you too, Mom." I gave her a hug, squeezing my eyes shut, savoring the moment.

We pulled apart, and Declan looked between us, like he was unsure what to do now.

"You guys better get moving." Mom glanced at her watch. It was early in the morning, and the sun was streaming in the tall windowed walls. PDX was primarily glass and metal. It was a pretty striking building inside. "And Declan, I expect you to look out for her."

"Of course." Declan nodded, a grin tilting his lips. Turning, he led the way to the security checkpoint. Thank-fully, the lines weren't too long.

Mom stayed with us as we waited. When we were next in line, she grabbed me, gave me another hug, and whispered in my ear to travel safe and have fun. This was the first time I'd been anywhere without one of my parents. It felt weird.

My throat constricted, and I could feel my eyes tear up. I couldn't cry. Not in front of Declan. It was only three freakin' days.

We made it through the TSA checkpoint, and as I put myself back together I looked back through the line and saw Mom standing there. I waved and turned back to Declan.

He met my eyes with his warm brown ones. "Let's go."

I nodded, tamping down my nerves. Depending on how things went between Declan and me, this trip could be awesome or utterly miserable. But he was smiling at me, so that was a good start.

"Do you travel a lot on your own?" I asked.

He shrugged. "Kinda. I get shuttled around between my parents often enough, I guess."

That had to stink. But it explained why his mom wasn't here.

We rounded the corner, our feet padding on the new teal carpet. The famous PDX carpet had been replaced, and really, it just wasn't the same. When we reached our terminal, I took a snap of my feet on the new carpet. I had to; it was tradition.

"Why?" Declan was watching me, one brow raised.

"It's just what you do when you're at PDX." I laughed and explained the whole carpet phenomenon.

He shook his head. "That's kinda dumb."

"Yeah, well, this is Oregon. We're weird." I grinned as I walked down a row of plastic chairs. Picking one near the windows, I sat and pulled out my iPad, waiting for our boarding call. I decided to try and avoid conversation altogether and read. I didn't know how to ask him if he'd talked to Quinn, and it seemed like a bad opener. Putting our issues at the forefront of this trip was not my goal.

My phone chimed and I pulled it from my bag.

> Phillip: Do you know how much it sucks that I'm stuck in class and you're jetting off to New York? :(
>
> Me: lol, lots! Have fun! Take notes for me. ;)
>
> Phillip: I hate you.
>
> Me: Love you too. ;)
>
> Phillip: Travel safe.

Chuckling, I slipped my phone back into my bag. When I glanced up, Declan was watching me from across the aisle. I looked down, unable to maintain eye contact. The way he was looking at me, it was as if . . . well, as if he were thinking about kissing me. I chewed the inside of my lip, willing myself to not think about that. I refocused on my screen, needing a distraction. It didn't last long. I peeked up, and he was still watching me.

"What?" I asked, setting my tablet in my lap.

"The way you smile when you're texting someone. It's cute. Makes me wonder if you smile like that when you text me."

I tucked my legs up to sit crisscross on my chair, feeling awkward and shy under his gaze. With a nervous giggle, I said, "Stop staring, you're making me feel weird."

He ran his hands through his hair, ruffling up the dark locks as he grinned, then stretched. The muscles in his arms pulled taut and his shirt lifted to expose the skin of his stomach. I clamped my eyes shut as images of him pressed against me flooded my senses. Good Lord, did it get hotter in here all of a sudden?

"Ladies and gentlemen, we will now begin boarding

Flight 1105 to New York. Please line up and have your boarding pass at the ready. Thank you for choosing Pacific Air."

I tucked my iPad away and stood, straightening my long, comfy tee and oversized sweater. Declan stood at my side, and we got in line. We were close to the front. A couple families with kids were before us. I was thankful we didn't have assigned seats. I needed to make sure I got one near a window so I wouldn't get air sick. Seeing the horizon was a must for my equilibrium.

Declan's shoulder bumped into mine and I looked up to see him looking straight ahead, a slight twitch happening on his lips. It must've been contagious, 'cause I was now smiling too. Leaning, I bumped him back. Then he bumped me again. So I bumped him. Then it turned into a silent bumper war. I was positive the people behind us thought we were stupid kids, but I didn't care. I was having fun. As he came back toward me, I leaned away and he nearly toppled over. I covered my mouth to muffle my laughter. He gave a shocked yip, then started laughing as he righted himself. This, the lightness between us, was nice.

It was our turn and the flight attendant took our boarding passes with a nod, giving us permission to board as she handed them back, wishing us a nice flight.

Walking side by side down the long boarding bridge, Declan held back so I could get on the plane first. I walked to the first row with the extra leg room. It was unoccupied and since Declan was tall, I figured he'd appreciate the extra space. I tilted my head so I could see him. "You mind if I take the window seat?"

His eyes darted up to mine.

Had he just checked out my tush?

Declan shook his head and gestured for me to take the chair I wanted. We both quietly sat. Out the window I could see workers in orange vests loading the luggage into the cargo bay. I saw our cellos, stacked together, waiting to be put on. I nudged Declan and pointed to where our instruments sat. Leaning around me, Declan's face came even with mine. Our cheeks brushed, and I so badly wanted to turn and place my lips on his. It'd been so long, and I was craving him. God, he smelled amazing.

"At least we know they've got them, and they're going to get on." He sat back and settled into his chair.

I followed suit and clasped my hands tightly in my lap. People filed past our seats, and with each additional passenger, we were that much closer to lift-off. Declan sat beside me, headphones on, head back, eyes closed. Me, on the other hand, my palms were sweating, my heart beating presto tempo, and my nerves were beyond frazzled.

My lids fluttered closed, and I focused on taking deep calming breaths. The steward shut and locked the door, went to the microphone, and began his spiel—which I paid no attention to. I was too busy focusing on calming my heart and lungs down.

The engines roared to life, and my eyes popped open. I gripped the armrests and prayed for a safe flight.

"Hey, you okay?" Declan removed his headphones and turned to me, concern evident in his eyes.

I shakily bobbed of my head, sucking in a deep breath. "Yeah, I just really hate flying."

He angled himself in my direction, leaning off the back of the seat, and pried my hand off our shared armrest and lifted the bar so it was no longer between us. My hand was still caught in his and he rubbed his forefinger against the inside of my wrist. It sent a ripple of pleasure through me. I loved it when his touch did that.

The captain came on the intercom, giving us the weather in New York and telling us what he expected of our trip.

"Is this your first time flying?" Declan asked.

A laugh squeaked from my throat. "No. I've flown before. I'm okay once we get up in the air. It's just the takeoffs and landings that are an issue."

He continued rubbing lightly, and I closed my eyes, focusing on the sensations he was creating as the plane moved to taxi on the runway. It wouldn't be long until we were airborne. I hated that moment when your body slammed back into the seat from the thrust of the plane.

"Pippa, look at me." Declan's voice cut through the cloud of my thoughts, and he squeezed my hand still clasped in his.

I opened my eyes as the plane gradually picked up speed and met Declan's milk-chocolatey eyes.

He looked at me seriously. "You're going to be fine. Just think about being in New York. You can do this. We're gonna have a fun time."

My head bobbed as I blew out a shaky breath. I hated that I had this reaction to something as normal as flying. But I couldn't stop the unwanted images of careening to the Earth, twisted metal, and a fiery inferno from popping into my mind.

I glanced around, looking for all the exits, making sure I knew where to go, just in case of emergency. My head felt like it was spinning, and I was breathing entirely too fast.

"You're looking pale." Declan fumbled with the pouch on the wall in front of him and pulled out the barf bag. "Do you need this?"

Lovely.

Inhaling, filling my lungs, I struggled to calm down. "No. I'm fine."

"You don't look fine."

"What if we crash?" My whispered voice sounded high and weird even to my ears. I was in full-on panic mode.

"We're not going to crash." Reaching up, he leaned closer to me and ran his hand through my hair, pulling the long strands over my shoulder. I closed my eyes, focusing on his touch.

The engines screamed, and we were jostled around as the plane gathered speed. My brow furrowed, but before I could lose it, Declan grabbed my face and kissed me. My eyes flew open as we were both thrown back into the seats, our shoulders hit the raised armrest, but I didn't care. His lips were warm and soft, and good heavens, how I had missed them. It was all I could focus on. I closed my eyes, wrapped my arms around his neck, and pulled him closer. Losing myself in him.

The tip of his tongue touched my lip, and I was a goner. I held onto him and kissed him like my life depended on it. I paid no attention to where we were, only to the fire now blazing inside me.

His fingers threaded into my hair and a low moan reverberated from his throat, sending tingles through every inch of me.

Beside us a throat cleared. We separated and looked to find a flight attendant smiling down at us. "Pardon the interruption, but can I get your drink order?"

Just how long had we been kissing?

Declan cleared his throat. "Um, Sierra Mist, please."

"I'll have the same," I mumbled and looked down at my lap, my face an inferno.

"Did it work?"

My brows drew together as I looked into his smiling face. "Did what work?"

"I was hoping to distract you."

Mission successful.

CHAPTER *Twenty-One*

Yeah we all shine on, like the moon,
and the stars, and the sun.

—*John Lennon*

The elevator doors opened onto a bright and industrial-looking apartment. We'd survived the flight and now we were at Declan's dad's house. In front of us, the New York skyline was on display through the large gridded windows. It was a breathtaking view. A slim woman in a snug black dress with brunette hair that rippled perfectly over her shoulder rushed over to us on bare feet. She smiled as she bounced a toddler on her hip. Next to me, Declan stiffened and didn't take a step forward. I clutched onto the strap of my cello and reached for my suitcase handle, looking between the two.

"You're finally here! We've been so excited." Declan's stepmom looked down at her daughter momentarily before she reached forward, holding her hand out to me. "You must be Pippa. I'm Missy. It's such a pleasure to meet you."

I shook her hand. "It's nice to meet you." Leaning a little closer to the little girl in her arms, I said, "And who might you be?" The little girl smiled and laid her head down on her mom's shoulder and sucked two of her fingers into her mouth.

"This is Carsyn." Missy brushed the dark bangs off her daughter's forehead. "Can you tell Pippa how old you are?"

A small slobbery hand popped up, showing me three fingers.

"Oh my, you're three? Such a young lady." I grinned and leaned back. "And I love your dress. It reminds me of Cinderella."

Carsyn held out the skirt of her sparkly blue outfit with a toothy smile.

"Cinderella's her favorite." Missy grinned down at her daughter.

A quick glance at Declan showed his irritation.

He sidestepped around Missy but stopped and ruffled his half sister's hair. "Hey, Carsyn."

Michael, Declan's dad, had picked us up at the airport. He now waited for me as I stepped off the elevator before following. I couldn't help but notice the concerned look that passed between him and his wife.

With a smile plastered on my face, I looked around the large room, trying to avoid the awkwardness. High ceilings, exposed brick, and duct work, it was like a large loft that they'd partitioned to break up the massive space. And it was spotless. If I hadn't seen her with my own eyes, I'd never guess a toddler lived here.

"Let's get you settled." Missy handed Carsyn off to her dad. "You'll be staying in Declan's room."

"Oh no, I couldn't. The couch would be fine, really."

"Declan doesn't mind. Do you, Sweetie?"

From the open kitchen, Declan cringed at the endearment. "No, of course not. It's not my room anyway. It's the guest room."

It was startling how he'd gone from charming and nice

on the plane to grumpy and angsty with his family. He wasn't this way with his mom, which made me curious about their backstory. There had to be a reason he'd done such a personality shift practically upon sight of his dad at the airport.

Missy smiled and held out a hand for my suitcase. I let her take it and she led the way across the sitting area to a small hallway. Glancing back at Declan before we turned from sight, I saw his father's finger waving at him as he whispered something close to his son's face. Little Carsyn lifted a finger and waggled it at him in imitation.

Turning away, I followed his stepmom. Missy didn't look much older than us. My guess would be early to mid-twenties. Which would probably bother me, too, if my dad married someone so close to my age.

"Okay, here we are." Missy opened the tall door, revealing a small room with a large window overlooking the neighboring building. It was sterile in black and white. A large bookshelf lined one wall full of old books and knickknacks. Nothing in here suggested this had ever been Declan's room. He'd been spot on calling it the guest room.

"Great, this is perfect." I turned back to face her. "And thanks again for letting me stay here."

With a wave of a hand, she brushed the idea away. "Of course. I'll let you settle in." Spinning, she closed the door behind her and left me alone with my thoughts.

The bed creaked as I sat down. A quick text to my parents and I flopped back, looking up at the high ceiling while blowing out a loud breath. A thought hit me. Declan's lain here, in this very spot. An unexpected curl of warmth spiraled from my stomach, which led me to think of his kiss on the plane. It'd been amazing. Just as kissing him always was. And I wanted more. I craved it. Him.

A soft knock had me standing and answering the door.

Declan's face greeted me, lips upturned and a twinkle in his eyes. "You want to go for a walk? Get outta here for a bit?"

"Don't you think we should get some practicing in?"

"I could really use a moment. Far away from my dad."

We'd just gotten here, but I could tell he needed to step away. His hair was more mussed than usual and his arms were crossed tightly over his chest—he looked stressed. The easygoing guy I knew was hanging on by a thread.

"Okay, let's go." We could practice later. I slipped into my fleece jacket and grabbed his offered hand, letting him guide me back to the elevator.

"We're gonna go for a walk. Be back in a bit," He called to whoever was listening.

"What about practicing? Don't you need to get some rest for tomorrow?" Declan's dad asked from the kitchen, his graying head popping out from behind the open refrigerator door.

"We'll work on it later tonight. I just need some fresh air," Declan answered.

"Don't stay out too long. We're going to head to dinner soon."

Declan nodded and pushed the elevator call button. "Okay, but don't wait for us."

"Well, since you'll be back in an hour, we won't have to wait, will we?" his dad countered.

The elevator doors opened and Declan released my hand and gestured for me to step inside. He followed, not bothering to answer.

We rode in silence. There was so much I wanted to ask, but I wasn't sure if I should.

"Want to go check out Central Park?" He looked down at me once we exited the elevator.

"Sure."

Grabbing my hand again, he pulled me out the lobby

door and across the street. The noise of the city hit my ears in a mix of horns and sirens. We wove through several yellow cabs and other vehicles that slowly moved in the backed-up traffic. "We're actually super close."

Standing on the sidewalk and looking up, I took it all in. The buildings seemed to go on and on. Seriously, how tall were they? There were tall buildings in downtown Portland, but this felt different somehow, more imposing.

Down two blocks of towering buildings and we were just about there. I could see the trees and a large patch of grass across the street. The sun peeked through the clouds, making this early spring day chilly. The grass wasn't a vibrant green yet, more sallow yellowy-green from being under snow all winter.

A gust of wind whipped past us head on, making Declan's scarf flap behind him.

"So . . ." I was hoping he'd start spilling the beans about his dad on our walk over, but he hadn't.

He looked at me, an eyebrow raised. "So what?"

"What's the deal with you and your dad?"

Declan blew out a long breath and raised a hand to scratch the back of his neck. "We don't get along."

With a soft scoff, I said, "Well, yeah, I gathered that. What happened?"

He inhaled sharply and bowed his head, tucking his hands into his pockets. "Long story short, my parents divorced because *I* caught my dad in bed with Missy."

"Oh, whoa." My eyes widened. I wasn't expecting that. Cheating, sure. Him catching them, no. "That explains a lot."

"Yeah, I came home early from my cello lesson after school. Mom was out of town on business, and I got home, expecting to be alone, when I heard a noise. I thought someone had broken in. I went toward the noise and, well . . . yeah, you can probably figure out the rest, I'm sure."

"God, Declan, I'm so sorry." I couldn't even imagine.

"He's just generally an asshole. As soon as he and Mom divorced, he totally focused on Missy and basically forgot about us. He married her right away, she got pregnant, and now the plan is three or four times a year, depending on his schedule, I'm forced to come out here and let him pretend to be a dad."

Reaching out, I grasped his hand and gave it a squeeze. A blast of cold air blew my hair in my face. I brushed it away and met his brown eyes once I was free. "I'm really sorry. I can't imagine going through all that."

He lifted his shoulder in a half shrug. "It is what it is. He's a dick. He's got his shiny new family, but thankfully I'm almost eighteen. I won't have to deal with it much longer."

"Wait." My brow raised, and I glanced at him, worried about his reaction. "If he didn't care about you, why would he bother with us at all this weekend? He has to care. At least a little."

"'Cause somehow it's helping him. He doesn't do anything for me unless it benefits him." His eyes were hard and cold. I didn't like seeing him like this.

I looked down at my shoes as we waited for the cars to ease up so we could dart across. "I got the impression that both your dad and Missy were happy to see you though."

Declan's lips tightened into a thin line. "Probably 'cause this gets them out of one of their visits with me. Or my mom gave him a break on the child support this month."

My brow wrinkled, still confused. That wasn't the impression I'd got. They'd both seemed genuinely delighted to see him. He, on the other hand, had morphed into moody, angsty Declan. "Maybe he's trying to make it up to you. Maybe he feels guilty."

His eyes met mine and he opened his mouth to say something, but stopped and shook his head, looking annoyed. "He should feel guilty. He's a cheater and a lousy father."

Biting the inside of my cheek, I debated whether or not I should say something, but ultimately decided to just go for it. "So maybe *let* him make it up to you. Then you guys might be able to have a better relationship. It's just a thought."

He made a noncommittal grunt and shook his head. Reaching up, he gave a playful tug on my hair. "I know you think you know everything, Princess, but trust me, you don't."

I grinned and let go of his hand, happy to tease with him. "I never said I knew *everything*. Just almost everything."

"Ah, I see how it is." His eyes softened and he smiled.

"Maybe just see what he does this weekend, and if he screws it up again, you can totally complain about it to me. I know how much you'd love to tell me I'm wrong."

With a sniff, Declan nodded his head. "We'll see. I might be getting lots of chances soon."

"What do you mean?"

"Nothing. Come on." Hand in mine, he pulled me across the street and through a small entrance into the park. Leafless trees surrounded us as the sun weakly filtered down. We walked into a quiet, circular area surrounded by dark benches. In the center of the pavement was a black and white inlaid mosaic with large letters spelling "Imagine" in the center. Fresh flowers wreathed around the tiny stones and formed a peace symbol; the red carnations popped out at me from the store-bought assortment.

"What's this about?" I gestured to ground.

"Oh, it's a memorial for John Lennon." He turned and gestured back to where we'd just come from. "Right over there is the Dakota Apartments where he was shot."

I glanced back at the castle-like building. Well, at least that's what it looked like the me. Dozens of dormers dotted the deep pitched roof, and rows of windows broke up the buttery exterior. It was lovely. "Oh, wow."

We stood to the side and took it all in. People rushed past us, faces buried in their cell phones. It made me wonder all the things I missed by not looking up enough.

Lately I'd been missing a lot. With everything going on with Quinn, I'd been in my own little bubble, focusing on the small things I could control and just trying to get by. I didn't want to ask, but I had to know if he'd talked to her. "So . . . did you talk to Quinn?"

"No." He shook his head. "When I tried, she said it was between the two of you and she didn't want to talk about it, then she walked away."

"That's probably for the best."

He reached up and cupped my cheek, giving me a tender look that melted my insides. "Don't worry about any of that right now. Come on, let's go over to Bethesda Terrace." He smiled down at me. "You can see the fountain. It's got to be the most iconic part of Central Park."

Tilting my head back to meet his gaze, I grinned and followed him down the winding path. The beginning of spring was showing all around. Buds and baby blooms blushed across the tree branches as fresh green shoots strained up from the rich earth. We stopped at the top of a tall staircase. Down below us I saw the famous fountain, the lake behind it.

Declan's warm hand still held mine, and a flutter of excitement made my heart race.

In a soft voice, he said, "Come on."

As we bounded down the steps, the wind rushed past our faces. Out of breath and laughter on our lips, we reached the fountain. I looked up at the tall bronze angel, wings spread, lilies in one hand. Four little cherubs were on the tier under her. She was lovely. I pulled my hand from Declan's and leaned on the concrete ledge to look down at the water.

"Here."

I turned to see him holding his hand to me, clutching something. I held my hand out, palm upturned, and he dropped a penny into it.

"Make a wish." He grinned, stepped to the edge of the fountain, and stood for a moment before tossing his coin in.

Standing beside him, I closed my eyes and listened to the sound of the water slapping and concentrated on my wish: *I wish we'd win tomorrow's competition.* Eyes still closed, I couldn't stop there. I tacked more onto the lone penny clenched in my hand: *I wish Quinn would forgive me. I wish I could be with Declan.* I sucked in a deep breath. Declan. *I wish for Declan.* Opening my eyes, I lobbed my coin, hoping to get it in the first-tier bowl. It fell short and plunked in the water below.

"What'd you wish for?" he asked.

My eyes widened, and I opened my mouth in mock horror. "Hasn't anyone ever told you? You can't tell people your wishes or they won't come true."

A low laugh shook his shoulders. "Fine, then I won't tell you what I wished for."

What *had* he wished for? Knowing that he would've told me, now I wanted to know. "What did you wish for?"

"Nope, not telling."

Smiling, I shook my head. "Fine." I turned to walk toward the lake but didn't get far. Declan's hand clasped my wrist and he spun me back around. His lips met mine as one of his hands tangled in the hair at the nape of my neck. Gentle at first, he then tilted my head and thoroughly kissed me. My fingers curled around the lapels of his jacket, and I pulled him closer.

Declan's free hand pressed onto my back, bringing my body flush with his. It felt as if he never wanted to let me go. Pulling back, he leaned his forehead against mine and breathed heavily. "You. I wished for you."

CHAPTER *Twenty-Two*

Music produces a kind of pleasure which human nature
cannot do without.

—Confucius

Declan and I stood enveloped in the darkness of the backstage area, cellos and bows in our hands, waiting for our turn. The big day was officially upon us, and in just a few minutes we were up. Closing my eyes, I pictured the music in my mind and fingered the notes on the strings as I mentally played through the piece. Footsteps sounded all around us. We were in Carnegie Hall, a musician's actual dream stage, Carnegie Hall. I couldn't believe I was going to get to play here. My earlier glance out the stagedoor informed me the lower seating area was nearly full, and the balconies were pretty packed as well.

Musicians wandered the outside hallways, finding small spaces to quietly rehearse. We'd been summoned into the blackened backstage area by a lady with a headset and thick-framed glasses. According to her list, there were two more groups, then it was all us.

"My, my, my, if it isn't the über hottie Declan Brogan."

I opened my eyes and watched Declan turn to face a short girl with pitch-black hair holding a cello of her own.

"Ah, Kara, I wondered if I'd see you here." The smile on his face didn't quite reach his eyes.

The petite girl sniffed. "Of course you'd see me here. Just one more place for me to kick your lame ass."

"Hmm, that's not how I remember it. I seem to recall me always kicking your ass. I *was* first chair when I left." He grinned. "But I'm guessing you've tried to forget that."

Her eyes slivered into slits as she pasted a fake smile on her lips and shook her head. "So, are you doing a solo?"

He shook his head. "Duet." Turning to me, he smiled. "Kara, this is Pippa Wyndham, best cellist in Portland. Pips, this is Kara Kennedy, most obnoxious girl in New York."

I nodded, a little shocked by his praise for me. "So you're Kara. Nice to meet you."

"He means I was his fiercest competition in New York." She looked back to him after glancing at me. "I just won this thing. The money and all the scholarships that follow behind are mine. You might as well go home. Later, losers."

We watched her saunter away and out the door. I couldn't stop my smirk. "Well . . . she seems *nice.*"

Declan shook his head. "Super humble too."

Another woman with long, thin blonde hair and a headset came over to us. "Are you Declan Brogan and Phillippa Wyndham?"

My nerves shot into overdrive and my stomach clenched with anxiety.

"We are." Declan nodded, answering for us.

"Fabulous! Follow me—you're on next."

Sucking in a big breath, Declan let me go ahead of him. I rushed to follow the woman clearly in charge. Lifting my hand in front of me, I watched it tremble. *I can do this,* I reminded myself. Once we came to a stop, I closed my eyes and prayed I wouldn't throw up.

"You okay, Pips?" Declan's voice reached my ears, and I could hear his worry. His hand came up to rub my back.

Opening my eyes, I looked up into his. "I think so. Just nerves."

This was a big moment. A big opportunity for us. And I definitely didn't want to screw this up.

Cello and bow in one hand, his other grabbed mine and held it tight. "We've got this. You know we do. We're amazing together."

My gaze fell to the ground and the tips of my black flats sticking out from my long slacks.

"Look at me." He let go of my hand and guided my face to his using my chin. "You're better than all these other players here. Hell . . ." He shook his head, a painful look on his face. "Even me. Let's go kick some ass."

A shocked smile stretched across my face, and I nodded as I blew out a breath. I never thought I'd hear him admit I was the better cellist.

Just then, blonde headset lady opened the door and ushered us through. We stepped onto the stage and I took in the honeyed wood floors, the ornate stage backing, the dimmed house lights, and the sea of people in front of us.

I met Declan's eyes and he held my focus for a moment and nodded in a silent message that I received loud and clear. We were gonna rock it. Since the performing groups were made up of all different instruments and numbers of people, we had to grab what we needed and do our own stage set up. We pulled chairs to the center of the stage and moved the stands off to the sides since we'd memorized our piece. Silently, we got settled and ready.

The world around me felt as if it were in slow motion. As Declan sat, I stood and, in a clear voice, announced us. Once I sat down, I took in the filled auditorium then spied the judges' table a few rows back from the front. The lights in the house were low, but four desk lamps illuminated their perch. Their crisp, white scoresheets appeared to glow. I looked to the side of the table and saw men in suits holding clipboards and pens, looking very official.

I couldn't believe we were here. To think we'd almost not made it. I thought back to the very first day when Mr. Woods paired us up . . . and now just look at us, playing in Carnegie Hall. It was a lot to take in.

My heart sped like a warped version of "The Flight of the Bumblebee." Declan cleared his throat, and I looked at him, nodding that I was ready. Just knowing he was beside me sent a wave of calmness through me. This was the moment we'd been working toward all year long. This was it. This could be the last time we played this piece together. It was both sad and freeing.

We started, our cellos harmonizing as the strains of our song wove their way through the magnificent acoustics of the hall. My mind flashed back to all the times before when I'd thought we sounded so perfect, but this was a million times different. I'd never heard us sound like this. So rich and full-bodied. It was beautiful. It was perfection. *We* were perfection.

Somewhere along the way, we'd become so tuned into each other that our duet had almost transformed itself into a highly choreographed dance. My eyes fluttered closed and I let the music wash over me, making the hair on my arms stand up from the chills I was getting. The crowd, the judges, the scouts, and the overconfident mean girl floated from my mind. I was in the zone, and Declan was with me.

We ended and the auditorium erupted in applause. I opened my eyes. The judges and scouts were busy scribbling things down. I looked over at Declan and he looked lit up inside. We'd done it. We'd kicked ass. Even if we didn't win the $10,000 dollars, I was proud of us.

Standing, we bowed, grabbed our things, and left the stage. Once we got backstage Declan turned and wrapped me in a one-armed hug. "That was incredible! You were incredible."

I smiled and held my cello to the side as he pulled me against his chest. "*We* were incredible."

He gave me one last squeeze and took a step back, his eyes searching mine, almost as if he were looking for something. "Pips, I . . . I really. . ." His words faltered and he looked away, shaking his head. "Thanks for doing this with me."

"Are you kidding? Of course! This was an awesome opportunity. If it wasn't for you, I doubt I'd even be here."

"Let's go pack up and find a seat."

Nodding, I led the way to the room where we'd been instructed to leave our cases. We packed up, then checked our instruments in the security station.

Cellos situated, we went to the main doors in the lobby. A young guy stationed there made sure people didn't enter during a performance. I could make out the strains of a small group performing. I leaned against the wall, waiting.

Declan stood in front of me, a strange look on his face.

"What's wrong?"

He sighed and slipped his hands into the pockets of his black trousers, raising his shoulders. "I just . . . oh, never mind, it's nothing."

I tilted my head to the side and watched him, wondering what was bothering him. Before I could ask any questions, the doors swung open and we were let in along with a few other people. We picked seats beside the aisle in the center section. The group that had just finished exited stage right as more musicians poured in from the left.

Resting my arm on the chair rest, I pressed against

Declan's arm and smiled. Even after all this time, whenever we touched it sent a thrill through me. I focused on the stage, trying to calm my galloping heartbeat. Honestly, I was having trouble sitting still. It was a blessing we'd performed near the end of the day. It meant we only had to listen to a few acts before we found out who the winner was.

Kara's sleek, long black hair was suddenly in my face as she leaned her head between us from the row behind ours, now talking to Declan.

"You guys weren't *that* good, you know."

I couldn't see Declan, but I could hear his reply as the musicians on stage were setting up. "True. We weren't that good. We were the best."

"You only wish." She scoffed. Our intruder leaned back into her seat where she crossed her arms over her chest and grumbled to the two other girls she sat with. The three of them glared at the back of Declan's head, looking supremely irritated.

Leaning toward Declan, I softly asked, "How did you put up with her? She's awful."

"It wasn't easy. And to think she's *almost* as competitive as you." He raised one eyebrow and sniffed as he turned his focus to the stage where the brass quintet began their jaunty jazz song.

My brow furrowed as I took in his smug profile. With irritation, I whispered, "So are you saying I'm difficult to put up with?"

He turned to face me, a half grin on his lips. "Absolutely. When I first met you, I knew you'd be a pain in my ass, one of epic proportions."

My mouth popped open, and I leaned away from him. "What? Please, you're lucky you met me."

He looked at me, clearly teasing and trying to get a rise out of me. "You quickly put me in my place and showed me how wrong I was." He reached over and threaded our fingers together, his thumb making soft circles on mine, which sent a scattering of shivers over my skin. "And you're right, meeting you was the best thing that's ever happened to me."

His words and his touch had me feeling lightheaded. I sucked in a breath and closed my eyes, thinking of how things would be different when we got back to Portland. I was going to *make* Quinn talk to me, even if it was the last thing I did. I was going to keep Declan. And I was going to end things once and for all with Noah.

"Alright, ladies and gentlemen, we're going to take a short break while our judges deliberate. Sit tight." A man in a sharp, three-piece suit held a microphone and gestured for the judges to follow him.

The five judges stood, slid down the aisle, and headed toward the door leading backstage. Declan gave my hand a squeeze. We were definite contenders to win this thing.

"What would you do with the money if we won?" I asked, facing him.

He raised a shoulder in a shrug. "I don't know. Probably use it for college. You?"

"College," I said with a knowing nod. "What do you think the scouts thought?" I used my head to gesture to the guys with clipboards.

"What makes you think they're the scouts?" Declan looked in their direction and scrutinized them.

"Well, duh, the clipboards." I laughed, realizing I might be wrong in my deduction.

"I see." A lopsided smile formed on his lips. I found myself wanting to lean in and kiss him, but our surroundings stopped me.

I needed to take my brain off his mouth. "So what happens after this?"

"Besides going back to my dad's and getting dinner?"

Shaking my head, I smiled. "I meant, what happens when we get back to Portland?"

Declan's mouth opened and closed as he shrugged. "Hopefully graduate and have one last summer of fun before we all head off to college."

Turning, I faced the stage once more. "We should start getting acceptance or rejection letters any day now."

It was early spring, and I knew people who'd gotten their letters. Even Phillip had gotten one from a school up in Washington. There was a huge chance Declan and I would be parting once the summer was over. The likelihood that we'd both be accepted to the same school was pretty slim. Despite our competitive issues, I'd miss him like crazy. My eyes watered, and I quickly blinked it away.

"Yeah, hopefully soon." His eyes locked onto mine. "I'm actually surprised we haven't heard anything yet. Doesn't leave a whole lot of time for making plans."

"No, it doesn't." My thoughts were stuck on the fact that we really only had a few months left together.

Declan leaned around so he could look at me. "You suddenly seem a million miles away. Where are you at?"

"Just wondering where we'll all end up in the fall. Do you have any backup schools if none of the music schools pan out?"

He nodded. "Yeah, Goddards is of course my number one choice, but I also applied to NYU and University of Oregon."

I grinned. "I applied to Oregon too. Phillip and Quinn did as well."

"Pips, I don't think you have anything to worry about. You'll get into Goddards." His eyes softened around the edges, and the way he looked at me had my heart doing backflips and my stomach all aflutter. "They'd be stupid to not accept you."

"You, too," I said, not able get my voice above a whisper.

Reaching up, he tucked a wisp of hair behind my ear that'd come loose from my messy bun. "Maybe we'll get lucky then. Maybe we'll both get in."

The door onstage swung open and our announcer now held a large index card along with his microphone. He went centerstage and waited for the judges to resume their seats.

Smiling, the announcer looked around the auditorium, his slicked-back hair glinting in the spotlights. "Ladies and gentlemen, in my hand, I hold the results for the 53rd Annual National Competition of Young Musicians."

CHAPTER *Twenty-Three*

A painter paints pictures on canvas. But musicians paint their pictures on silence.

—*Leopold Stokowski*

Silence filled the auditorium. People stood along the sides and at the back, waiting for the announcer to reveal the winners. Smiling, he looked around the room, then to the card in his hand, then back to the audience, trying to build anticipation. Really, he was just being obnoxious. "In third place and winning $500 each, the brass quintet from New Jersey."

He rambled a list of names, and five guys made their way to the stage, accepted small trophies, smiles on their faces, and stepped to the side.

"In second place and winning $1000, violinist Mikheala Price." He clapped, the thick paper making a crinkly sound in the microphone. A slender, dark-skinned girl, dressed in an ankle-length velvety black dress, climbed the stairs to the stage, accepted her prize and handshake, then moved to stand next to the quintet.

"Alright." The announcer straightened his jacket and

looked once again at his notes. "It's the big one folks. The one we've been waiting for all night. In first place and each taking home $10,000 is . . ."

Declan squeezed my hand. I sucked in a deep breath and held it, willing the announcer to read faster.

"The cello duet of . . . Declan Brogan and Phillippa Wyndham."

The air left my lungs in a rush; I couldn't believe he'd actually said our names. Declan stood, hand still in mine, and pulled me to the aisle and up onto the stage. I couldn't hear anything over the applause. My knees felt weak, and I was shaky all over. From the stage, the lights were at full power now, and I had to squint to see the audience. We each were handed a silver musical eighth-note trophy. A woman with envelopes passed them out to all the winners. I couldn't stop smiling.

This is it. The start of everything.

The moments after flew by, as if in fast forward. The announcer said something that I paid no attention to, the house lights turned on, and the auditorium began to empty. On stage, people were congratulating each other and hugging perfect strangers. A large guy from the brass quintet wrapped his arms around me and bounced me up and down. He let me go, and the judges came up and shook our hands, offering compliments. The scouts, only one of whom had a clipboard, came and introduced themselves to all of us. I barely had a moment to breathe.

"Lovely job, I'm sure you'll be hearing . . ."

" . . . consider teaming up."

"Congratulations!"

My head swam with all the information I'd just taken in. We won. It still didn't feel real. I looked up at Declan and he was smiling, looking at his trophy. The crowd now filed from the room in long, snaking lines up the aisles. It was officially over.

"Let's go grab Francesca and Booth." I beamed up at Declan. Loopy smile on his lips and his eyebrows raised, he still looked shocked.

Nodding, he followed behind me. As we neared the secure instrument room his hand settled onto my back. We handed the attendant our check-in slips, and the college-aged girl handed over our instruments.

"You two won, right?" she asked, smiling.

I nodded.

"Congrats. I heard you were fabulous."

"Thanks," Declan and I said in unison.

We reached the front of the lobby, and standing there waiting was Declan's dad. Beside me Declan stopped walking. I looked back at him then at his father.

"Missy was here. She watched you perform, but she had to take Carsyn home. She was getting fussy. You guys . . . you were incredible."

"Um, thanks." Declan's voice sounded surprised. "I didn't expect you'd come."

Michael smiled at his son. They were almost the same height, Declan had the slight advantage. "Of course I'm here. I wouldn't miss this. I'm so proud of you guys."

"Thanks." I smiled up at him. Glancing at Declan, his brows were furrowed, and he looked irritated.

"I've got the car. I thought I'd give you a lift home." Michael gestured toward the door.

Declan shrugged. "Sure, why not?"

We followed his dad as he guided us to where he'd parked. We put our large cases into the cavernous trunk and climbed into the backseat of the black luxury car.

I watched the bright lights of the city stream by the windows, glowing in the darkness of the night. It all seemed so dazzling and alive. I could see myself living here. Going to school here. Making a life for myself here. I eyed Declan, a soft sigh escaping my lips. We only had tomorrow left. Part of me worried that once we got back to Portland, all this magic might end.

For now, I'd enjoy the moment I was in and not dwell on the possibilities of tomorrow. At least not yet.

♫

I leaned toward the bathroom mirror and slid the lipgloss wand across my lips. Tonight Declan was taking me out to dinner, then we were heading to Broadway's Gershwin Theater to see *Wicked*. Excitement bubbled inside me. I'd always wanted to see this show. My absolute favorite thing about the theater was the music. I loved being in the orchestra pit for school plays. I couldn't imagine being in a show of this scale.

My long hair fell over my shoulder and onto the navy tunic dress I was wearing. Small pink roses dotted the silky fabric. Paired with leggings, it was sweet and simple. I added a long matching sweater and some tall brown boots. I hadn't brought anything super fancy with me other than my performance clothes, and I didn't want to wear those. I hoped I wouldn't be too underdressed.

Finished getting ready, I grabbed my bag and headed out to the kitchen. As I rounded the corner of the hallway I saw Declan and his dad talking near the elevator. Declan wore dark jeans and a gray sweater. With his disheveled hair, he looked fabulous.

As I got closer I could see that Declan's brow was furrowed.

"It was a great opportunity. She had to take it, son."

Declan looked down at his shoes and shook his head, muttering, "Whatever."

His dad looked up and saw me approaching. Smiling, he

patted Declan on the shoulder. "We'll talk more about this tonight. Looks like Pippa's ready to go."

When Declan looked up at me, he wasn't smiling. Instead, he looked disappointed. As I got closer he forced a small smile. "You look lovely. You ready?"

I nodded as I glanced between him and his dad. "Is everything okay?"

Declan's head bobbed, but he didn't say anything.

"You two have a great time tonight."

Silence accompanied us down the elevator and into the cab. On the ride to the theater, Declan stared out the window, looking lost in thought. I didn't know what to say, and I hated that. His mood didn't improve upon exiting the car either.

We stood in front of the theater. The *Wicked* poster with Galinda whispering into Elphaba's ear took up the centers of the tall black columns rising from the awning.

This was fantastic. Inside me, crackles of excitement popped and frizzled. Now if only I could get Declan on the same page. Or at least get him to talk to me about what was going on.

"Where do you want to go grab a bite to eat? There's a little place just around the corner that's pretty good." Declan broke his silence.

"Sure." We walked side by side, but he didn't grab my hand. He seemed so far away.

Declan stopped outside a steakhouse. "Does this look okay?"

I looked at the menu in the window and nodded. Throughout dinner Declan barely spoke a word. Every attempt I made at conversation fell short. After we ate and got our check, I was well on my way to annoyed. Pulling out my wallet, I tossed down half the amount of the check and stood, ready to go. I'd been so excited. This was the first anything-like-an-actual date we'd had, and it was going horribly.

"Pippa?" Declan quickly stood and stopped me. "What's wrong?"

My brows shot to my hairline. "Why don't you tell me? You haven't been here all night."

A sigh blew from his lips, and he gestured for me to sit down. "Please sit, I'm sorry."

"What's going on?" I lowered myself back down and waited.

His hand ran through his hair then looked up at me. "My mom called me with some news, and I'm not sure what it'll mean for me."

"What kind of news?"

"You know how I told you my mom kind of gets sent wherever her job needs her?" At my nod he continued, "Well, she's being sent away from Portland."

There's that feeling when you're on a roller coaster and your stomach feels like it jumps into your throat. Well, that perfectly described what was happening inside me right now. "What does that mean?"

He shook his head. "I don't know. I didn't get much information other than the offer came about suddenly. We're gonna talk more tonight."

"Does this mean you're moving? There's only three months until graduation."

He shrugged and opened his mouth, but no words came out.

His mom had to let him finish the school year in Portland. Surely she wouldn't move him twice in his senior year. Right?

"You ready? We should get to the theater." He grabbed the cash I'd plunked down and handed it back to me. "I got this."

I didn't have it in me to fight. With the money tucked safely back in my wallet, I followed him out the door. His mood totally made sense now. What if he left? I didn't want to think about not seeing him every day.

His warm hand slid into mine and gave it a squeeze. "Let's have some fun."

Around us, the streets were lit by flashing neon signs and bright lights. My head tilted back, and I met his eyes. "Okay."

Inside the theater, emerald green rugs greeted us and we padded over them to the darker green carpet. We passed the trinket booth and made our way up the stairs to the mezzanine level and found our seats in the front row of the balcony. I leaned on the balcony's edge and took in the curtain. It was a map of the emerald city, lit up with green twinkle lights. Above it was a large metal dragon with huge, outstretched wings.

"This looks so cool!" I could no longer contain my excitement.

"Have you seen *Wicked* before?" Declan copied my pose and watched me with the first genuine smile he'd worn all evening.

Shaking my head, I answered, "I read the book, but I've never seen the play."

"You'll like it."

"Have you seen it?"

He nodded. "A couple times. It was a field trip at the conservatory where I studied. My parents also took me when I was younger."

"Why didn't we go see something else then?"

"Dad knows the owner of the theater."

"Ah." I smiled and looked around. "That explains the awesome seats."

His lips curled into a smile, and he reached and grabbed

my hand. "I'm glad we're here. It's a good way to end the trip." He raised my hand to his lips and kissed the back of it.

Tomorrow was Monday, and we were leaving on an early morning flight. I didn't want to go back to reality. There were too many things still to be dealt with. And now with the addition of Declan possibly leaving, I didn't want to face any of it at all.

"I don't want to go home," I whispered.

Declan leaned so his face was closer to mine. "Me, neither."

Around us the seats were filling, and all the intermingled conversations formed a low roar. I wanted him to kiss me. I didn't care that we had an audience.

His hand came up and cupped my cheek. A smile on his lips, his gaze darted between my eyes and my mouth and back. "I seriously want to kiss you."

I tilted my body toward his and gave him a look that suggested kissing me was exactly what I wanted him to do. He pressed a chaste kiss to my lips and pulled back, making a huff of air leave me. That wasn't nearly enough to calm my hunger for him. His face still close to mine, he ran his fingers through my hair, the long strands slowly slipping through his grasp.

What looked like a dad, mom, and daughter slid past us to their seats, forcing us to sit back, stopping what was sure to be an amazing kiss to make room for them. Declan squeezed my hand and chuckled. The moment was definitely over. What I wouldn't give to be alone with him. I almost wanted to skip the show to go find a quiet, dark corner and just make out all night.

The lights flickered, and the seating bell chimed as the orchestra finished their warm-up and tuning. The audience took their seats and stilled as the house lights went out. In the darkness, the eyes of the large, winged dragon glowed a fiery red, and smoke plumed out his nostrils. Stage lights went on, the orchestra began, and the curtain lifted. Clockworks framed the stage, and the backdrop was a giant clock face. It was incredible. Bubbles appeared, and there was Galinda in her own bubble, singing and slowly floating down to the stage. I was immediately enthralled in the wonder of it all.

♪

Declan and I stood outside the elevator to his dad's apartment. He pressed the button and we waited. I looked back over the chic gray and cream lobby to the doorman and regretted that the next time I came down here, we'd be leaving for good. Tonight had been amazing. It was something I'd never forget. Especially the cab ride back. There'd been some epic kissing in the backseat and it'd been perfect.

It'd definitely taken my mind off Declan's immediate future, but now that we were here, it slammed back into me. I didn't want him to leave Portland.

The elevator slid open and Declan gestured for me to go first. As the doors closed behind us Declan descended on me again, kissing me breathless. His hands rested on my hips, and he guided them to the mirrored wall where he pinned me with his body pressed against mine.

My head reeled as we kissed, and my pulse soared. I slid my hands under his sweater, their coolness meeting his warm skin made him gasp. With a groan, he deepened the kiss.

"God, I don't want the night to end," he muttered against my lips.

"Me, neither." The breathless voice that left my throat didn't sound like me. My fingers splayed on his skin as the elevator dinged, and the door opened.

Declan leaned back, his eyes squeezed tight and his breath coming in heavy pants. "Damn."

I reached up and straightened his hair and smiled. "Come on."

He let me pull him from the elevator and into the apartment. I yanked him toward the guest room. Once there, he pressed me into the door and resumed kissing me. Never had I felt anything like what Declan made swirl inside of me. It was probably a very good thing we weren't alone. 'Cause I was getting the distinct impression that we wanted the same thing.

"Declan?" a masculine voice called through the apartment.

"Yeah, Dad?" Declan pulled back, his eyes heavy-lidded and trying to control his voice.

"Come into the office so we can finish our talk."

A heavy sigh blew through his lips. "Yeah, I'll be right there." Reaching up, he swept my hair away from my face. "In case I don't see you again tonight, sleep well and I'll see you in the morning."

I nodded. As he turned away I clutched his arm and pulled him back. On my tiptoes, I planted one last kiss on his lips. "Tonight was amazing. Thank you."

"I'm glad." With a kiss to my nose, he sauntered down the hallway, his hands tucked in his pockets.

Unable to tear my eyes away from him, I stared at his backside until he turned the corner. My teeth caught my bottom lip as I fought back a smile. Inside the guest room, I flopped onto the bed. A giddy giggle escaped me. The show had been incredible, the music simply magical, and Declan . . . I couldn't have asked for a better date.

A muffled voice broke through my stupor of happiness. Standing, I crept to the door and pressed my ear against the cool white wood, hoping to hear something. I could make out two distinct masculine voices talking loudly, but it wasn't clear enough to decipher their words. Cracking the door, I listened carefully.

"But that's not fair." Declan sounded frustrated.

"Well, I'm sorry, but that's just how it is."

"What if I don't want to do this?"

His father's gruffer voice countered. "You don't really have a choice. You know your mom feels awful about this. This isn't what she wanted from this Portland move. If it's any consolation, it's a temporary position. She'll most likely be going back there once this is over."

"Declan dear, it could be fun." Missy's voice broke through.

I heard a derisive laugh. "Yeah, I highly doubt that. I'm outta here. And don't bother calling me 'dear.' We all know you don't mean it."

The click of the elevator call button being pressed repeatedly told me he was leaving.

"You're not going anywhere," his dad said. "I know it's not ideal, but we have to work this out."

"I'm nearly eighteen. Can't you just get me an apartment out there until I go to college?" Declan pleaded. "I can't come back here. Not now."

CHAPTER *Twenty-Four*

Music can change the world.

—*Beethoven*

My legs hung over the corner of the bed as I looked at the door. My bags were packed, and I was ready to go back to Portland. Hearing Declan and his dad talking last night had me a little nervous to see what would happen to him and us. How much longer would we have together? At least we'd have the plane ride to talk about it and try to make plans. Sucking in a deep breath, I blew it slowly out. Waiting was the worst. I checked my phone again, but nothing had changed since the last time I'd checked it three minutes ago. I'd sent a text to my mom and hoped for a reply, but she was three hours behind me right now, so I doubted she'd seen it yet.

A soft knock had me tossing my phone aside. "Come in."

Declan's eyes had dark bags under them, and he looked miserable. Once inside, he closed the door behind him. "How'd you sleep?"

"Okay. You?" From the looks of him, not well.

"I actually didn't sleep much." He lowered his head as he

rubbed the bridge of his nose. "Um . . ." A deep breath left his lips. "I have to tell you something. Uh . . . I'm—I'm not going back to Portland with you."

My eyes widened, and my brow furrowed. "What do you mean? Not at all?"

He shook his head, his eyes not meeting mine. "No, Mom's job is taking her to Shanghai for the next eight months. She leaves tomorrow. So . . . I get to stay here with my dad and go back to the conservatory. She's sending my things."

Air came in and left my lungs, but I didn't feel like I could breathe. "So, this, this right here, right now, is the last time I'm going to see you?"

He nodded.

Tears prickled and built, but I tried to fight them back. I pressed my palms to my eyes, nowhere near ready to say goodbye to him. Not wanting to face my world at home without him. I dropped my hands, sucked in a shaky breath, and shook my head, struggling to process.

Declan's dad appeared behind him. "You about ready to head to the airport, Pippa?"

No, I'd just been hit by a wrecking ball. How could I possibly be ready?

The chipperness in his voice was like nails on a chalkboard. I was the furthest thing imaginable from a fan of Declan's parents at the moment. How could they do this to him this close to graduation? He couldn't even give us a freaking moment alone to talk. Nodding, I grabbed my cello and threw it over my shoulder, followed by my carry-on, then I grabbed my suitcase handle, ready to drag it behind me. "Um, yeah, I guess."

As I followed his dad out the door, my eyes met Declan's, looking for something, I didn't even know what. His hand grasped my upper arm, and he stopped me.

"I'm so sorry."

I shook my head, trying to put on a brave face, because I knew this had to be way worse for him than it was for me. "It's not your fault." I pulled up to my tiptoes and placed a soft kiss on his lips. "I'm going to miss you. We'll keep in touch, right?"

He nodded, his mouth downturned.

"Bye." I walked to his dad who was watching us, then I gave Declan a wave. I didn't hear his footsteps following me. I wished he'd at least come with us. I didn't want to go to the airport with just his dad. The thought of getting on the plane by myself had me near tears.

Missy stood by the elevator with Carsyn. "It was so lovely to meet you, Pippa. If you end up in New York for college, I hope we'll see a lot more of you."

"Thanks. And thank you again for letting me stay here."

She nodded. When I looked back, Declan just stood there watching me like a statue, his brows lowered and a look of pain on his face. The elevator opened with a soft ping. I took one last look back and lifted a hand to wave again. My heart now held a large, jagged crack down the middle.

I stepped out of the apartment and into the elevator. The doors slowly slid together and I heard Declan shout, "Wait!"

His father pressed the open door button, and the next thing I knew, Declan held my face in his hands and was kissing me. In front of his family. I dropped everything but my cello and covered his hands with mine, kissing him back like it was the last time I'd ever get to do it. Because it might be just that. I didn't care that his dad and stepmom were right there watching us. All that existed in that moment was Declan and me.

Declan pulled back and leaned his forehead against mine. "Enjoy every moment you have left in your senior year.

You deserve it."

I nodded as a tear ran down my cheek. Declan wiped it away with his thumb before taking a step back. I couldn't speak, even though there was so much to say.

His dad looked between the two of us and cleared his throat. "Um, okay, I'll see you guys later."

Declan took a step back into the apartment, and the elevator doors closed between us. With a slight jolt, his dad and I made the descent to the main floor. I bit my bottom lip and looked up at the ceiling, willing myself not to cry. I missed him already.

We'd started the year with me hating him and being so sure he was the enemy, thinking he was here to take everything away from me, and now . . . now the thought of him not being there physically hurt. My chest and lungs ached at the very idea of not seeing him every day.

"Are you okay?" Declan's dad asked as the door opened to the street level.

Smiling too brightly, I nodded my head. "Yeah, I'm good. Um, why didn't Declan come with us?"

His dad cleared his throat. "Oh, ah, Missy and I didn't think it was a good idea."

Why the hell not?

"O-okay." I nodded, feeling even weirder with him now than before.

We climbed into the car and made a silent trip to JFK international. He was on his phone the entire time before he dropped me at the departures area, then had his driver speed off. I checked in, got through security, and found my gate. Sitting down, frazzled and lonely, I sent a quick text to Mom to let her know I was getting ready to get on my flight and to update her on the situation. My phone rang in record time.

"Hi, Mom."

"Are you telling me Declan's not with you? He's not coming back to Portland at all?"

I ran my free hand through my hair as a tall guy, probably just a little older than me, sat across from me. He was actually pretty cute, but I didn't care. He flashed me a smile. I weakly returned it, then looked to the ink stain on my favorite pair of comfy jeans. "That would be what I'm telling you."

"Are you going to be okay?" The worry in her voice came through loud and clear on our connection.

"Not really, but I don't really have much of a choice, do I?"

I heard the key cover on the piano close with a bang. "I don't want you traveling alone."

"Well, what am I supposed to do?" My voice rose an octave. Annoyed by her irritation. It wasn't my fault.

"Don't take that tone with me, young lady. I get that you're having a bad day. I'm trying to sort this out. Give me a second to think."

Closing my eyes, I leaned my head back. "Mom. I'll be fine. I can handle this. I'm almost eighteen. Just make sure you pick me up."

She sighed. "Are you sure? You know you're not a good flier."

"I know, but what's the alternative? You flying to get me? Don't be silly. You just got back from LA. I survived the flight here, I can survive the one back."

"All right, fine. I'll let you deal with this. Call me if you need anything and travel safe. I'll see you tonight. I love you, Sweetie."

"Love you too, Mom."

We hung up and I slipped my phone into my carry-on. The fear, already settled low into my stomach, was sending out curly fingers of dread to twine through my whole system and make me nauseous and shaky.

And this time I didn't have Declan to take my mind off things.

♫

Mom's hand reached for mine as she drove down the freeway. It was good to be home. I rolled my head from side to side, my shoulders killing me from how tense I'd held them throughout the flight. I'd survived, without using the barf bag, and I was actually pretty proud of myself. I hadn't even cried. I'd been close, but I'd put on a brave face and gotten through it. This little adventure made me realize I was tougher than I thought I was.

And I was certainly tough enough to get the bottom of this Quinn debacle. The thought of still having to deal with it made me want to scream, but I had to get it over with. Because I was done—with her if necessary.

"You okay?"

I nodded. "Just tired."

"Well, let's get you home so you can relax. And to celebrate your big win, I'll make your favorite."

"Enchiladas?"

"You bet." She smiled and turned off the freeway.

Thoughts raced through my mind as we turned on the street with the high school. I looked at the old brick building and had trouble imagining it without Declan. Which was hard to stomach, considering I'd spent the first three years there without him just fine.

We pulled onto our street, and I saw Quinn's house. The light in her window was on. "Mom, stop."

Mom slowed and edged her way to the curb. "You going to go talk to Quinn?"

"Well, she won't take my calls, she's avoiding my texts and emails and visits. Maybe tonight she'll be willing to talk."

"Okay, good luck. I'll see you at home."

I hopped out of the car and stood on the sidewalk, watching Mom turn into our driveway a few houses down. My eyes darted to Quinn's room. School would have been out only a few hours, and I could imagine her up there working on her homework, sprawled on top of her bedspread.

Up the front steps I went and rang the doorbell. Footsteps clomped around inside. The door opened and Mrs. Green greeted me, grin on her face. "Hey, Pippa, I've missed seeing you around the Oak."

I looked down at my shoes and twisted the toe of my left foot, feeling guilty. "Yeah, I know it's been a while. Do you think Quinn will maybe talk to me?"

"I sure hope so. Go on up." She patted my shoulder and stepped out of the way so I could enter.

The wooden stairs creaked as I made my way up them. I stopped at Quinn's door and knocked softly.

"Come in."

I pushed the door in just as she pushed herself up to sit on her bed.

"Pippa." She looked surprised to see me. "What are you doing here?"

"What do you think I'm doing here? Still trying to get you to talk to me."

Quinn's gaze dropped to her lap. She played with the hem of her top, rolling and unrolling it.

"Look, I'm sorry you got hurt. You have to know I never wanted that to happen."

She shook her head, still not meeting my eyes. "I know."

"Then why did you freeze me out? You're my best friend."

"I was jealous."

My head jerked back. "What?"

She looked up at me then squeezed her eyes shut as

she said, "You were getting everything you wanted. You got Noah!" Her eyes went wide, and she shook her head. "You wanted him for years and suddenly, poof, he was all yours. Wish granted. You know how long I've wanted that with Phillip? God! And then once you had Noah, you turned the tables and caught the attention of the one guy who showed even a little bit of interest in me."

"Quinn, I didn't go after Declan." I put my hand over my heart. "In fact, I told him several times that we couldn't see each other because you had feelings for him. What more did you want me to do?" Tears welled in my eyes.

"I don't know." She looked away and took her glasses off to rub her eyes. "I realize I wasn't being fair. I know it. I just couldn't help it. From the very beginning I could tell you were falling for Declan, and I knew he was totally in love with you. I just . . . I wanted something like that for myself."

I flopped down in her beanbag chair and looked up at her as she stood up beside her small aqua desk. I was completely taken aback. "Love? Really? You think he loves me?"

"Seriously, Pips? He's totally gone on you, and you know it. Jesus, you're practically the only thing he talked about all Winter Formal."

I couldn't stop my lips from lifting. I hadn't dared to put the term *love* on how I felt for Declan. And I still wasn't sure I was ready for that. Could he really feel that way about me? It didn't really matter anymore, did it? He was stuck in New York, and I was clear across the country. "Why didn't you answer any of my texts or calls?"

"I wasn't ready to admit I was wrong." She sat her glasses atop a pile of books on her desk. "I missed you."

"I've missed you, too."

"And Lexi's been driving me bonkers lately." She laughed, then scrunched her nose and sighed.

I chewed the inside of my cheek, not sure I should even broach the Lexi issue. "About Lexi . . ." I sighed. "I'm so freaking tired of you playing us off each other and using us as backup for whoever you're mad at in the moment."

"I don't do that." Her brows drew together.

My head tilted to the side. She couldn't be that blind, could she? "Seriously? Anytime you're mad at me, you whip Lexi out to be rude and snotty to me, and she replaces me as your friend."

"And you don't do that with Jenna?" One of her bushy brows rose as she eyed me defensively.

"No, I don't. Jenna likes us both. She always wants us to make up. Lexi *hates* me. She'd be beyond thrilled if you and I never made up. There's a huge difference there."

"What's your point?"

Angling myself to face her, I met her hazel eyes. "I'm not saying you can't be friends with Lexi, of course. I'm just trying to tell you that I'm sick of you swapping us out. I don't want to deal with that anymore. I get that you might get mad at me in the future, but don't pull Lexi into it anymore. You've even said yourself that she's obnoxious. And I'm seriously so over it. We're either friends or we're not."

She was quiet a moment, as if processing my words. With a sigh, she stood up. "Ugh, I should probably apologize to Declan tomorrow, shouldn't I?"

My throat tightened, and I struggled to suck in a breath. I hadn't expected her switch back to our initial subject. "Um, that'd be kinda hard."

"Why?"

"'Cause he won't be there."

Her forehead wrinkled. "Why not?"

I explained his new situation thanks to his mom's job.

She came and sat beside me, half on the bean bag, half off, and put an arm around me. "Are you okay?"

Shrugging, I tilted my head from side to side. "Not really, but there's nothing I can do about it."

"God, Pips, I'm sorry." She wrapped me in a hug. "And I'm sorry I was such a jealous bitch." She squeezed me even tighter.

"I'm sorry I hurt you." I smiled as a tear slipped down my face, followed by several of its watery buddies. "So are we friends again?"

"Always."

It sucked that Declan was gone. That I'd probably never see him again. But, at least one good thing came out of it—Quinn and I were back on track. And right now, I really needed my best friend.

CHAPTER *Twenty-Five*

*My heart which is so full to overflowing, has often been
solaced and refreshed by music when sick and weary.*

—*Martin Luther*

It'd been a week since I'd left Declan behind in New
York. We'd texted a little. He was busy picking up his life
at his old school. I was busy too, mostly moping and being
miserable. Mr. Woods had thrown an impromptu party for
the orchestra to celebrate our win the day I got back. He'd
gotten a cake, and when I saw it, I'd nearly burst into tears.
Declan's and my name were both on it. It'd been awful. It
capped off a horrible day spent explaining why he wasn't
there. Pure torture. All week, I'd been answering questions
about him. I was relieved it was Friday.

As I left school and walked to my car, trying to settle
back into my routine, Noah ran up to my side and fell in step
with me.

"Hey, Pips."

"Noah, how's it going?" I still hadn't had *the* talk with
him. It'd only been the past week that we'd fallen back into a
somewhat friendly relationship, and I didn't want to screw it

up. But even with Declan gone, I didn't want to date Noah. I didn't want anyone anymore.

He slicked a hand through his short blond hair. "Good. Um, hey, you think I could come over tonight so we can talk?"

"Sure, what about?"

"Nothing much, just stuff I don't really feel comfortable talking about with other people around." He started to back away then stopped. "Don't let Phillip know, 'kay? I'll be over around eight."

My head bobbed in agreement. Thankfully he hadn't tried to ask me out again since he'd witnessed Declan kissing me. I hoped he wasn't planning on trying again tonight. I just had to make sure I straightened things out between us first thing. Dating wasn't my priority. My focus was back right where it should be, on my cello and college, which is where it probably should've stayed this entire time.

Okay, maybe not. The truth was, Declan made me better with my cello. I only hoped I'd had the same effect on him.

At my car, I pulled a yellow sticky off my window. It had a smiley face on it and said, "Congrats again!" Under that was a loopy heart and Jenna's name. I smiled and stuck it on the strap of my backpack. Jenna had been trying everything all week to perk my spirits up. And it was actually starting to work. I pulled out my phone and shot off a quick smiley text to her.

I hopped into my car and buckled in. On the street, the city bus came to a stop, its breaks hissing and squealing. I smiled at the memory of Declan it conjured up.

A pang of longing hit me, and I inhaled a sharp breath. I hadn't expected it to be *this* hard. Thoughts of him seemed to pop up when I least expected them. And they always left me a little breathless from the sudden ache in my chest.

I drove home and walked in the back door. The gentle strains of a sweet song hit my ear. Mom must be in the middle of a lesson. Dinner bubbled on the stovetop. I lifted the lid on the pot and wrinkled my nose. Stew. Not my favorite. Maybe there were some enchiladas left in the freezer.

My phone chimed and I grabbed it. I had an email. From Juilliard.

Phillip strode through the back door, scowling. "Your friend is a gigantic pain in the ass."

"Oh my God!" I grinned, so not listening to my brother.

"What?" He came and peered at my screen, reading my email.

Still beaming, I looked up at him. "I got accepted into Juilliard. Holy cow!"

"That's awesome!" He dropped his backpack and wrapped me in a hug. "It's not your first choice though, right?"

Shaking my head, I reminded him it was Goddards.

"Congratulations, you deserve it, you little cello badass." He raised his fist for me to bump it, and I did. We both laughed. "Okay, enough about you." He gave me a teasing wink. "We need to talk about Quinn."

"What? Quinn?" My brows rose in surprise. "Why?"

"Because she's being irritating and all . . . weird and, I don't know, it's like she's mad at me."

"Well, what did you do?"

He scoffed. "Nothing."

I shrugged my shoulders. "What happened?"

He kicked his backpack out of the way and opened the fridge door and pulled out a soda and the glass container of cut up strawberries. "I tried to talk to her today after school and she got pissy with me. For absolutely no reason." He sat on the bench and popped the lid and stuck a large berry chunk in his mouth.

"You must've said something to tick her off?"

"I just asked her if she was coming over this weekend and she was all," in a high pitched voice, he repeated, "'Why?

What does it matter to you if I come over? It's not like you'd care one way or the other.' Then she just stomped off."

"Ask her out." I sat in the chair across from him and rested my chin in my hands. "You like her, she likes you, what are you waiting for?"

His finger ran around the lip of his can. "It feels weird. What if she says no?"

"Seriously, Phillip? Come on, do you really think she'd turn you down?" I gave him an incredulous look. Just the idea of her turning him down was insane. "Suck it up and call her now."

"Look what happened with you and Noah."

A soft smile made the corners of my lips twitch. "Noah and I weren't right for each other. You and Quinn, I think you guys might stand a chance. I mean you both want to go to the University of Oregon. You've both got your future plans figured out. You both love me. You're good to go. Besides, since when have you been scared to ask a girl out?"

"I'm not scared." As he tilted the can back to his lips it made a metallic crinkle as it popped under his fingertips. Setting it down with an empty rattle, he looked at me. "But, it's different with Quinn. If we don't work out, she's your best friend, so I'd still have to see her."

I slid my phone across the table, her contact already pulled up.

"Fine." He dialed. His eyes widened and I assumed it meant she'd picked up. "Oh, uh, no . . . it's not Pips, it's Phillip."

The picture of Quinn doing a silent happy dance flitted through my mind, and I grinned. If these two could finally get together, it'd be awesome.

"Yeah, sorry, um, Pips just passed me her phone." He scratched his scruffy cheek and stood up to pace. "Look, um . . . would you want to go to the movies? Maybe grab some dinner?"

I gave him a thumbs-up and he waved me away, looking irritated by my cheerleading.

"Just the two of us, yeah." He nodded. A heavy sigh left his smiling lips. "Great. Does Saturday evening work? Cool, I'll pick you up at seven then."

He hung up the phone, huge grin on his face, but I could tell he was trying to play it cool as he handed my phone back.

Pretending to be him, in a low voice I teased, "Gee, thanks Pips, for helping me get off my ass and ask Quinn out. I probably never would've done it without you."

"Shut up, whatever." He laughed, a sense of relief about him.

I stood and went up to my room. Pulling up Quinn's contact info again, I called her, knowing she'd want to talk.

"Pips?" she answered, her voice cautious.

"Yeah, it's me."

"Oh my God!" she shrieked. "Am I really going out on a date with your brother?"

Laughter left my lips. "Sure looks like it."

She launched into thoughts of what she was planning to wear, and I listened and mmhmm-ed at all the right spots, but my mind drifted to Declan. I wondered if he liked being back at his old school. Did he have a girlfriend there from before? Were they back together now that he'd returned? I'd never asked if he'd been with someone in New York. I didn't like thinking of him with someone else. Of him kissing anyone the way he'd kissed me. I didn't like it one little bit. But there was nothing I could do to change it.

♪

My desk lamp glowed down on the book I was reading for English. Beside me, my phone pinged. I glanced at the illuminated screen and saw Noah's name and his message scrawl across the top of my lock screen.

Noah: I'm out front can you meet me?

Me: Be right down.

As I left my room, Phillip's bass thumped through his closed door. I made my way down the stairs and before I could reach the doorknob, Mom stopped me.

"Pips, where you going?"

I popped my head into the living room where she was sitting on the couch reading. Dad was working late. "Noah's out front. He wanted to talk to me and didn't want Phillip to know."

"Why?"

My shoulders lifted. "I was just about to go find that out."

Her lips momentarily pursed. "Okay. See you in a bit."

I stepped out the front door and slid the long sleeves of my black t-shirt down. A cool breeze made the evening chilly. Noah sat on the white porch swing, slowly rocking.

"What's up?"

He slid over and patted the seat next to him. "I wanted to talk to you about something."

"'Kay." I went and sat down, crossing my arms over my chest.

"What are you doing after graduation?"

"I'm not sure." I looked over at him and shrugged. "I just got my acceptance letter from the University of Oregon, and Juilliard wants me, but I'm really waiting to hear from Goddards. What about you? Have you decided on anything?"

He cleared his throat. "I don't know. Um, honestly, I only applied to Oregon State because a coach there was really interested in me. I don't know if I want to go. I have no clue what I want to do with my life, Pippa."

"Well, you've got time. College is four years."

His shoulders lifted, and his face screamed confusion

and worry. "I envy you. You know what you want and have since you were little."

Angling myself toward him, I tucked my legs together on the bench and leaned against the side rail. "I would've thought you'd get a basketball scholarship."

"I had scouts looking at me and talking to me, but I'm kinda thinking I want to take a few years off. Work, save some money, then I'll go back to school. I just need a break."

"But if you did that, wouldn't you essentially be saying goodbye to basketball?"

He rubbed a hand over his face. "Yeah, probably."

"Why don't you want to talk about this with Phillip?"

Shaking his head, he looked at me. "'Cause you're the only one who won't judge me. Or think I'm stupid."

"Phillip wouldn't think that."

A cool wind whipped around us, forcing my hair behind me. Lifting my face, I enjoyed the sweet scent it carried past me on the current. Spring was the best season, especially in Oregon.

Noah closed his eyes and pushed out a heavy sigh. "Maybe not, but he's always pestering me to figure it out and to make plans. I just didn't feel like another lecture from him."

"Have you heard back from OSU?"

"Yeah, I got in, and the coach there is saying I got a scholarship, but I haven't seen any paperwork about it, so I don't know how much yet."

My mouth popped open. "Noah, that's awesome! Congratulations!"

He threw his head back and let out a soft growl. "But I don't know if that's what I want. School isn't my thing. You know that. I just barely skate through as it is. College is bound to be harder, right?"

I shrugged. "Probably."

"Pippa, I don't know what I want to do with the next ten minutes, let alone my whole future. It'd just be wasted on me."

"Okay, first, no education is ever wasted. Second, you're eighteen. You don't have to have all the answers right now. You can figure out a major while you're there."

A smile turned up a corner of his lips. "I guess you're right."

"Think of it this way, if worse comes to worst, you go there, decide you don't like it, and leave, right?"

"I'm not sure how it all works, but yeah, I could do that, I suppose." His eyes shifted and met mine. "Thanks for . . . this."

"Of course, what are friends for? You know Jenna's heading to OSU in the fall too, right? She got her letter just the other day."

"That's cool. It'll be nice to see a friendly face there. Hey, if you got into the UO, did Phillip?"

I nodded. "Yeah."

"That's awesome, it's where he wanted to go." He rubbed his hands along the top of his thighs. "So . . . how's Declan?"

My lips twisted in a crooked pucker. "Um . . . I haven't really heard much from him. He's probably busy getting back into his old life."

"Well, isn't this cozy?" Lexi stood just off the porch in our front yard, a smirk on her face. "Looks like you've forgotten Declan in a blink of an eye."

I inwardly groaned at her sudden appearance. Where the hell had she popped up from?

Noah turned to face her. "What are you doing here, Lexi?"

She raised a leash and put on a superficial happy face. "Walking Shasta."

The black lab looked gray around the muzzle and

plopped down at her feet with a heavy sigh.

"Sorry to interrupt. I just heard you talking about Declan. You haven't heard from him. I wonder why?" Lexi turned her focus on me.

I wasn't about to talk to her about Declan. "That's none of your business."

"Maybe he's dating someone else, too." She looked pleased with herself. "Come on, Shasta, let's go visit Quinnie. We haven't seen her in a long time." She sauntered off and looked back at me with a wave.

She was so not my favorite person.

"God, she's cold." Noah shook his head and watched her before turning back to me. "For your sake, I'm sorry he's gone. I know you must miss him." Noah's words sounded sincere and when I glanced at him, he looked genuine.

Running a hand through my hair, I grabbed it and started braiding it over my shoulder, needing something to keep my hands busy. I really didn't want to talk about Declan with him. "It is what it is, I guess."

He patted my knee. "So, any chance you'd want to go out this weekend?"

I looked up to the starry sky and shook my head. "Well, first, I need to talk to you about something."

"What's that?"

"I owe you an apology for this whole Declan thing. I was so confused and just caught up in it all, and I don't think I was very fair to you."

"How so?" He leaned a little closer and perched his elbows atop his thighs.

"I should have been more open with you. I like you, I do. But, I think it's more like a—"

"Please don't say brother." A pained look crossed his face.

I laughed and shook my head. "I actually wasn't going to say that. I was going to say like a best friend. You're someone

I like hanging out with and who I know I can count on, but that spark just isn't there for me. And I'm sorry I didn't realize that sooner and dragged you into my confusion."

Noah's hand reached out and grabbed mine, giving it a quick squeeze. "It's okay. I definitely figured it out when I saw you and Declan kissing. We definitely didn't have what you guys had."

"So we're okay, right?"

"Of course." He chuckled. "So, I guess that means no on this weekend."

"Want to get a group together and do something?"

He nodded. "Sure. We can do that." Noah stood and reached a hand out to me to help me up. "I'll probably see you tomorrow."

"Yeah." I pulled my hand from his and tucked it in my pocket, watching him walk away. It was amazing to think back on just how much had changed this year. My life may have been held together by tatters at the moment, but I was slowly mending them. At least out of all this Quinn and Phillip were finally getting somewhere. That was a victory worth celebrating.

CHAPTER *Twenty-Six*

Playing lifts you out of yourself into a delirious place.

—Jacqueline du Pré

Two weeks and I'd be a high school graduate. Holy cow. I'd heard from every school, except Goddards. All of the music schools were highly selective, but I'd amazingly gotten into Juilliard, with an incredible scholarship. Berklee College of Music accepted me, but the scholarship offer was only so-so. In their letters they'd referenced my NCYM win and expressed how much they'd love to have me. NYU Tisch ended up waitlisting me. Still, my hopes were pinned on my number one choice, Goddards.

In the past few weeks I'd done little else but practice. It helped me deal with the emotions I had running through me. Mom, sick of the sad music I was stuck on, offered to take me to the music store and get some more lighthearted music, claiming she couldn't handle the slow, sad, gut-wrenching pieces anymore. But that's where I was emotionally.

It'd been forever since I'd heard from Declan. I tried to tell myself he was busy and getting back into his regular

268

routine and life, but it wasn't helping. It didn't take that long to text someone, so why wasn't he at least messaging me? I pulled my phone from my pocket as I walked down the hallway to my math class. My day almost finished, I just had orchestra after this, thank goodness. Text messaging screen up, I couldn't take the silence anymore; if he wouldn't text me, I would send him one. I had to at least know where he'd gotten in.

Me: Have you heard back from any colleges?

My phone slid back into my back pocket; I wasn't expecting a quick reply. Even when he was here, he hadn't been a fast replier.

The door to my math class was wide open. I walked in and took my seat. The bell rang, and Mr. Adams called the class to attention.

"Alright, seniors, today's your lucky day. You don't have to sit through my lesson. Instead you're down on the field for a run-through of graduation. Let's head out there."

Quinn, who was standing in the hallway outside her history class, waited for me to get to her side. "Let's go practice walking."

Now she wasn't just *my* best friend. It was finally official, she was Phillip's girlfriend. After their first date, there'd been no separating them. They were always together. It was kind of cute. Disgustingly cute, actually. Seeing them made me miss Declan even more.

Lexi, on the other hand, was staying clear of Quinn. Not that I was complaining about it, but once she found out Quinn and Phillip were a thing, she nearly disappeared. Granted, she knew that Phillip didn't like her at all, strictly because of how she'd treated me. It may not be much, but it felt like a small victory.

We walked down the stairs to the back doors and

out onto the field. I could see Phillip and Noah standing together. When they spied us, Phillip waved and walked over to Quinn, draping an arm around her and pulling her into his side.

"Hey, babe."

"Hey." She curled into his chest, a content look on her face. I was happy for them. Really, I was. The ache in my stomach was probably just something I'd had for lunch. I didn't want to think it was because of who I was missing.

The principal called our attention and did a quick run through of how things were going to be laid out and what was expected of us. It was long. It was boring. It was thankfully a beautifully warm sunny day, so I didn't care.

A soft buzz from my back pocket captured my attention. My heart jumped in an excited beat.

> Declan: Only one. Juilliard. You?

> Me: All but Goddards.

> Declan: And?

> Me: I got in at UO, Juilliard, Oberlin, and Berklee. Wait-listed at NYU.

> Declan: Congrats.

> Me: How've you been?

> Declan: Good.

> Me: I miss you.

My fingers just typed it out and hit send before I could stop myself. My heart rate sped up as time came to a standstill.

> Declan: Please don't hate me, but I can't do this. Now that I'm not in the picture, you and Noah deserve a

real chance. I think you guys could be really happy together. It's why I haven't been in contact. And I won't be anymore. Take care, Pippa.

I couldn't breathe. All the air had been sucked from my lungs, and I couldn't seem to fill them again. My vision blurred as I stared at the screen and his parting words. That was it. It was officially over. And it hurt like hell.

I tucked my phone back in my pocket, feeling numb. I still didn't know if he'd even gotten in to Juilliard or not. Physically, he was thousands of miles away. Emotionally, it was more like a million.

♫

The dark, foreboding clouds rolled overhead as our large graduation class filtered to our seats on the football field. I glanced around the stands, wondering where my parents were. Phillip walked in front of me, his white robe flapping in the breeze. We were going to get rained on. There was just no way around it. The principal told us it was supposed to hold off until later this evening. One glance at the storm curling in the sky above us told me that it'd arrived early.

I sat in my foldable metal chair and prayed I wouldn't get struck by lightning. The alternating red and white graduation robes created a cool checkerboard effect. The valedictorian had just started her speech when a solid drop hit my leg, feeling cool on the bare skin my sundress left exposed underneath my robe. I ran my finger over the darkened red spot, my mind drifting. I hadn't heard from Declan, and I certainly hadn't tried contacting him again. At first, I hoped he'd change his mind, and I'd waited for his text telling me so. It never came. I had no choice but to accept that he didn't even want me as a friend anymore.

"As we leave these hallowed halls of Marshland High,

we go on to bigger and brighter futures than many of us ever dreamed of." Our valedictorian, Angela, addressed the group, looking up at the sky with a wary glance.

A look over at Phillip made me sigh. He and Quinn were definitely heading to UO this fall. Her for English, him for business. Noah was heading to their rival school, OSU, with Jenna. Me? I was still in limbo. Just waiting to hear from Goddards.

It was killing me. Added to Declan's decision, I'd been stuck in the funk to end all funks.

Angela's speech continued and I tried to focus. " . . . we worked hard. We never gave up, 'cause our amazing teachers wouldn't let us. And most importantly, we're heading off a little wiser and more determined to pursue our dreams than ever before. In ten years, when we come back for our reunion, I can't wait to see what every single one of you has achieved."

More drops hit me. It wasn't heavy yet. The valedictorian finished up her speech, and we all clapped. The principal took over and began handing out diplomas. Or rather the diploma holders. We received the actual piece of paper once we returned our rented graduation gowns.

It took forever for them to make their way to the "W" section. I'd cheered for Quinn and Noah at their turn. Our row stood and formed a line to the side and waited to be called. We all looked speckled with raindrops, but at least we weren't drenched. I looked up at the school I'd just spent the last four years at, and I couldn't believe it was over. These halls held more memories and laughter than almost any other place. This was the end of an era, and the gravity of the moment suddenly hit me. My eyes watered as Phillip's name was called. I stood at the front of the line on the side of the stage and waited for my brother to go through all the motions.

"Phillippa Wyndham," Principal Nacer called me up. I stepped up the three steps, walked toward him, shook his hand, and held my diploma case, posing for a quick photo. I went down the line of people congratulating me and shaking my hand. At the end was Ms. Peters, my old English teacher. She winked at me and whispered, "Congratulations, Pippa."

Smiling, I nodded and went back to my seat. Thoughts of Declan threatened at the periphery of my mind, but I pushed them out. I had to move on. I couldn't dwell on what might have been. I'd probably never see him again. It was time to get over him. He clearly had gotten over me.

I noticed everyone around me was standing, so I followed the crowd.

"Students, it's official, you are now graduates. Please move your tassel to the left." Principal Nacer grinned at us.

Reaching up, I pulled the red tassel to the other side of my cap and cheered along with the rest of my classmates.

"I present to you Marshland High's graduating class of 2018! Congratulations, graduates!"

We threw our caps in the air and cheered. I kept an eye on my cap and caught it on its way down, not that I threw it super high to begin with. I wanted to keep it. Phillip reached over and gave me a hug. We ventured into the melee and found Quinn and Noah. Quinn wrapped her arms around my brother and planted a big kiss on him. Noah shook his head and gave me a quick arm around-the-shoulder squeeze. Once the new lovebirds parted, Quinn came to me and gave me a hug.

"Come on, Mom and Dad will want pictures." I tilted my head toward the stands to show the direction we should go. Falling into step behind Quinn and Phillip, Noah and I followed.

In the distance, our parents stood together on the black rubbery track, talking and laughing. Mom wiped under her eyes with a crumpled Kleenex.

"Here they come! The graduates!" My dad raised his arms in the air, as if he'd won a prize, and walked toward us. He grabbed Phillip and me, draping an arm around each of us. Mom was right behind him and we ended in a giant family hug.

"Did you ever imagine the day these two would be all grown up?" Dad asked.

Mom's eyes watered, and she had trouble speaking. "It seems like it was just yesterday you two were toddlers and I was trying to keep you little mischief-makers out of trouble."

"Yup, I guess we're empty nesters now, right?" Dad's eyes glinted.

At that Mom started crying. "Stop it, Sam. We still have the summer."

I gave Mom a bear hug. "I'll always need you, Mom."

She leaned into me and squeezed me tighter. Over her shoulder I saw Noah and Quinn, both with their parents, doing the same as we were. A pang of bittersweet happiness hit me. This was the last time all of us, the class of 2018, would ever be in the same place again.

"I want a group photo," Mom announced, pulling out her cell phone as she wiped at her eyes.

"Oh, me too." Quinn's mom Sarah grinned, her face lighting up. I admired Quinn's mom. She'd raised Quinn all by herself and was getting ready to put her through college, thanks to her successful diner.

I stood between Phillip and Noah. Quinn was on the other side of my brother, his arm around her.

"Say freedom," Dad instructed us.

"Freedom!" we shouted, grinning and laughing. The lineup of our parents turned into a blur of flashes. And just like that, our high school days were over. We'd never be the same.

CHAPTER *Twenty-Seven*

Music is a moral law. It gives soul to the universe, wings to the mind, flight to the imagination, and charm and gaiety to life and to everything.

—*Plato*

The graduation after-party had been a blast, but I was exhausted. I sat in my car in the driveway and heaved a sigh. High school was officially over. I wondered if I'd feel much different tomorrow. My keys slid out of the ignition into my hand and I carried them to the door, locking the SUV as I walked away.

Inside the house, I tossed my cap on the table. The lights were dim and I couldn't hear the sound of the television. Phillip's car wasn't here, so he must still be out partying. A large white envelope sat propped up on the counter and caught my attention. I ventured closer and saw it was addressed to me, but the address was off and it'd been misdirected. No wonder it took so long to get here.

It was from Goddards.

A large envelope was better than a small one, right?

My hands shook with a mixture of terror and excitement

as I ripped through the flap. I slid out the pages, a glossy brochure was behind the letter.

I read aloud. "Dear Ms. Wyndham, Congratulations! We are pleased to offer you a spot in our class of 2022 . . ." A happy shriek left my lips and I covered my mouth. Tears fell down my cheeks as the kitchen lights flicked on. Mom and Dad stood on the back stairs behind me.

"Congrats, Pips." Mom came over and hugged me.

I sobbed. Happiness, relief, excitement, and shock flooded my system. I was going to Goddards. New York was my future. Thoughts of Declan hit me. Where would he end up? Not that I should care anymore.

"Congratulations." Dad enveloped us both in a bear hug. "I don't think anyone ever doubted you'd get in. You were destined to go there."

"Thanks." I stepped back as we broke apart and wiped at my tears with my hands. I finished reading the letter and my mouth popped open. "Oh my God, I got a full scholarship." The paper shook with my hands.

"That's amazing!" Mom reached over and grabbed a napkin from the holder on the center of the table. "We've got a lot of planning to do to get you ready to move . . ." She choked up. "To move you across the country." Now she joined me in my cryfest.

Laughing through my tears, I wrapped her in another hug. "I love you."

"Love you, too, pumpkin."

"Ladies, as much as I hate to go, I have an early morning so I'm heading back to bed. Don't stay up too late. Congrats again, Pips. I knew you'd do it."

Dad went back up the stairs, leaving Mom and me in the kitchen.

"Ice cream?" she asked.

I nodded and sat at the table, flipping through the brochure and re-reading the letter, just to make sure it was true.

She got two bowls out and the carton of Moose Tracks from the freezer. "We need to start a list of things you'll need."

The back door sprang open and in walked Phillip, grinning like the cat who got the cream. He'd clearly had a good night.

"Well, well, well, where have you been?" I raised a brow and took in his disheveled hair and starry-eyed look.

He sat beside me and Mom pulled out another bowl. "I was just taking Quinn home."

"Translation: you made out on her front porch for the last hour."

"Yes. As a matter of fact, you're spot on." He made a face at me and grabbed one of the bowls Mom brought over. I took the other and thanked her, which prompted Phillip to remember his manners. "Thanks, Mom."

Once we were all sitting down, we filled him in on my news.

"That's great. Really. Who knows, maybe you'll hook back up with that Declan guy there."

I shook my head. No one knew about his text. Not even Quinn. "I doubt it. He's moved on and probably already has his plans sorted out. And they most definitely don't include me."

Mom shrugged. "Well, sometimes things happen for a reason. Plus, I'd think the chances of you guys running into each other in New York for some cello thing would be pretty high even if he's not at Goddards."

He didn't even want to be friends.

"He might not be staying in New York. He applied to Oberlin, in Ohio."

Mom closed her eyes tight and rubbed at her temples. "Oh, ow, brain freeze." Once she stopped squinting and could see again, she continued, "If it's meant to be, it'll happen. Just like it did for your father and me. And like

Phillip and Quinn."

My eyes involuntarily rolled. "Please, I made that happen."

"Yes, dear, but remember, they had a hand in it too." She looked at me like I was getting a bit full of myself, taking credit for it all.

"I'm heading up." I smiled at them, grabbed my shiny new acceptance letter, and climbed the stairs to my room. I laid down on my bed and read it over again, still completely floored. I pulled out my phone, took a quick snap and sent the picture to my grandparents.

Holding the phone over my head, I flipped through the pictures in my gallery, stopping at the one of Declan and me at the competition. Right after we'd won. We looked so happy. I was glad I had this. It was a good way to remember him. I flicked my finger across the screen a few more times and stopped at the Winter Formal pictures. Despite having other dates who were in the photo with us, Declan and I were leaning into each other. I remembered the way his hand felt on my back and how that'd been the night of our first kiss. My fingers itched to send him a text about my acceptance. He was the person I wanted to tell most, but I couldn't.

Placing my phone and papers on my nightstand, I changed into my flowery pajama shorts and a gray tank top. A quick trip to the bathroom to brush my teeth and wash my face and I was climbing into bed. My mind swirling with New York possibilities. My dreams were coming true.

♪

"Come on, Pips, it's not a date, just a movie. Trust me, I get it, you're not interested." Noah stood on my front porch giving me the stink eye. "I just really don't want to be the third wheel."

"I can't. My mom and I were gonna go shopping for the stuff I'll need in New York." We'd been avoiding it all summer long, but we were getting down to the wire with only a few weeks left.

"Can't you do it afterward?"

Sighing, I held up a finger and poked my head into the music room. "Mom, Noah wants me to go to the movie with Phillip, Quinn, and him. Do you mind if we go shopping tonight?"

She shook her head, a pencil held between her lips as she looked over some sheet music.

"Thanks." I turned back to Noah. "Fine, you big baby, I'm going."

"Thank you so much. I owe you for this."

Sniffing, I shook my head. "Big time."

Noah shoulder bumped me and we stepped off the porch. Quinn and Phillip were standing by the car kissing . . . of course. It seemed like it was seriously all they did these days. It was rare that they came up for air. Quinn made very little time for me, and honestly, seeing how I was leaving in the fall, I could kind of understand it. Still, it sucked a bit, especially since I wouldn't be able to see her much once I left Portland.

"You talked her into it." Phillip slung an arm around Quinn's shoulders and leaned in to kiss her one last time before guiding her to the passenger side door and opening it for her.

"Yes, thank God. Otherwise I'd have had no one to talk to while the two of you tongue-bathed each other."

My faced scrunched. "Ew. That's a disturbing mental image. Thanks a lot."

Noah laughed and waited for me to climb in the back seat as Phillip ran around to the driver's door.

"So, Pips, you excited for Goddards?" Noah asked, sliding in next to me.

I nodded. "Yeah, I leave in three weeks, which is insane.

This summer just flew by." I'd spent it playing cello, reading books, and basically relaxing. Jenna had resumed her role as counselor at her horse camp, so she was never around, and I missed her.

"I can't believe you'll be all the way in New York." Quinn turned around in her seat and shook her head. "And Noah'll be in Corvallis. Ugh, we're all getting too far apart."

Laughing, I said, "Please, Corvallis isn't far from Eugene, an hour at most."

"Yeah, but we won't see each other every day, and Noah and Jenna will be our rivals." Quinn's bottom lip popped out.

Shaking my head, I patted her shoulder. "Somehow, I think you'll manage to stay friends."

How would life be when I returned for breaks? Would they all move on and forget me? It was hard to imagine not being around them every day. At least we had our phones and could still text and video message. Declan and I hadn't talked, emailed, texted, nothing. Not that I was expecting anything; it just hurt. I still struggled with his sudden change.

The chatter in the car surrounded me, but none of it really sunk into my consciousness. Instead, I was off in deep thought. Mucking through the drama that my own mind was creating. What would I do if I ran into Declan in New York? What would we say to each other? How awkward would it be? What would I do if he wasn't single?

One thing was certain, since he'd moved on, I could and *would* do the same.

We pulled into the parking lot of the theater and hopped out. At the window was Lexi. I'd almost forgotten she got a summer job here.

"Hey, Lex." Quinn greeted her with a smile. "How's it going?"

"Okay. I heard you were heading to University of

Oregon in the fall."

She nodded and wrapped an arm around Phillip. "We both are. Where are you going?"

Lexi handed over their tickets after my brother slid some cash through the pass-through. "I'm heading up to Bellingham. I got into Western Washington University."

"That's great! Your grandma lives up there, right?" Quinn stepped to the side as Noah and I stepped up.

Lexi nodded. "Yeah, she does. It was good seeing you."

"You, too." Quinn and Phillip went over to the doors, waiting for Noah and me.

Focus shifted on us, Lexi said, "I guess you guys finally got it figured out, didn't you?"

"Um, one ticket please," I asked and slipped my money through.

"Every time I run into you, you're with Noah." She slid my ticket out and started ringing up my sidekick.

My brow furrowed. "Well, we're friends, so we tend to hang out occasionally."

Rolling her eyes, she gave Noah his ticket. "Okay, whatever, Pips."

Some things never change apparently. I looked up at Noah, and we both chuckled. Now that he'd finally resigned himself to just friendship, we were back to normal, and it was a nice feeling. I'd missed it. We joined up with the rest of our party and went inside. It was good that I'd gotten out. There wasn't much time left for me here, and I knew that once I was gone I was going to miss these three like crazy. Yet, as much as I'd miss them, I couldn't deny that I was beyond excited for the fall and for my new life to finally start.

CHAPTER *Twenty-Eight*

Love, love, love, that is the soul of genius.

—*Wolfgang Amadeus Mozart*

My few boxes had been shipped yesterday and were now winging their way to New York. All that was left was to get me there. I stood at the TSA line with my parents, Phillip, and Quinn. Thankfully there was no major PDA going on. I looked at Mom, who was dabbing her eyes with a tissue. Dad had his arm around her, his face getting red.

"You stay safe out there, alright?" he ordered me. "You have your pepper spray in your checked bag, right?"

My head bobbed. The lump in my throat made it impossible to speak.

Mom grabbed me, wrapped me in a hug, and held me tighter than I think she ever had. "Call me when you land. And when you get to school. And then when you settle in your dorm, FaceTime me." She stepped back with a decisive nod.

"I will." I looked around to the faces that I knew and loved. "I'm gonna miss you guys."

Quinn hugged me and whispered in my ear, "What am I going to do without you? I hope you find someone as awesome as Phillip. Thanks for making this happen. I'll never be able to repay you."

Next was Phillip. He wrapped me tight and dug his chin into the top of my head. "Gonna miss you, Pippy." I didn't even care that he'd used my most hated nickname.

"Miss you too, Phil."

The person in line behind us cleared his throat and gave me a grumpy look. I signaled him to pass me as I gave everyone one last long hug. "I'll call, and I'll be home for Thanksgiving, which will be here before we know it. I'll see you soon. I love you guys."

Phillip and Quinn had their big move-in day next week. I was glad they got to be here to see me off and weren't already down in Eugene.

I slid my shoes off, gathered the stuff in my pockets, and placed my carry-on into the gray plastic trays for the x-ray machines. Stepping through the metal detector, I gathered my stuff and slid to the side to put myself back together again. When I looked up, my little tribe was smiling and waving. God, I already missed them. Mom was now full on crying. Lifting my arm, I waved back, then walked away and around the corner.

My big solo adventure had started. And I didn't even care that I had to fly.

♫

My half of the dorm room was now completely unpacked, cozy, and decorated. I shared the room with a flautist named Grace. She seemed sweet. Our little room was part of a large suite. Kind of like a quad. We had communal living spaces with a living room and partial kitchen—meaning it had a small fridge, a sink, and someone had brought a hot plate. Branching off from that were four bedrooms and two bathrooms. Each room slept two people. It was a pretty sweet arrangement. Also, big bonus, the building was essentially brand new.

I sat on my bed, clutching a pillow to my chest, and watched as Grace flipped the pages of her magazine. She hadn't unpacked yet; she said she needed to recover from traveling. She'd come from Connecticut.

Lying back, I shot another text to Mom. When I'd arrived yesterday, I'd been exhausted. No unpacking got done, aside from digging out bedding. I'd just FaceTimed my family and crawled into bed and slept. My shoulder muscles were still achy from being so stressed while traveling.

But now that I'd gotten settled in, it felt great. My cello stood in the corner by the window, my music stand nearby. I had a locker in a nice climate-controlled room, but I just couldn't bring myself to store her there. Not yet at least. It was like she was my security blanket. This was my first time on my own, and despite my nerves, I was seriously having a hard time not smiling. This year was going to be amazing.

"So, do you have a boyfriend back in Connecticut?" I turned on my side to face Grace.

She shook her head, her blonde hair swishing around her face, not looking up from the glossy pages. "Nope. You?"

"No. I'm about as single as they come."

Meeting my gaze, she laughed. "Well, you're in good company then. I was dating a guy, but he was going to Spain with an exchange program, so he broke up with me 'cause he wanted to basically be free should a better opportunity come along. Yes, those were his exact words."

My nose wrinkled in distaste. "Ick."

"Yeah. I figured I was better off without him. I'm just hoping to find me some sexy musician here, although I wouldn't turn down a drama guy. Have you seen some of these dudes on campus? So freaking hot." Goddards only had a few major programs: drama, dance, instrumental, and vocal. Though their majors may have been few, there definitely wasn't a shortage of hot guys.

"I've noticed a couple who were pretty good looking." I grinned. For the first time in like . . . ever, I felt free to actually have a life, one outside of my cello. I'd made it. I'd reached my primary goal. Now maybe I could have an actual well-rounded, normal life without the guilt of not constantly being focused on my cello and school. Although my education was still my primary concern, I didn't feel like I had to fight tooth and nail to keep it. Well . . . yet. Goddards was an entirely different beast, and that free feeling could very well vanish with the start of classes. And at the moment, I didn't even want to contemplate what it'd take to get into the New York Philharmonic. But that was down the road. My next dream.

"We'll have to see what we can do about getting some dates soon." Grace winked at me, a wicked grin on her face. "You about ready for dinner?"

"Sure." I grabbed my meal card, tucked it in the pocket of my black shorts, and slipped into my sandals. Summer in New York was hot. Not only that, it was muggy. It was kind of disgusting, especially when compared to Oregon summers. Thank goodness the dorm had air-conditioning. This would take some getting used to.

Grace led the way, calling out and asking if anyone wanted to join us. A quiet brunette named Harriet popped out from her room and fell into step behind me. From what I could remember her telling me, she was from Montana. I think. She really hadn't opened up much. I did know that she played the oboe though. But she'd already stashed it in her locker.

When I'd landed in New York yesterday, I'd come so close to calling Declan, but I stopped myself. He didn't want to talk to me, and it'd just be painful if I tried.

"So, are you guys ready to start classes tomorrow?" Harriet asked quietly, her fork lightly scraping against her plate as we sat at a table in the small cafeteria-type eatery on the street level of the building. Windows wrapped around the walls, and you could watch the cars zip by.

I nodded. "I've been ready since I got my acceptance letter. I'm so excited."

"What's your first class?" Grace asked and took a bite of her pepperoni pizza.

Swallowing, I answered, "Chamber orchestra. You?"

Harriet chimed in. "I've got a small group session."

Grace smiled. "Same. Small group."

We ate and chatted, getting to know each other better. By the end of dinner I knew that Grace was an only child. Harriet was a middle child. And they were blown away that I was a twin.

"You have to introduce me to your brother." Grace laughed as she looked at a picture of Phillip on my phone.

"He's already got a girlfriend."

"Bummer." She handed back my cell. "Well, ladies, we're about to start our new lives. Hopefully there'll be loads of cute guys in them. Let's head back to the quad."

We stood and left the dining hall. As I passed through the glass doors behind my roommates, a cute blond guy slipped past me and gave me a smile. I turned to watch him, and he did the same. He definitely held promise. It was well past time to face reality and let my dreams of Declan go. A renewed perk in my step, I caught up with Grace and Harriet.

"You guys totally missed that cute guy."

"Where?" Grace flipped to walk backward and check out what she'd missed, a twinkle in her eyes. "We could go back."

I pushed her to keep going. "No, there's a whole year to worry about guys."

"Okay." Her voice was singsongy. "But you may have just missed your chance."

Shaking my head, I said, "I'm sure I'll survive somehow."

Up ahead was a tall slender guy with messy dark hair. My heart skipped a beat and I stopped walking. From behind he looked like Declan. My lungs stopped their steady rhythm, leaving me breathless.

What if he's really here with me?

I wasn't sure how to react. This totally blew my just formed *really*-letting-him-go plans out of the water. We got closer to where he was standing, and I noticed a cello case next to him. I sucked in breath. Should I say something? Just ignore it? My heart felt like a hummingbird.

"Pips, Earth to Pippa." Grace waved a hand in front of my face.

Harriet was looking in the direction I'd just been staring. "What just happened?"

The guy turned around to look at us.

It wasn't Declan.

My stomach sank with disappointment. "Oh, um . . ." I shook my head and looked down to the wildly patterned carpet. "I just saw someone I thought I knew."

Grace hit the button to call the elevator again, as if that would speed it up. My energy now drained, all I wanted was to take a hot shower and crawl into bed. I hadn't realized it until just this moment how big a part of me was really hoping to run into Declan here. I wanted to see him again, to perform with him again, to kiss him again. There were so many things I wanted to do with him again—a few new things as well. And none of them were going to happen.

Shaking my head, I heaved a deep breath. It was silly to think he might be here. It was the not knowing where he'd ended up that was by far the worst.

♪

Chamber orchestra met in Zeissel Hall. It was a small auditorium with sound panels covering the walls. I smiled and took a seat in the audience, following what the other students were doing. I couldn't believe I was really here. I sat my cello case in the chair next to me as more students filled the room. An elderly man walked down the aisle and climbed up the stairs onto the pale wood stage.

"Students, please take out your instruments and come take a seat. Anywhere you want for now. We'll deal with who sits where later."

I stood and spread my cello case over the arms of two chairs and pressed my body against it so it wouldn't tip forward and drop as I pulled out Francesca and my bow.

"This time it's gonna be me in first chair, Princess."

My heart stopped beating, and my head snapped up to the smiling voice coming from the row behind me.

"Declan?" My mouth opened in shock; I probably looked like a fish out of water, but I was seriously having trouble believing what I was seeing.

"When I got in, I figured you must've too." He ran a hand through his hair. It was longer than I remembered. It looked amazing. *He* looked amazing. "It's good to see you again."

Was it really?

My eyebrows pulled together, and I shook my head, trying to process his sudden appearance and what this meant. Half of me was ready to burst out of my skin from sheer happiness at the sight of him. The other was dreading being around him when he'd made it clear he didn't want anything to do with me. "Why—"

"Come on, students, let's get started. You can chat afterward." Our instructor clapped his hands and called to the stragglers. Which was the two of us and one other girl.

I climbed onto the stage, my brain struggling to keep up with my churning emotions. I didn't know whether to cry or smile. Declan carried Booth and came up the stairs behind me, quickly catching up to me with his long stride.

Two chairs stood empty in the back row. A slight smile

settled onto my lips as I sat.

He was here. Really here. I could reach out and touch him. Which I seriously wanted to do right now. Just to reassure myself he was real flesh and blood.

I looked up and saw him beside me, the grin he had on was adorable. The only thing I wanted to do was talk to him. To find out what he'd been up to. How things had turned out with his dad. And most importantly, why he'd sent that awful text cutting off all contact with me.

"As some of you may know, I'm Professor Sweets. This is my twenty-ninth year at Goddards, and I must say that I'm very excited to work with such a promising group of musicians." He went on to talk about what we'd be playing this year, his general philosophy, and how we'd be testing for chair placements.

Thankfully, class wrapped quickly. I stepped off the stage and packed my cello away. I hadn't really needed it after all. The closures on my hard-shell case snapped shut and I pulled the strap over my shoulder.

Declan was standing there, waiting for me. "You want to go grab some coffee? Maybe go for a walk in the park?"

I glanced at my watch. I had two hours until my next class so I nodded. "Um, sure. I guess so."

He smiled and gestured toward the door. We walked down our separate rows of chairs until we merged at the joint aisle at the end. Looking up at him, I kept my expression guarded. The last thing I wanted was for him to know just how thrilled I was to see him.

We stashed our instruments in our lockers before we walked to a corner coffee shop, making small chitchat about the weather and school in general. Thankfully the line wasn't too long. In minutes he had a cup of black coffee, and I had an iced tea. We slipped back out the door and walked a couple blocks, past the Hayden Planetarium, and into

Central Park. The trees were laden with green leaves, and sunlight speckled down, dappling the pathway.

"So, Princess, how's your brother?" He took a sip, a small drip falling onto his black t-shirt, which he brushed off. Hearing him calling me Princess again felt good. I'd actually missed it.

"Good. He's at University of Oregon with Quinn. They're finally *together* together." We walked up the steps into Shakespeare's Garden and I smiled at the lovely rustic fences made from gnarled branches. Dotted along the pathways and tucked into the bushes were small plaques with quotes from The Bard.

"That's good. I bet Quinn's over the moon."

I swallowed my drink and smiled. "Oh, she's shot so far past the moon."

"And you guys are okay now?"

Nodding, I said, "Yeah, after I got back from the NCYM, we had a long talk and got it all out."

"I'm glad."

"So how did things work out with your dad?" I sipped my iced tea, enjoying the coolness in the muggy air. I couldn't begin to fathom how Declan was managing a hot drink.

His shoulders raised in a shrug. "Better than I thought. I'm glad to be out of there, but we at least came to an understanding. He apologized for . . . everything. And he really made an effort. I also may have made more of an effort with Missy. Turns out she's not as terrible as I once imagined her to be."

"I'm glad. I was worried about you." I didn't dare look his way, even though I could feel his eyes on me.

Declan cleared his throat. "So, how's Wonder Jock?"

"Oh, um, Noah's at Oregon State, in Corvallis. Jenna's there too." I glanced up at him, but he didn't look at me.

"Got a really great basketball scholarship. Hasn't a clue on a major yet, so he's just taking all his core classes."

"I'm happy for him." There was no mocking in his tone this time. "It must've been hard for you to leave him behind?"

My nose wrinkled. "Not really, why?"

He shrugged and ran a finger over the edge of his coffee lid. "I just figured since you guys were dating, it'd be hard to part."

"Noah and I aren't dating. Despite what you tried to tell me to do." A soft laugh left my lips.

His eyes snapped to mine. "You're not? Did you break up before you left Portland?"

I shook my head. "Declan, Noah and I were never together. We weren't right for each other."

"But I heard that you'd . . . that you guys started dating right after you got back, after our competition."

I shook my head again. "Wait, is that why you sent that text?"

His mouth opened and closed a few times before he answered, "Partly. I just figured if there was even a chance for you and Noah, it wouldn't be right for me to still be in the picture. I knew he wouldn't appreciate it. And it's not like I was there to do anything about it."

"Okay, there are just so many things wrong with that idea that I don't even know where to start." My face scrunched at his logic. "Where did you hear that we were together?"

"Lexi emailed me after I'd already decided to send you that text. She just confirmed my suspicions."

I didn't realize he and Lexi were friendly enough to email each other.

"Lexi?" My brows shot up. "You listened to Lexi? You know, even if I *were* dating Noah, I'd like to think that you and I'd still be friends. Still talk to each other. I mean, if all else fails, I'd always think of you as my obnoxious competition, and someone I very much wanted to stay in touch with."

He gestured to a bench in an alcove of trees and bushes. "So then you guys never . . . got together?"

"No." As I sat beside him, I studied my fingernails, my ponytail slipping over my shoulder. God, how I'd missed him. Did he seriously have to look as good as he did? "I couldn't."

He blew out a heavy breath. "You don't know how awful it's been thinking of the two of you together—him touching you and kissing you." He ran his hand over his face before stopping to pinch the bridge of his nose. "It practically killed me." A slow smile made his lips curl. "I'm really glad you're not with him."

I sucked in a sharp breath, hope welling inside me. "What about you?"

"There's no one else."

He moved his hand to cover mine, which I flipped over so we were now palm-to-palm. "So then, there's been no rekindling anything, with anyone, happening on your end?"

"Not even a spark." He threaded our fingers together. "I guess this means we're both single."

Slowly, I raised my gaze from our joined hands to meet his eyes. "It does appear that way."

He leaned closer, his warm breath caressing my skin and sending a wave of goosebumps to cover my body.

"Pippa, you have to know that there's no one else for me but you. I missed you more than I even thought possible." He reached up with his free hand and slid it behind my neck, gently guiding my face closer to his. "Truth is, I've fallen in love with you."

Love?

My eyes widened, and I couldn't suppress my grin. He

loves me.

He pulled apart enough to study my face. With a nervous smile he added, "I get that you might not feel the same as I do—"

"I do, Declan." I curled my fingers in the thin t-shirt covering his chest, wanting to yank him closer. "It's why I couldn't be with Noah. He wasn't you. *You're* what I want."

He lit up and pulled my face within millimeters of his. Lips barely a whisper apart, he said, "Thank God for that."

Our mouths pressed together and fireworks shot off inside me. It was just as hot and sexy as I remembered. He seriously knew how to kiss. And I knew with absolute certainty that I'd never get tired of these feelings. In fact, I was looking forward to exploring more of them with him.

Musically and physically, we just sparked and ignited. We melded together, strengthening each other, making us better than we ever were apart. For a long time, I used to believe that my cello was the key to my future. Now I knew better. Yes, my cello would be a huge part of it and unlock numerous doors, but I'd enjoy it all so much more with Declan by my side. I wanted him in every aspect of my life with every fiber of my being. Well . . . all except one spot. He still wasn't going to get my first chair.

Acknowledgments

Kristin Kisska, Victoria Van Tiem, Amy McKinley, and B, you guys are rock star critique partners! I'm so lucky to call you talented ladies my friends. Thank you with all my heart. I couldn't have done it without you.

Jessica Watterson, you are a superhero of the agenting world! I couldn't be more grateful to have you on my team. Thanks for always having my back and looking out for me.

The Life Raft ladies: Amanda, Anise, Kimberly, Tara, Samantha, Colleen, Heather, and Kelly. You ladies never fail to make me smile, and you give wonderful advice. I'm so glad we found each other on this crazy journey.

Gina Denny, thanks for taking the time to help and answer my research questions.

To Cherrita, Dayna, Kayla, and the rest of the amazing ladies at Amberjack, you guys took Pippa and Declan and made them sparkle. I'm forever grateful. You were all truly so delightful to work with!

For my parents, I know I've said it before, but I'm blessed to have you guys. I thank my lucky stars for you both.

To my hubby and kidlet, you both inspire me in so many ways every single day. Bug, I love brainstorming with you.

You've got such a wonderfully creative brain, and I know it's going to take you far. And Ryan, I can't thank you enough for being so supportive and helping me pursue my dreams. This wouldn't be possible without either of you.

And last, but definitely not least, you, my dear readers. You guys are some of the sweetest and kindest people I've ever come into contact with. I love hearing from you! You never fail to give me a dose of the warm fuzzies. Thank you for being your awesome selves, never change.

ABOUT THE *Author*

Emily Albright was born in Salt Lake City, and her parents moved her all over the continental US growing up. As a result, she now knows several places that she could never move to. As an only child, often in a new city, Emily spent all of her time lost in the worlds of her favorite books and making up imaginary places and friends to keep her company.

A graduate of the University of Oregon, she received a degree in Journalism and Communication. She now gets to spend her days going back to her roots, dreaming up heroes and heroines and putting them in awkward or sometimes swoony situations.

Emily now makes her home in the Pacific Northwest with her handsome husband, her amazing daughter, their crazy cock-a-poo, and an incredibly tolerant senior feline. She has no intention of ever leaving the PNW . . . well, unless she could somehow finagle a free and adorable cottage in Scotland, but that seems highly unlikely.

When Emily isn't writing, she's usually reading, and when she's not reading, she's binge-watching Netflix or her DVR. She always has a glass of tea at her side and usually something furry cuddled up to her.

In addition to *Perfect Harmony*, Emily is the author of the series *The Heir and the Spare*.